SANGRIA AND SECRETS

PERIDALE CAFE
BOOK 31

AGATHA FROST

PINK TREE PUBLISHING LTD

Published by Pink Tree Publishing Limited in 2024

All characters and events in this publication, other than those clearly in the public domain, are fictitious and any resemblance to real persons, living or dead, is purely coincidental.

Copyright © Pink Tree Publishing Limited.

The moral right of the author has been asserted.

All rights reserved. This book or any portion thereof
may not be reproduced or used in any manner whatsoever
without the express written permission of the publisher
except for the use of brief quotations in a book review.

For questions and comments about this book, please contact
pinktreepublishing@gmail.com

www.pinktreepublishing.com
www.agathafrost.com

WANT TO BE KEPT UP TO DATE WITH AGATHA FROST RELEASES? *SIGN UP THE FREE NEWSLETTER!*

www.AgathaFrost.com

You can also follow **Agatha Frost** across social media. Search 'Agatha Frost' on:

Facebook
Twitter
Goodreads
Instagram

ALSO BY AGATHA FROST

Peridale Cafe

33. Cruffins and Confessions (coming soon)
32. Lemon Drizzle and Loathing (coming soon)
31. Sangria and Secrets
30. Mince Pies and Madness
29. Pumpkins and Peril
28. Eton Mess and Enemies
27. Banana Bread and Betrayal
26. Carrot Cake and Concern
25. Marshmallows and Memories
24. Popcorn and Panic
23. Raspberry Lemonade and Ruin
22. Scones and Scandal
21. Profiteroles and Poison
20. Cocktails and Cowardice
19. Brownies and Bloodshed
18. Cheesecake and Confusion
17. Vegetables and Vengeance
16. Red Velvet and Revenge
15. Wedding Cake and Woes

14. Champagne and Catastrophes
13. Ice Cream and Incidents
12. Blueberry Muffins and Misfortune
11. Cupcakes and Casualties
10. Gingerbread and Ghosts
9. Birthday Cake and Bodies
8. Fruit Cake and Fear
7. Macarons and Mayhem
6. Espresso and Evil
5. Shortbread and Sorrow
4. Chocolate Cake and Chaos
3. Doughnuts and Deception
2. Lemonade and Lies
1. Pancakes and Corpses

Claire's Candles

1. Vanilla Bean Vengeance
2. Black Cherry Betrayal
3. Coconut Milk Casualty
4. Rose Petal Revenge
5. Fresh Linen Fraud
6. Toffee Apple Torment
7. Candy Cane Conspiracies
8. Wildflower Worries
9. Frosted Plum Fears

Other

The Agatha Frost Winter Anthology

Peridale Cafe Book 1-10

Peridale Cafe Book 11-20

Claire's Candles Book 1-3

BEFORE YOU READ...

Hello everyone, and welcome to another Peridale Cafe book! Except this time, we'll be leaving the cafe and heading back to Savega in Spain. For those of you who may remember, Savega is where Julia's Great-Aunt Minnie runs the La Casa hotel!

And if you don't, I don't blame you. 2020 was a long time ago! Savega, Minnie, and La Casa were first (and last) seen in the 20th Peridale Cafe book, **Cocktails and Cowardice**, which you can read on Amazon.

If you want a little refresher (contains spoilers for **Cocktails and Cowardice**), read ahead...

Julia and Barker, and Dot and Percy, travel to Savega for their joint honeymoon in Savega. Things start off well with a lovely family reunion with Minnie, but things aren't all they seem. The quaint Spanish town has been

Before you read…

overrun with shops selling knock-off goods, and a mysterious figure known as The Buyer has taken over the town. And if that isn't bad enough, Dot and Percy are soon taken by The Buyer and held captive in a villa deep in the valley. Julia and Barker, along with the Spanish police raced against the clock, digging through the clues to uncover the identity of The Buyer to save Dot and Percy from meeting a sticky end.

Now, several years later, they're ready to return… everything will work out just fine this time… ***won't it***?

(Stay tuned at the end for two BONUS Sangria recipes!)

1

The first morning of spring bathed Julia's Café in a refreshing sunlight, casting aside the shadowy remnants of a long and bitter winter. Julia South-Brown, perched at her usual table by the counter, pondered the future of the land behind the café that had become the village's battlefield. Her new red, shiny suitcase, packed for the upcoming week abroad, stood guard beside her. On the table, a steaming cup of her favourite peppermint and liquorice tea sat next to the ballot sheet detailing the potential futures of the field—all four options whispered promises of change.

She sipped the minty sweet tea as her pen traced every option on the ballot sheet: the simplicity of leaving it be, the promise of a public garden, the vibrant vision of an outdoor market. Yet, it was the image of children's laughter in a play park—something the village hadn't had since Julia's childhood—that made her pen hover

over the checkbox. She could hear Olivia laughing from the swings on a not-too-distant summer afternoon.

That's what the fight against the developers had been for.

Her daughter's future.

Months of battles with James Jacobson over the fate of this land weighed in her memory, but now its destiny lay in Peridale's hands. They had Julia's step-mother—though they were almost the same age—Katie to thank for this second chance. More specifically, the centuries-old loophole and the tangled Wellington-Howarth family tree that had led Katie to becoming the land's rightful heir.

And while Katie manned the café for the next week, she'd be encouraging people to cast their votes in the box next to the charity tin on the counter. In typical Katie fashion, she'd bedazzled the box in glittery pink paper.

Putting down her tea, Julia leaned back in her chair and peered through the beaded curtain into the café's small kitchen. Barker and Katie had been deep in conversation about something altogether more serious for as long as Julia had been weighing the ballot options with her tea.

"... and I know it might seem like a maze with no exits, Katie," said Barker, Julia's husband—his voice still held a tinge of the soft authority from his detective inspector days. "I promise, I'm not giving up. Your mother is out there somewhere. We will find her."

Katie let out a small sigh, lacking in her usual girlish

optimism. "I believe in you, Barker. It's just... with Father dead, I thought maybe she'd have come looking for me by now."

An empathic ache twinged in Julia's chest; Katie's journey to find her birth mother—one that had started with the recent ringing in of the new year—had been arduous and fraught with dead ends. Whoever or wherever she was, the mysterious Mrs Wellington listed in Katie's birth certificate over four decades ago had yet to reveal herself from the mists of time.

Glancing down at the options again, Julia patted the pocket of her vintage floral dress, feeling the outline of her passport. Maybe the week in Spain would give Barker new ideas for how to approach the tricky case. She knew he was looking forward to having more time to work on his latest book. A week soaking up the Spanish sun was just what they needed. Between Barker's hunt for Katie's mother, his overflowing PI caseload, and drafts for his third novel, there hadn't been many romantic evenings together since the crack of New Year's Eve's fireworks.

And the holiday wasn't just a chance to reconnect with her husband, but also with her eccentric Aunt Minnie. Great-Aunt Minnie, to be exact. They'd exchanged birthday and Christmas cards along with a few letters here and there, but Julia hadn't been back to her aunt's hotel since her ill-fated honeymoon two-and-a-half years ago.

The bell above the door announced Percy as he barrelled in, pulling Julia from her pen tapping. Urgency eclipsed his usual jovial grin, his round cheeks rosy and red bowtie askew.

"*Julia*! Don't suppose you have a moment?"

Behind him, the airport minibus—pre-booked by Julia's gran weeks ago—screeched to a halt.

"What is it?" Julia glanced at the clock among the framed pictures showing the café over the years. "We're setting off for the airport in five minutes."

"That's just it," he said, beckoning Julia to the door. "Your gran... she... she's said she isn't coming."

Julia had feared something like this might happen.

"Ah."

"Nothing I've said is changing her mind." Nibbling his lip, he glanced through the window and across the green to their cottage. "Ethel's trying now, but I'm afraid my Dorothy is only getting more wound up. Would you—"

"Of course. Is this about what happened last time?"

Percy offered a solemn nod, and a chill not even the thoughts of the Spanish sun could soothe skated down Julia's spine. She abandoned the list—there would be time to decide when they returned. For now, she had to make sure her gran wasn't giving up the chance to face her demons.

Surviving a harrowing kidnapping during their joint honeymoon at Minnie's hotel had etched deep scars.

But what was that old saying?

Lightning wouldn't strike in the same place twice.

2

Dot peeked through the lace curtains at the minibus across the green. The memories of her last visit to Savega continued their taunting dance, flooding her with a paralysing dread.

They almost hadn't made it out alive.

"*Dorothy?*" Ethel called, rapping her knuckles on the other side of the locked bedroom door. "Please tell me you're packing in there."

"I... I'm... *thinking* about it." Dot stared at the half-empty suitcase on her bed. "Please, Ethel, just... leave me be."

Dot let the curtain flutter back into place and sank into the floral armchair by the window, her heart hammering. She couldn't bear to look at the minibus anymore. How could they tempt fate after the horrors of their last experience? And how had she allowed Minnie's invitation, promising the 'fantastic relaunch of La Casa Hotel', to sweep her away?

She clenched her eyes tight as glimpses of their days held captive flashed through her mind—the sweltering villa hidden deep in the valley with barred windows, the scratchy rope binding their wrists, Percy's pained groans after she sliced open his leg on that window during their escape.

She shuddered, wrapping her arms around herself. How could she have agreed to this trip? And not just agreed—she'd *planned* the whole thing. What had she been thinking? That she'd feel peachy on the day? That their therapy two years ago had rid her of the cobwebs? She'd spent months painting a rosy picture of tapas under strings of lights, sangria by the sea, siestas, and endless games of cards by the pool.

Wishful thinking.

A gentler knock at the door pulled Dot from her thoughts, and when she didn't answer, the handle rattled.

"Go *away*, Ethel. I told you, I—"

"It's me, Gran," Julia's soft voice called through the door. "Let me in."

Dot pushed herself from the armchair and crossed the room with some reluctance. That's where Percy had run off to—to fetch the cavalry. But there was nothing anyone could say to change her mind. She let Julia in and returned to the armchair by the window.

"Looks like you've almost finished packing," Julia said, as optimistic as ever. "Want to talk about it?"

Dot shook her head, unable to put her fears into words as Ethel and Percy followed Julia in. Their dogs,

Lady and Bruce, were close behind. Bruce stayed by Percy's feet, but Lady trotted over with her usual elegance. Standing on her hind legs, the white-haired Maltese rested two paws on the chair arm and stared at Dot with her 'treat time?' eyes.

"I *cannot* leave," Dot said, stroking Lady's soft ears. "Someone needs to stay behind for the dogs."

"You know Evelyn volunteered to house sit. She's downstairs at this very moment." Ethel shook her head —she made no attempt to hide that she thought Dot was being silly. "The minibus you booked is waiting."

Dot shrank further into her chair. Percy's face softened with understanding as he sat on the ottoman and took her hands in his. He was the only one who understood what they'd been through, and yet even he was excited for a second round in Savega.

"We'll be in Minnie's lovely hotel, surrounded by family."

"*And* friend," Ethel cut in.

"And friend," Percy corrected. "No one can hurt us there. We don't even have to leave the room if you don't want to."

Dot could stay trapped in her room at home, thank you very much, and at least she'd have the comforts of Peridale to stop her from going insane.

"You've talked Savega up so much," Ethel said, verging on begging now. "The food, the winding streets, the little shops near the marina. And the beach—you said there was nothing better than strolling along the shore at sunset."

"Tickets are in the bureau downstairs," she said, fiddling with her brooch. "I'm not stopping anyone else. In fact, I *want* you all to go. Give me some peace and quiet for a change."

"I'm excited to experience it with *you*," Ethel said. "For your many, many faults, it won't be nearly as fun without you. Will it, Percy?"

"Not one bit."

A ghost of a smile flickered across Dot's lips, but the dread snatched the excitement away just as fast.

"This was never going to be easy," Julia said, squatting next to Lady. "But we'll all be with you. Every step of the way."

Dot let out a shaky breath, glancing between their supportive faces. The sound of laughter drifted in through the open window, drawing her back to the curtains. Her other granddaughter, Sue, and Sue's husband, Neil, were with their young twins, loading suitcases into the minivan. Was Dot really going to let fear stop her from sharing their joy?

"This holiday doesn't have to be something to dread," Julia assured, joining her at the window. "It can be an opportunity."

"An opportunity?"

"A chance for closure," she said. "To replace those dark memories with new, happy ones. To walk those winding streets and see that valley again without fear holding you back. You *escaped* that place and survived."

Ethel slid her arm around Dot's shoulders. "And *I*

wasn't with you last time, was I? I'll show them what's for if anyone tries anything."

"And break a hip in the process?"

"Oi!" Ethel squeezed her shoulder. "You're much, *much* older than I, Dorothy. And I'm being serious. I know we've had our quarrels, but that's all behind us now. You're as good as family to me, and family looks after each other."

"We're all in this together," Julia added.

Percy gave Dot's hand an affectionate pat. "Plus, think of all those new outfits you've bought. Such fashionable ensembles longing for their chance to shine under the Spanish sun. You shouldn't deny Savega the chance to see your exquisite taste, my love."

Dot couldn't help but chuckle. Trust her husband to make her laugh when she was feeling her worst. She drew a balancing breath as she let the fear wash over her. She turned from the window to see the outstretched hands of Ethel and Percy. Their compassion shone in their eyes, bolstering her courage. Gripping their hands, Dot rose from her chair on unsteady legs.

"Fine, but I'll need your help packing my case if we don't want that minibus to leave without us."

"Already on it, my love," Percy announced, hurrying to the wardrobe. "Ethel, shoes are under the bed. Julia, you go to Barker and get your cases in the van and tell the driver to wait for us."

"You won't be the last," Julia said, checking her watch. "Jessie and Olivia haven't turned up yet. I'll find them."

Julia left, and they had Dot's case packed and sealed within minutes. After dragging it down the stairs between them, it joined Percy and Ethel's, waiting by the door. Evelyn, as promised, was cross-legged in a bright sangria red kaftan on the sofa.

"Look after them, won't you?"

"Like they're my own children," Evelyn said, crouching to let Bruce's excited tongue lap at her chin. "I sense we're going to have the best time. How about a tarot reading for the road to settle your nerves?"

Dot sighed. She'd never been one for Evelyn's mysticisms.

"We don't have time. The minibus is—"

"Will only take a second," Evelyn insisted.

She produced a deck of cards from her kaftan, shuffling before offering them out. Percy drew first.

"*Ah*! The Three of Wands appears," she announced, "promising adventure and growth on your journey. It's a call to embrace new experiences, as your path brims with possibilities. And Ethel?" Ethel drew. "The Three of Cups! The joy of friendship shines. This journey will not only bring fun and laughter, but it will also strengthen the bonds between the three of you. Together, these cards assure a memorable holiday, filled with exploration and the warmth of companionship. The cards *never* lie!" She turned to Dot with a grin. "Your turn."

With heavy reluctance, Dot drew a card from the deck and handed it to Evelyn. The mystic's face dropped as she glanced up at Dot with a worried wobble in her bright eyes.

"Well? What is it?"

"The cards aren't *always* right. How about you pick another—"

Dot snatched the card. She turned it over, her heart sinking at the sight of a man lying face down by a body of water with many silver swords poking out of his back.

"You just said the cards *never* lie. What does it mean?"

"The Ten of Swords could mean *many* things," she said, taking the card and slipping it into the deck as the minibus horn honked outside. "*Ah!* Won't want to miss your flight, will you? Have a *splendid* holiday! I'm sure it'll be... absolutely fine."

Dot huffed, tempted to press Evelyn further. She'd never believed in her so-called predictions—Evelyn would claim it was going to rain only after the first drop had fallen from the black clouds above—but it wasn't like Evelyn to withhold her readings. Before Dot could confront her, Percy and Ethel whisked her over the threshold with their cases.

"Everything will be fine," Percy assured her, squeezing her hand as Barker and Neil loaded their cases into the boot. "And look, Jessie and Olivia still aren't here, which means we're not the last to— *passports!*"

Percy dashed back into the cottage, and with the image of the ten swords haunting her, Dot might have followed if Ethel hadn't pulled her onto the bus.

"Don't let Evelyn's cards unsettle you," Ethel whispered as she buckled her seatbelt next to Sue and Neil, both of whom offered a giddy wave. "We're all going to have a fantastic time, swords or no swords."

Dot nodded, trying to dismiss the ominous card from her mind, but as Percy boarded and the minibus pulled away, she couldn't resist a final glance back at the cottage, where Evelyn stood waving, her red kaftan billowing in the wind like a bright, foreboding flag.

Jessie glanced at her watch, sinking further into Dante's side on the worn sofa as she watched Olivia shred last week's 'PEOPLE OF PERIDALE TO DECIDE FIELD'S FATE' front page. She couldn't tear herself away from the small room above Katie's nail salon, the tiny headquarters of *The Peridale Post*. There were no deadlines to keep her there today, yet she was five minutes late to meet the airport minibus.

She snuggled up closer. "I wish you were coming with us. You were so excited about it. *I* was so excited about it. Our first holiday as a couple."

Dante wrapped an arm around Jessie's shoulders. "I know, and I'm sorry. I wish I could join you, but you know how it is." He nodded across the office at their editor. "Veronica has given me an excellent opportunity here at *The Post*. She's already had me working on more interesting stories than I ever got at the *Riverswick*

Chronicle. And technically, I'm still in my trial period, aren't I?"

Veronica peeled a satsuma one-handed, hunched over her desk with her nose and giant pink specs inches from the screen. After everything Jessie and Veronica had been through using the pages of the paper to fight the likes of Greg Morgan and James Jacobson over the past year, Jessie knew matters of the heart didn't sway Veronica's judgments.

Not that Dante had asked for time off.

"Not to be too soppy," she said, "but it won't be the same without you there."

"Be soppy." He gave her a sad smile and pulled her in close. "You know I'll miss you too. A week is the longest we've gone without seeing each other. The second you get back, let's plan something together, just the two of us. Anywhere you want to go."

"Anywhere?" She thought about it for a moment. "Let's go to the moon."

"Anywhere on *this* planet."

"Now, you never specified—"

A sudden crash made them jump apart. Jessie looked over to see Olivia frozen with wide eyes, the pot of pens she'd knocked off the desk scattered across the floor. Veronica glared over the top of her screen as Olivia looked around with a sheepish grin. Jessie couldn't help but laugh. She got up and helped Olivia collect the pens, keeping one eye on the clock—their time was nearly up.

After returning the pens, Jessie approached

Veronica's desk. "You can dock my wages for the interruption."

"Don't worry, I will," Veronica said with a wry smile. "Shouldn't you be setting off? Your flight is at noon."

"On my way."

Veronica glanced up from her work, offering Jessie a satsuma segment. "Send a postcard or something. We'll be able to struggle on with you."

Jessie grinned. "You'll be shutting the place down by tomorrow without me here to steady the ship." She cocked her head to the side, tossing back the segment. "You ever think about getting away for a bit? Even an unstoppable force like you needs a break now and then."

Veronica dismissed the idea with a wave of her hand. "'The world's mine oyster, which I with sword will open.'"

"Huh?"

"*The Merry Wives of Windsor*," Dante answered for her. "Act Two, Scene Three?"

"Scene *Two*," Veronica corrected, her tight smile growing, "but well done, Dante. It's nice to have someone in the room who picks up what I'm dropping. It's my way of saying: I'm exactly where I need to be." She nodded at the paper-strewn desk. "Besides, if I go on holiday, who'll run this place?"

At the honking of a horn, Jessie peered out the window through the neon pink glow of the Katie's Salon sign below. Outside, a minibus crawled to a halt, exhaust fumes rising in the morning air. Her dad, Barker, waved to her with one hand, shaking his phone with the other.

Jessie checked her phone to see six missed calls, three from each parent.

"Get some sun," Veronica ordered, returning to her screen after tossing back her final satsuma piece. "You've earned it, and we'll try not to burn the place down while you're gone."

Scooping Olivia up from her nest of shredded newspaper, Jessie hurried down the narrow stairs and into the salon. The scent of nail polish mingled with hairspray, and Katie's shy new apprentice, Clarice—a fifty-something career changer with heavy make-up to rival Katie's—glanced up from painting Shilpa's nails as Jessie ran to the front door; Clarice had yet to say two words to Jessie or Veronica.

Dante followed Jessie out onto the pavement with her suitcase. As she leaned in to kiss him goodbye again, her phone pinged with a new message. Pulling back, Jessie glanced at the screen. The text was from Johnny Watson, the former editor of *The Peridale Post*.

JOHNNY

Hey! Hope things are alright in Peridale. Dropped you an email about a something I think you'll be interested in…

Frowning as Julia took Olivia from her, Jessie tucked her phone away. She'd have to look into it later. She gave

Dante's hand one last squeeze, then wedged herself into a seat beside Ethel, who patted her knee in greeting.

As the minibus pulled away from Mulberry Lane with the chatter of excitement buzzing through the cramped bus, Jessie pulled out her phone again. She hadn't heard from Johnny in a while.

Before she could open the email, Dot leaned over Ethel.

"Dear, would you look something up for me?" she whispered. "Find out what the 'Ten of Swords' tarot card means."

Ethel groaned. "Not more of this nonsense."

Jessie closed the email app and opened a search browser instead. Johnny's email would have to remain a mystery until later.

"Ten of Swords," Jessie said as she scanned the summary at the top of the search window. "Something to do with betrayal, defeat, backstabbing, and hitting rock bottom..."

"That's it!" Dot cried, patting the back of the driver's headrest as they turned the corner of Mulberry Lane. "Turn this minibus back around. I'm going home!"

"Gran, remember what we said," Julia said, twisting in her chair from the front seat. "Nothing is going to ruin our family holiday. *Nothing*."

Jessie hoped so.

Even without Dante, a break would be nice.

3

The plane rocked side to side as it descended through cotton wool clouds, eliciting more whimpers from Olivia. The little one had cried for most of the flight, much to the annoyance of the other passengers crammed into the stuffy cabin. Julia bounced her on her lap, while Barker rubbed the toddler's back, but nothing could console her.

She peeked through the narrow chairs to the row behind them, where her gran clutched the armrests with white knuckles. Her face was pale, and her lips were a tight line—any other onlooker would think she'd never flown.

"Not much longer now," Julia said, smiling through the gap. Dot attempted to return the smile, lips only budging at the corners. "We'll be landing soon."

"Very soon," Percy announced, nose pressed against the windowpane. "I think I see Minnie's hotel! Tiny, of course, but I'm sure that little white box is La Casa."

Still bouncing Olivia, Julia leaned over Barker to peer down as the woolly clouds whisked away, revealing the view. The familiar Sierra de Almijara mountains came into sight, their scrubby slopes giving way to neat rows of olive groves and vineyards. Nestled in the valley below was the town of Savega, its white-painted buildings glinting in the blinding afternoon sun. The view impressed Julia anew, even two and a half years later.

The brakes squealed as the wheels bounced on the tarmac. Olivia and Dot let out loud wails in similar pitches as their fellow passengers sighed in relief that the turbulent descent had ended.

Despite the relief, Olivia's wails turned into choked cries, and the young woman in the row in front swished her blonde ponytail around to stare through the gap between the chairs. She angled her judgmental glare over the rims of her face-covering sunglasses for at least the twentieth time since she'd muttered that she had 'drawn the short straw' by having to sit near a baby on a plane.

"What's her *problem*?" the girl demanded at a mortifying volume. "Get her under *control*. She's ruined my peace this entire flight."

"She's a baby," Jessie called across the aisle. "What do you expect?"

"I expect not to be tortured, and I know *everyone* agrees with me."

Julia shot the young blonde woman an apologetic

look while jiggling a still-crying Olivia, relieved that no one spoke up to agree with the woman. She had noticed similar glances from all directions every time Olivia tested her lung capacity. She attempted to whip up the perfect apology, but her hopes of defusing the situation vanished when she noticed the woman's phone drift in front of her chin.

"Are you recording this?"

"It's the only way *you* people ever learn," she replied with casual iciness. "Do you think it's fair that I'm expected to suffer through an entire flight because you were *selfish* enough to bring a newborn on a plane?"

"She's not a newborn," Barker replied, blocking the camera lens with his hand. "Now, if you don't mind, we didn't give you permission to film us."

"*I* don't need *your* permission. I have rights."

"Are you out of your mind?" Jessie snapped.

"I was about to ask the same thing!" Dot called from behind, finally distracted. "Pipe down, Blondie."

Julia and Barker exchanged confused looks as the phone—and the woman's grin—lifted. Having seen enough clips of disastrous social situations on planes that often resulted in someone being dragged off by air traffic control, Julia bit back her defences.

Ethel reached around the girl's arms to turn off the reading light above, knocking the phone from her hand as quick as a whip. It bounced into the aisle.

"Oops, how clumsy of me!" Ethel exclaimed. "I'm *so* sorry."

"You *idiot!*" she cried. "Pass me my phone."

Ethel stretched out her hand as though her arm was half the length. "Would you look at that? Can't reach."

The woman shot to her feet, but a steward called out, "Miss, sit down! The seatbelt sign is still on."

"But my phone!" she exclaimed, growing shriller by the second. "Don't you know who I am?"

Jessie laughed and said, "No, we don't."

"I'm *Chloe Saunders!*" the woman announced, and when no one reacted, she added, "I have one *million* followers, and I need to get my—"

"Sit down, *please.*"

The woman dropped back into her seat as Julia met Sue's eyes, raising a questioning eyebrow. Her sister shook her head and glared at Chloe's blonde ponytail. The stares directed at Julia throughout the two-hour flight now redirected to Chloe Saunders and her million followers.

"Could we have done anything differently?" Julia whispered to Barker as he watched the luggage van pull up under the wing.

"Would it have made any difference?"

Even from the little Julia knew about the woman, she wasn't sure it would have. Given how often Chloe had turned to stare throughout the flight, it was almost as if she'd been waiting for her moment to erupt and record to put them on display. Peridale had its fair share of strange characters, but thankfully, no 'influencers' who recorded their every interaction.

"Forget about her," Barker said, unclipping his seatbelt as the sign above changed. "We're here to relax. In ten minutes, we'll never have to see Chloe Saunders and her million followers ever again."

After wiping a sheen of sweat from her forehead, Dot handed over her first euros at the checkout of the airport's book shop. She had spent the last ten minutes deliberating over which book to purchase before settling on a small leather-bound book decorated with images similar to Evelyn's tarot cards. Tucking the book into a brown paper bag, Dot hurried over to the baggage claim where Percy and Ethel were watching for their cases.

"What's in the bag?" Ethel asked.

"Oh, just a tourist book. For the sights."

"The sights?" Ethel arched a brow. "We're staying with your ex-sister-in-law, aren't we? She'll know the sights." She snatched the bag and pulled the book from the paper with an exaggerated sigh. "Oh, Dorothy! You've never believed a lick of Evelyn's hocus-pocus predictions before. Why start now over a silly card?"

"I know, I know." Dot frowned, taking the book back. She flicked through the pages as she searched for the Ten of Swords entry. "But a little research wouldn't hurt, oh..." The pages were all in Spanish, the words indecipherable to Dot's untrained eye. "Maybe Minnie can translate when we get to the hotel."

"Or do yourself a favour and throw it into that bin over there," Ethel said. "And if you're suddenly a believer of Evelyn's ways, maybe there's a reason you can't read this. Maybe you're not *supposed* to know."

"But Jessie said betrayal... backstabbing... *defeat*..."

"And *I* say you're on holiday!" Ethel said, snatching the book back again. She crammed it into her beach bag, holding the straps tight around her shoulder. "Now, forget all this nonsense and try to enjoy yourself. We've flown all this way, and—*ugh*..." She rolled her eyes, nodding down the line of people waiting for the first bags to emerge at the carousel. "Little Miss *Million Followers* is still lingering around like an unpleasant smell."

The insufferable Chloe from the plane had staked her claim right at the front of the crowd. Dot watched in disbelief as Chloe ignored a polite airport employee, ushering her back behind the yellow line. She kept peering at the conveyor belt while pretending not to hear the flustered man.

"I'm crossing my fingers that she's staying anywhere but Savega," Percy said, shaking his head. "What a little madam!"

"I hate to be the bearer of bad news, but I saw her booking confirmation on her phone when she wasn't pouting for the camera," Ethel replied with a huff. "Unfortunately, she *is* staying in Savega. How big is the town?"

"Quite small," Percy said. "We'll just have to do our

best to stay out of her way. I doubt that girl has ever stayed anywhere under five stars before."

"Let's hope Minnie's renovations haven't bumped the place up a few stars," Dot said, stepping towards the carousel as the cases shuffled out. "Finally, some *good* luck! Looks like our cases are the first ones out."

After dragging their cases off and backing away from the fray, Dot fanned herself with a brochure, watching with some delight as Chloe grew increasingly frustrated at being left waiting.

"Serves her right," Ethel muttered. "Might teach her some manners."

Percy shook his head as Chloe shoved past an old couple to reposition herself closer to the spot where the wall spat the cases out.

"I doubt it," Dot said. "She seems determined to be awful."

"She's done one good thing," Ethel said. "She's distracted you from all this nonsense."

As they followed Julia and the others, dragging their cases through the terminal, Ethel pulled the tarot book out of her bag and dropped it into a bin by the bookshop.

"Ethel! That cost my fifteen euros."

"A small price to pay for your peace of mind," Ethel said, looping her arm through Dot's as Percy hurried to keep up behind them. "Now, it's time to forget all about swords and kidnappings and focus on the three S's. Sun, sea, and—"

"Oh, Ethel, don't be so crass."

"Sangria!"

Julia gazed out of the van's window, taking in the terracotta rooftops and vibrant flowers of Savega. As they navigated through the winding streets, the familiar sight of the shop where her gran and Percy were taken loomed into view. In the daylight, it was just another ordinary shop, but its past held a terror that couldn't be painted over. Sensing the unrest radiating from Dot, Julia stretched her arm across the space separating the front and back seats, her fingers enclosing around her gran's trembling hand in a comforting squeeze.

On Julia's knee, Olivia's cries escalated, her cheeks growing redder. They had tried everything—soft toys, songs, silly faces—but nothing could appease her post-flight irritation.

Sue flipped through the pages of *Hola!*, glancing at the glossy photos of celebrities lounging on yachts along the Costa del Sol. She had already made it clear she wanted to do nothing but recline on deck chairs with the sea breeze whipping through her hair, a fruity cocktail in hand. Beside her, Neil leaned back in his seat and let out a contented sigh, already several pages into the novel he had borrowed from the library.

In the seat next to the driver, Jessie's fingertips traced invisible shapes across the fogged-up windowpane, her mind wandering the ancient side streets and hidden corners of the town. Ethel adjusted her oversized sunglasses and craned her neck to take in the view as if scoping out the perfect sunbathing café to spend her days—somewhere quiet with a steady stream of tourists and locals to people-watch and gossip about.

Julia glanced back at her gran, who was staring at her hands knotted in her lap. Percy gave Dot's arm a supportive pat.

Next to Julia, Barker glanced at the view between scribbling in his notepad. For once, he wanted Julia's feedback on some new chapters and character developments for his latest book: *The Man in the Field*. This was unfamiliar territory for them—normally, she only got to read the finished novel—but she appreciated Barker's vote of confidence in wanting her input during the drafting process.

When the central square's fountain came into view, ringed by lively cafés and restaurants, Julia sighed in relief. One more turn and they would be at Aunt Minnie's hotel, finally able to stretch their legs after the long journey.

Julia smiled as the minibus pulled up outside the whitewashed walls of La Casa. She craned her neck, taking in the stunning mountain views framing the boutique hotel.

"Well, it doesn't look any different," Dot remarked, "and—oh no, is that *her*?"

A sleek black car pulled up just ahead of them, and the driver jumped out to open the back door of a private transfer car, and out stepped Chloe Saunders.

Julia's cheeks prickled with fresh embarrassment.

"Don't you know who I am?" Chloe demanded as the driver hurried to unload her excessive luggage. "Get my bags out *carefully*. If there are any scratches on my luggage, you're as good as fired."

"Maybe she's staying at the hotel next door?" Sue suggested.

But the driver—as carefully as carrying fragile glass—placed Chloe's three suitcases on the doorstep of La Casa. Chloe waved the driver off, throwing a colourful twenty-euro note at him. As the tip fluttered to the ground at his feet, Julia sighed, resigning herself to the likelihood that their paths would cross again during their stay. She could only hope that Chloe would keep her diva antics to a minimum so they could enjoy their family holiday in peace.

"Let's get checked in, shall we?" Percy announced, clasping his hands together with an eager smile. "Sangria all round?"

"Now we're talking," Sue replied. "I need a glass of something after that flight... no offence, Julia."

"None taken," Julia said as she held Olivia's hand to help her down the stairs towards the hotel's shaded entrance while the twins, Pearl and Dottie, ran ahead. "And just like that, Liv's tears have stopped."

Chloe shoved past them, spewing insults under her breath. Before Julia could open her mouth to respond, the double doors of the hotel swung inwards. An elegant woman with flowing white hair emerged, the soft jangle of her artisan jewellery announcing her presence. She moved with poise, her flowing white dress a stark contrast to their travel-rumpled group.

"Has Minnie had some work done?" Dot muttered.

The woman let out an airy laugh. "Oh, I'm not Minnie. I'm Dahlia Hartfield, her new business associate." She bowed her head. "I've been assisting with the rebranding of La Casa."

Despite the awkward introduction, Julia warmed to Dahlia's friendly face. It seemed to melt away the tension left in Chloe's wake, and her jangling jewellery captured Olivia's attention.

"*Chloe*! How lovely to see you again," Dahlia said as Chloe glanced up from her phone. "I'm delighted you made it."

"I just had the flight from *hell*." Chloe glared at them, and Julia fought the urge to smile an apology. This time, she narrowed her eyes, tired of the entitled antics. "Next time, it's first class or *nothing*. Have my bags taken straight to my suite—I need to freshen up before I create my content."

Dahlia laughed. "No suites at La Casa, I'm afraid, but I'm sure you'll find your room comfortable. I *personally* oversaw the redesign."

Chloe huffed, shoving past Dahlia and abandoning her bags on the doorstep, and Dahlia's smile faltered before she turned back to the group.

Julia stepped forward, returning Dahlia's warm smile —she smelled strongly of lavender and patchouli.

"It's lovely to meet you, Dahlia. I'm Julia, and this is my husband, Barker."

Barker gave a polite nod.

"Ah, yes. Minnie has told me so much about you both," Dahlia said, shaking their hands. "And this must be little Olivia. What an angel."

Olivia blinked sleepily as Dahlia gave her pudgy hand a gentle shake before moving on to greet Dottie and Pearl. Julia noticed her grandmother's guarded expression as Dahlia took both of her hands.

"You must be Dorothy and Percy! I've heard all about your terrifying ordeal here. But not to worry—the new La Casa will be a sanctuary of serenity for you both, I'm sure."

Dot managed a thin smile. "Well, let's hope so. This is our friend, Ethel White."

Dahlia beamed at Ethel, who was busy taking in the surroundings behind her shades. She then turned to Sue and Neil.

"Susan and Neil? So wonderful to meet you and your girls." Finally, Dahlia turned to Jessie, who had been typing on her phone until this point. She glanced up, surprised. "Jessie, yes? I understand you've been doing well, carving out a journalism career for yourself." Jessie nodded, tucking her phone away. "We were expecting your partner too?"

"He couldn't make it," she said. "Work stuff."

"What a shame," Dahlia said as she stepped back and swept her arm towards the open doorway. "But I'm sure you'll have a wonderful time, regardless. Please, come in, come in! I'm thrilled to welcome you all to the new *and* improved La Casa Hotel."

Julia took in the lobby of La Casa, struggling to orient herself in the unfamiliar space. The cosy, rustic charm she recalled was gone, replaced by a stark white box of a room. The scents of fresh paint and new wood mingled in the air. There were no pictures or flowers to welcome them, only a white marble blob of a sculpture with no definable lines. She drew in a slow breath, trying to steady the uneasy flutter in her stomach.

Beyond the bare dining area, where a lone woman with clear-rimmed glasses sat typing on a laptop, the view opened onto the lush green valley just as she remembered. Julia clung to the sight, letting it wash over her like a visual exhale. That, at least, was unchanged.

Two white-clad staff members emerged, gathering up their suitcases and spiriting them away down the white halls. Julia shifted closer to Barker, desperate for something familiar amidst the foreign space.

"Please, help yourself to cucumber water," Dahlia offered, motioning to the glasses poured on the concrete block that had replaced the reception desk. "As you can see, La Casa has been transformed into a place of rejuvenation and wellness."

"Feels more like an asylum if you ask me," Dot muttered.

Dahlia either didn't hear or pretended not to, pressing glasses of cucumber water into each of their hands when nobody reached out for them.

"We've eliminated all unnecessary clutter to limit overstimulation," Dahlia explained. "In a world constantly vying for our attention, La Casa has become a place where the senses can truly rest."

Julia forced herself to take a sip of the water, which the cucumber had soaked in for far too long for her tastes.

"The water itself has special rejuvenating properties, drawn from our new natural mineral spring," Dahlia continued, her voice as soothing as an audiobook designed to send you off to sleep. "You'll soon experience its healing benefits for yourselves when we—"

"My room?" Chloe interrupted, her demand echoing in the white space.

Julia studied Dahlia and Chloe, detecting a strained familiarity between them. Before she could reflect further, the kitchen door swung open. Julia leaned forward, hoping to see Aunt Minnie or Lisa emerge. Instead, a handsome dark-haired man came out carrying a tray of appetisers.

"Ah, I'd like you all to meet Luca Valenti." Dahlia gestured to the man with a flourish. "A world-famous holistic chef. Luca had kindly agreed to design the new menu, which he'll be cooking for us all week."

Luca saw Chloe, and an uncomfortable tension crackled between them. His jaw tightened, restraint narrowing the dark lashes over his golden eyes.

"What is *she* doing here?" he snapped.

"Good question," Dot said, sniffing at the cucumber water with a wrinkled nose.

"Please, not in front of Minnie's guests," Dahlia said,

shooting Luca a pointed look. "There'll be time for reconciliation later."

What needed reconciling?

Luca smoothed his features with visible effort and nodded. As Julia and her family sampled the nutritious-looking appetisers he had brought out, Chloe wandered over to the patio on the other side of the dining room, absorbed in her phone. Luca disappeared back into the kitchen.

As strange as their interaction was, another question nagged at Julia.

"Where's Minnie? Is she here at the hotel?"

Dahlia's smile grew. "She's taking one of her mineral baths in the lower levels to prepare for your arrival. The spring water is wonderfully restorative. Minnie will join you all for dinner this evening to welcome you."

"Well, I certainly hope she hasn't changed as much as this hotel," Dot said, placing her glass on the concrete desk. "And where's Minnie's daughter? I thought Lisa would meet us at the airport."

"All in good time, all in good time," Dahlia said. "Now, as I was saying earlier, your visit here coincides with our relaunch. This is the test run week for the relaunch, to be precise. Which means you'll get a sneak peek at the new La Casa before we officially unveil it to the world."

Ethel cocked a thin eyebrow above her oversized sunglasses. "We're guinea pigs?"

"Honoured guests, I assure you."

Julia studied the woman more closely, searching for

any cracks in her polished, gracious mask. She couldn't deny a nagging sense of something being not quite right. She didn't hold a relaxing bath against her great-aunt, but she had expected to be greeted by her at the hotel like last time.

Her gaze drifted out to the pool area as a man with a lean build and a long silver beard settled into a yoga pose on the water's edge. Each movement seemed effortless yet controlled as he transitioned from one pose to the next with meditative grace, ignoring Chloe's impromptu selfie photoshoot on the other side of the pool.

"That's Ian Fletcher," Dahlia said, following Julia's gaze. "Ian is a very popular fitness guru and lifestyle coach. I've invited him here to design a yoga and exercise program."

Dahlia then introduced the woman at the laptop as Doctor Helena Ford, a leading expert and proponent of holistic medicine. Doctor Ford glanced up from her work and offered a polite smile at the mention of her name. Unlike Ian, she didn't ignore Chloe, and her gaze lingered on the influencer for a moment as she tilted her face to catch the sun across her features at the best angles.

"You'll have a chance to meet everyone officially at dinner tonight," Dahlia said, guiding them down the nearest corridor. "Shall I show you to your rooms? I'm sure you're all eager to freshen up."

As they moved deeper into the bowels of the hotel, the unfamiliar walls closed in around Julia. The same stark white paint and minimalist décor stretched on endlessly ahead, and she couldn't help but agree with her grandmother's 'asylum' comparison.

"Is it just me," Barker said, leaning in close, "or is something really off here?"

"You took the words right out of my mouth."

Something strange *was* happening at La Casa, and it wasn't just the new décor. This Dahlia Hartfield was walking around as if she owned the place, and they had still seen no sign of her great-aunt Minnie.

4

Dot stood motionless by the large window, gazing out at the lush hills rolling into the distance. The glass felt cool against her fingertips as she leaned forward. Somewhere out there, among the scattered whitewashed buildings and groves of olive trees, was the old villa.

She had spotted the turnoff on the winding road on their drive in from the airport—just a flash of crumbling brick walls blanketed in ivy before they turned a corner. But it was enough. Enough to send her mind careening back through the dark corridors of memory.

"Tea, Dot?"

Percy's voice made her flinch. She turned to see him unpacking their suitcases and placing clothes in the small pine dresser by the bed, the only furniture in the spartan room.

"I'm not in the mood," she said, attempting a smile.

"My Dorothy is *always* in the mood for tea." Percy

paused, a pile of folded shirts in his hands. "You're looking for it, aren't you? The place."

Dot stiffened, clutching the windowsill behind her. She should have known she couldn't hide anything from him. Everyone pretended to understand what they went through during that time, but only Percy truly knew.

"I'm admiring the view," she lied. "Trying to cleanse my eyes of all the white paint."

After they returned to Peridale, there had been nightmares. Panics that left her breathless. Mornings when she couldn't get out of bed. She had seen doctors and therapists on those doctors' orders. She did her homework, practiced her breathing exercises, took her pills, and got well enough to be taken off them. After months of hard work, she felt cured. The old Dot—cheerful, energetic, unflappable—had returned.

Until this trip loomed on the horizon.

Back to this beautiful, terrible place.

As soon as the tickets were booked, the darkness began creeping back in a little more each day. The hollow feeling returning to the pit of her stomach. The vice-like pressure in her chest. And now, being here, she wasn't sure she could keep it at bay.

"Well, I could use a nice cuppa," Percy said, breaking her spiralling thoughts. "And I'm going to make you one too, and—*oh*... only herbal tea. Hmm... I suppose it'll have to do."

Dot turned back to the view outside. The sun had begun its descent towards the ridge of mountains in the distance. She listened to the faint sounds of Percy filling the kettle in the bathroom to ground herself.

She allowed her gaze to sweep across the landscape once more. It *was* beautiful here. The golden light filtered through groves of trees. The hazy shadows lengthened across the vineyards. Birds swooped and dived over rooftops.

She took a long, deep breath and released it. She was here now. There was a plane that could take her home from the airport every three hours if things got too much.

The kettle whistled, and before Percy could grab it, the adjoining door swung open and Ethel burst in, a welcome burst of colour in her summer get-up.

"No *proper* tea!" Ethel exclaimed. "Not a drop of *real* milk to be found, and no sugar either? This place is nothing like you described."

"Because it isn't anything like I described."

Percy handed Dot a steaming mug before sinking down onto the edge of the bed.

"You're right, Ethel," Percy said. "It's not just the appearance of the place that's changed. The whole atmosphere is... off. It was a warm spring day when we arrived, yet I feel a chill inside that I can't shake."

Dot wrapped her hands around the warmth of the mug, seeking comfort more than warmth. She felt that chill, too.

"The Minnie we knew would have been waiting at the door," Dot said, "ready to envelop us in one of her big hugs. She wouldn't have missed greeting her family for the world, not even for a long soak in the bath." She shook her head, perplexed. "It makes me wonder if that Dahlia has done away with her altogether. There's something unsettling about her. Far too smiley."

"Minnie didn't mention her in her letters?" Ethel asked.

"Not a word. Just mentioned she was excited to show us all the changes at the hotel and assured us we'd have a great time here."

Dot took a long sip of her tea, hoping to calm her nerves, but it was overly fruity and bore no resemblance to the quality tea she kept in her cottage cupboards.

"How about we find a shop for some supplies?" Ethel suggested, breaking the silence with a slap of her knees. "If we're to spend a week in this sanatorium, we'll need some contraband to see us through."

"Excellent plan," Percy remarked. "I believe I spotted a shop on the corner as we drove in. I'll finish unpacking here."

Leaving Percy to transfer his neatly folded underwear from the suitcase into the drawers, Dot and Ethel stepped out into the hallway, closing the door to their stark white room behind them. Dot smoothed her pleated navy skirt and straightened her collar, endeavouring to maintain an air of normalcy despite the unease churning within.

"Tea supplies, and then straight back," Dot stated.

"Pull the other one, Dorothy. We both know that's not the real reason we're venturing out. The tea can wait. We're off to find Minnie."

"It would be nice to know what's happened to this place straight from the horse's mouth."

"Precisely. And if she's no longer in the bath, something tells me she's squeezed into a suitcase at the back of Dahlia's wardrobe." Ethel gave Dot's stiff collar an appraising glance. "When are you planning to change out of that stuffy old uniform? You're on holiday, and I'm well aware you purchased half the contents of that catalogue."

Before Dot could protest that her uniform helped her feel like herself, Ethel unpinned the brooch from her collar and affixed it to the breast pocket instead.

"There, that's better." Ethel gave a satisfied nod. "You always appear as though you're being choked. Let that lovely, long neck have some air."

Dot ran a hand over her exposed collarbone. "Long?"

"Like a freakish giraffe."

"You're just envious because your shoulders start beneath your droopy earlobes."

"And there's the Dorothy I know." Ethel winked, linking their arms together. "I was starting to worry you'd left her at home. Come on, giraffe. We'll uncover this mystery. Just like we always do. Dot and Ethel, on the case."

After they descended the stairs, Ethel glanced around the open lobby area.

"Hard to believe this is the same hotel from your stories of Minnie entertaining all those Hollywood stars from back in the day."

"Parties would go on into the night. She had

photographs with everyone." Dot smiled at the memories. "Minnie was quite the 'good-time girl', as they used to say. She loved having a crowd around her, playing poker, and dancing until sunrise."

"That's the holiday I was hoping to have."

"I suppose it's what we make of it, right?"

"I suppose," Ethel agreed with a nod. "Glad to see you've cheered up a bit."

"Merely... distracted." At the bottom of the stairs, Dot paused, peering down a dim corridor. "Dahlia mentioned 'lower levels' earlier. But I didn't go down to any kind of basement or cellars when we were here before."

"Could have been code for 'I buried her under the patio?' Brookside style?"

"I thought she was in the suitcase at the back of the wardrobe?"

"Maybe she chopped her up? You said she was quite the plump lady."

Dot and Ethel made their way into the open dining area adjacent to the lobby. The long wooden tables and mismatched chairs that once filled the space were gone, replaced by small round tables with two chairs each.

At one of these tables sat Ian Fletcher, the Gandalf-looking meditation guru they had seen earlier. He sipped tea with his eyes closed, seemingly lost in thought. At the table next to him sat Helena, the Doctor, still on her laptop.

"You know, I still cannot *believe* Dahlia invited *her*

here," Helena said out of the blue. "After everything she wrote."

Ian cracked one eye open. "Yes, but she does have over a million followers. Her blessing could make this place."

"Or *break* it. Dahlia is playing a dangerous game."

Dot and Ethel exchanged puzzled glances.

Noticing their presence, Helena ended the conversation with Ian, who returned to his meditation.

"We're looking for the mineral baths," Ethel called out. "Could you point us in the right direction?"

"I'd be more than happy to take you," Helena said, closing her laptop. "I've done more than enough work for the afternoon."

The doctor led them across the lobby to a spiralling stone leading into darkness.

"Watch your step," Helena said, flipping a light switch.

Dot gripped the railing as they descended, the temperature dropping with each step underground. They followed it round for what felt like an age until they came out in a vast cellar with high arched ceilings lined with half a dozen baths made of stone.

"There was a terrible flood down here last year," Helena explained, her voice echoing off the cold stone walls. "Minnie thought she might have to close the place down. But when we tested the water, we found it was actually a mineral spring."

Ethel's eyes widened. "A natural spring? Right under the hotel?"

"I've tested the samples myself, and the results are extraordinary."

Steam rose from the baths that glowed an unearthly teal under the dim lights. Dot frowned, peering into the nearest bath. The water seemed to glow with a hypnotic shimmer, but there was something unsettling about this cavernous underground spa.

"Minnie?" Helena called out. "You have visitors."

Dot followed Helena's gaze to the far wall, where she could just make out a figure reclining in the last bath at the end. As they drew closer, Dot gasped. It was Minnie, and she was immersed up to her shoulders in the mineral water, head tilted back and her eyes closed.

"Is she... *dead*?" Dot whispered.

"She's in a deep state of relaxation," Helena said. "This water is extremely therapeutic, and Minnie can't seem to get enough of it."

She waved her hand in front of Minnie's face, and Minnie's eyes fluttered open behind a pair of swimming goggles. Seeing them, she sat up with a start, water sloshing over the sides.

"*Dorothy!*" Minnie cried, pulling off her goggles. "What on earth are you doing here?"

"We've come to see you, of course!"

Minnie climbed out of the tub, revealing a much thinner frame than Dot remembered. She pulled a plush white robe around herself and tied it into a knot that showed off a trim waistline.

"You must have caught me dozing off," Minnie said, shaking her head. "I lose all track of time in these healing waters. This must be the friend you wrote about?"

"Ethel White. Charmed."

Dot studied her sister-in-law in dismay. Minnie's signature bouffant hair was gone, replaced by a simple bob. The heavy makeup and bold prints she favoured were nowhere to be seen either. Even her voice seemed lighter, missing its usual theatrical flair. She seemed almost a different woman.

"Well, it's wonderful to see you both," Minnie said, fussing with drying her hair with a towel. "Will you be joining me for a soak?"

"I'll pass for now, thank you," Dot said. "You're looking... well, Minnie. How have you been keeping?"

Minnie smiled from ear to ear. "Never better! I can't wait for you all to experience our relaunch."

Dot glanced around uncertainly. "Where's Lisa? I assumed she would be helping you run the place."

At the mention of her daughter, Minnie's expression cracked, and she looked away. With a forced smile, she peered down at her wristwatch.

"Goodness, is it that late already? I must get ready for dinner."

With that, Minnie hurried off towards the stairs, the white robe billowing behind her. Helena followed close behind, leaving Dot and Ethel at the lower levels.

"This place must be ancient," Ethel said, whistling as she looked around. "Are you sure you don't want a little dip?"

"Forget the water. What was that about?"

"Maybe she's just nervous? Big relaunch, and all." Ethel shrugged, looping her arm through Dot's. "Time to find some proper tea and milk. I think we could all use a nice hot cuppa after the day we've had."

Dot nodded in agreement and glanced around the eerie underground spa once more before following Ethel up the stairs. There were mysteries lurking in this place, but they would have to wait.

For now, tea was just what they needed.

Jessie wandered into the plaza on her own before dinner. Back in her travelling days with her brother—Alfie was working in a bar somewhere in South America the last time they spoke—exploring the streets of a new place alone was one of her favourite things to do.

Just like the hotel, the plaza had changed a lot. Last time she'd been there, the streets had been lined with dodgy shops selling fake designer tat, run by a gang. The same gang who had snatched Dot and Percy. And now that they had been chased out of town, the locals had returned with their quaint cafés, lively bars, and souvenir shops selling handmade local treasures. Unlike the changes at La Casa, these were an improvement.

She paused to admire the magnificent fountain in the middle of the plaza, the water sparkling as it danced in intricate patterns. She perched on a shady bench beneath a tree near the fountain and pulled out her phone. Taking a deep breath, she opened the email from Johnny Watson and read:

Subject: Exciting Job Opportunity at Wander Magazine!

Hi Jessie,

Hope you're keeping well down there in Peridale. I've been following the stellar work you and Veronica have been doing with the paper. The coverage of James Jacobson and Greg Morgan has been nothing short of impressive. You've done more than I ever could. Couldn't be prouder.

Now, the reason I'm reaching out to you today is that a fantastic opportunity has come up with one of our brands here, Wander magazine. Given your flair for adventure and your knack for vivid storytelling (I've seen your posts from your travelling days on social media; they're brilliant!), you immediately sprang to mind.

We're on the lookout for a Travel Journalist to join our team, and I couldn't think of anyone better suited than you. This role is all about living on the move—reviewing boutique hotels, immersing in local cultures, sampling cuisine, and basically giving our readers a taste of what the world has to offer through your eyes. It's not just wandering; it's Wander-ing with purpose (cheesy, I know.)

The perks? You'd get to see the corners of the earth, have your experiences published, and get paid a pretty penny whilst at it. The salary package is generous with ample room for progression. The last person in this role has gone on to present a popular 'stay vs go' travel TV program, so who knows where this could take you!

I understand it's a lot to consider, given your commitments back home, so I'm giving you a week to mull it over before we cast the net wider and 'go live' with the job post. But let me tell you, Jessie, this job has your name written all over it.

Leah sends her love—tell your mum we'll be back to visit soon. Anyway, I don't need to tell you twice how action-packed and rewarding this position would be. I'm sure the wandering spirit in you is already packing your bags.

Drop me a line with your thoughts, or if you need more information. No rush, but also... don't keep adventure waiting for too long!

Best, Johnny

P.S. It really has been a joy to see how you've kept the spirit of *The Peridale Post* alive and kicking. Proud is an understatement!

Jessie read through the email once, then again.

She sat staring into the rippling blue water of the fountain. She had never imagined her life taking this direction. She'd never expected to become a journalist at all. Johnny had been the one to nudge her into it when he'd helped her through her dreaded Shakespeare coursework. Veronica, her tutor before she quit teaching to run the paper, hadn't let her turn down the job.

She'd only been at *The Post* for a year.

Leaving hadn't crossed her mind.

And she was still doing the odd shift at the café between articles.

A travel journalist? She did love exploring new places, trying new foods, meeting new people. Her recent articles showcasing small businesses in Peridale after the heat of writing scathing exposé pieces for much of last year had been a joy to research and write. Imagining that kind of work on a global scale made her stomach turn over.

Jessie sighed and clicked her phone off. She couldn't make the decision right now. This opportunity had come out of the blue. She needed time to think it through, weigh the pros and cons. And she needed to talk to Dante.

A commotion across the plaza caught her attention, and Jessie looked over to see Chloe Saunders shouting at someone half-hidden in the shadow of a building.

As if Jessie needed another reason to dislike her.

"Don't push me," Chloe was saying, jabbing her finger toward the hidden figure. "Don't think I won't tell the world the truth about your food."

A man responded, but his voice was too low for Jessie to make out the words. Chloe's face twisted into a spiteful smile.

"Oh, now you're threatening me? Want to see how that'll go?" Chloe's face changed like the flick of a switch, and she stumbled backwards. Feigning distress, she cried, "Someone help! This strange man is harassing me!"

Jessie watched as the man turned and hurried away, his shoulders hunched. Chloe stared after him, a smug grin breaking across her face. She shook her head, chuckling to herself as she turned her attention back to her phone. Jessie stared after the man, sure she'd seen him earlier at the hotel. What was the name of that chef that Dahlia introduced them to?

Jessie's phone began to buzz in her pocket. She glanced at the screen, half expecting it to be Johnny with a follow-up—it was Dante calling.

"Hey," she said, injecting lightness into her voice. "Sorry, I meant to let you know we got here. How's Peridale?"

"Same as when you left it." Dante's voice came through,

sounding stressed. "Veronica's got me running around the village gathering quotes to see which way the vote for the field is swaying. She keeps texting me with new tasks."

Jessie chuckled. "She does that."

"I'm sure I'll get used to it. How's Spain?"

"Spanish," she replied, looking back to where she'd seen Chloe; she'd vanished. "It's nice. The weather is lovely. The hotel is a bit odd. You're not missing much, to be honest, and..." The job offer was on the tip of her tongue. "Yeah, that's it."

"You good?" he asked. "You sound off."

"Must be a bad connection," she lied, her eyes clenched shut, uncertain of what to tell him—the email had turned everything upside down. "Just about to have dinner, so I'll call you later, okay?"

There was a long pause.

"Yeah, sure," he said. "Just about to pop into the café to see if Katie will let me have a sneak peek at the votes so far. Veronica reckons the gardens will win, but I've put my money on the market. How did you vote?"

"To leave it as is," she said. "Speak later."

Jessie ended the call, a surge of guilt flooding her chest as she gripped her phone. Home, Peridale, and Dante—it all seemed so distant now. She envisioned herself travelling the globe, writing exotic stories for *Wander Magazine*. Was that what she wanted?

And why hadn't she told him?

She turned to head back to the hotel, colliding with someone walking backwards. The blonde woman spun around, her phone held aloft. It was Chloe, and she had been taking more selfies.

"Watch where you're going!" Chloe snapped.

"Me?" Jessie retorted. "You were the one looking at your phone."

"Well, I'm not the one who walked right into someone. People need to pay more attention."

"Who are 'people'?" Jessie bristled at her condescending tone. "Those without followers? You think that matters?"

"It does."

"Look, we both weren't paying attention. There's no need to be rude about it."

"Ugh, typical," Chloe said, rolling her eyes dramatically. "I don't have time for this. Some of us have content to create. Don't you know who I am?"

Jessie stepped aside to let Chloe pass, her patience wearing thin.

"No, I know exactly who you are, Chloe," Jessie said, her voice tinged with an acidic bite. "You're an entitled brat who thinks she can treat people however she wants."

Chloe's eyes widened in outrage as she sputtered for words. Before Jessie could react, Chloe drew her hand back to slap her. Somehow, Jessie reacted in time to grab Chloe's wrist. She strained against Jessie's grip as though still trying to make contact, so Jessie squeezed harder.

"You're hurting me!"

"You tried to slap me."

"This woman is assaulting me!" Chloe cried, pulling

her hand away. "Don't just stand there! Someone do something."

But the people around didn't react as Chloe searched the crowd for allies. Dot and Ethel emerged, their plastic shopping bags swinging from their wrists.

"Clear off!" Dot exclaimed, brandishing her shopping bag at Chloe. "We saw you try to slap her."

"What gives you the right?" Ethel chimed in. "Go on, you heard her. Clear off!"

Chloe gawked at them for a moment before whipping around and marching back towards the hotel.

"Are you okay, dear?" Dot asked, placing a hand on Jessie's shoulder.

"I'm okay, really. Just a bit shaken. I think I might have hurt her more than she hurt me."

"Good!" Ethel said with a firm nod. "Might teach the girl a lesson. What a troublemaker she is. Her actions will catch up to her."

Jessie pondered Ethel's words. Chloe did seem to thrive on conflict: first on the plane, then the tense encounter with the man Jessie suspected was the chef, and now this unprovoked aggression.

"I hope you're right," Jessie said as they followed Chloe's path back to the side street leading to La Casa. "With her attitude, it's only a matter of time before someone fights back."

5

Julia surveyed the elegant patio with unease. The twinkling lights in the valley below were a comforting sight, yet the atmosphere around the table felt as sterile as the bare table setting. Like the rest of the hotel, the colour had been drained. White plates on a white tablecloth, with only glasses of icy water to drink.

So much for the sangria Minnie had promised in her letters.

At the head of the table, Dahlia Hartfield scanned the patio as though everything was as perfect as could be. Beside Dahlia sat the peculiar wellness staff—Ian Fletcher, the fitness instructor, and Doctor Helena Ford. Julia studied their serene expressions. Their fixed smiles evoked tough days in the café when a plastered-on smile couldn't quite mask the ache in the arches of her feet.

Dot leaned over to Julia and whispered, "Once again, where's Minnie?"

Julia shrugged, as perplexed as her gran.

"And what's this food?" Ethel moaned, poking at the wet lettuce on her plate. "If I'd known we were going to be eating rabbit food, I'd have smuggled a few packs of bacon in my case."

"Packing meat, Ethel?" Percy shook his head. "Sounds like a case of food poisoning waiting to happen, dear."

"Not if you freeze the bacon and then pack it just before you leave. It thaws out by the time you've arrived."

"Not one of your worst ideas," Dot said, pushing her plate away. "But you're right. A little meat would be delightful right about now—"

A clinking glass drew their attention back to Dahlia, who was glowing with evangelical passion as she rose from her seat.

"Welcome, everyone!" she said, extending her arms in another billowing white dress. "Even though we're a few short, I'd like to thank you all for coming to this dinner to celebrate the reason we're all here." She poured herself a glass of icy water. She lifted it to the glow of the twinkling lights strung above them and tilted her head as though she could see something they couldn't. "What if I told you that the secret to a more vibrant life is as simple as the water you drink?"

"I'd say you're talking rubbish," Dot said.

"Today, I want to share with you the miraculous benefits of the elixir held within this hotel's *very* cellar. What does this look like to you?"

Ian and Helena turned to the family with their frozen smiles while they all looked at each other in silence.

"Water," Dot replied, her tone as cold as the ice bobbing in the water. "Unless you have a jug filled with gin? In which case, I'd like to swap."

"Very humorous," Dahlia said with an empty chuckle. "And no. There is no alcohol at La Casa because, as you pointed out, we have water, and what more could we need?"

"Is that another trick question?" Dot muttered.

"This water isn't just any water," Dahlia said, steaming ahead. "This water, which burst forth like a miracle in the cellar under our very feet, is packed with essential minerals that are the cornerstone of wellness: magnesium, sodium, potassium, zinc, and sulphur."

As Dahlia sipped the magical elixir, Julia grew uneasy. Glancing at Barker, she could tell he shared her scepticism.

Dr Helena cleared her throat and said, "Dahlia is right, and if you'd let me explain further, I can help demystify those confused looks on your face."

"Do we have a choice?" Dot said.

"Let's start with magnesium, the master mineral that powers over three hundred biochemical reactions in your body," Helena said after an encouraging nod from Dahlia. "From energising your day to soothing your muscles and bolstering your heart's health, magnesium is an unsung hero." She adjusted her glasses, pausing for a sip. "And let's not overlook sodium, often misunderstood, but in just the right amounts, sodium is not your foe, but a vital friend. Then, there's potassium, the heart's guardian, and zinc to fortify your immune system. And the cherry on top is sulphur. Who doesn't want glowing skin, lustrous hair, and strong nails?"

"This is not *just* water," Dahlia announced, raising the glass in a toast. "This is the potion of life. Embrace the journey to wellness, one sip at a time."

Julia studied the other guests' reactions. Sue, a former nurse, looked like she was trying to keep an open mind, while Neil seemed indifferent, absorbed in his novel stashed under the table. Jessie listened closely, ever the journalist, though her right eyebrow had a defiant arch. Barker suppressed a fluttering yawn as he watched over Olivia picking at her food.

"Sounds like snake oil to me," Dot announced after a gulp of water. "You're to tell me one sip of this water can do all of that?"

"Not just a sip," Dahlia said, her enthusiasm indomitable. "We also recommend relaxing soaks in the water to allow your body to absorb every drop of these magnificent minerals."

"If something sounds too good to be true..." Dot said.

"I *assure* you, we have the science to back it up," Helena said. "I oversaw the tests myself. This spring is remarkable, and—"

Just then, Chloe Saunders sauntered in, silencing Helena with a snort. She plopped down on a chair beside Ian. He inched away, angling his whole body from her presence.

Dahlia's placid expression faltered, and she welcomed their latecomer with strained graciousness. Chloe rolled her eyes and pulled her phone up in front of her face.

Just then, Luca emerged from the kitchen, balancing plates on his arms. His face fell at the sight of Chloe tapping away at her phone. With strained politeness, he served each guest, working his way around the table.

When he reached Chloe, his hands quivered. Soup sloshed over the rim, spilling onto her dress.

"Ugh!" She jumped up. "You idiot, you could have burned me!"

Luca slammed down the dishes, his composure shattered. "It's gazpacho! It's cold! What is your problem? You will not do to me what you did to Ian."

Ian Fletcher choked on his first slurp of the cold soup. Pulling his napkin from his lap, he folded it into a neat square, laid it by his plate, and stood up.

"If you'll excuse me," he said. "I'm not very hungry after all."

Julia and Barker exchanged puzzled glances as Ian disappeared inside, his steps careful but quick. Luca followed, leaving questions about what Chloe had done to Ian hanging in the air. Given Dahlia and Helena's avoidant gazes, it was clear they knew what the chef was alluding to.

Before Julia could ponder further, Dahlia waved her hand as if to disperse the tension in the air, and said, "You'll all get to know Ian better during your stay. I'm sure you'll all want to join him for a yoga session by the —*Ah*! Minnie! You made it."

Minnie bustled onto the patio, wrapped in a plush white robe and towel turban. "So sorry I'm late, darlings." She air-kissed Dahlia before plopping down in Ian's empty chair. "I lost track of time again and couldn't pull myself away from the water. I never feel better than when I'm soaking up those minerals."

"I was just telling our guests all about it. Why don't you tell them how we came to transform La Casa?"

As Minnie settled in, Julia took a sip of her gazpacho, the cold soup refreshing on her tongue. Luca was a talented chef, even if his creations strayed from the hearty baked goods and simple casseroles Julia was used to.

"I was seconds from closing the doors to La Casa forever," Minnie said, sighing as she towelled off her shorter hair. "When the cellar floor burst with water and flooded the place up to my knees, I threw my hands up in despair. After everything that happened here last time you were all here, I didn't think I had the energy to pull this place back from the brink." She reached across the table and clasped Dahlia's hand. "How fortunate I was that Dahlia was a guest here at that moment. She helped me see the flood as a new beginning rather than a disaster."

"The health retreat was all my idea," Dahlia said, bowing her head. "After we had the water tested, of course. Minnie was sceptical, but then she started following my patented *Blisselle* program."

"*Blisselle?*" Jessie spoke up.

"My award-winning wellness app," Dahlia said. "I encourage you all to download it and see for yourselves."

Chloe snorted, shaking her head behind her phone.

"My results speak for themselves," Minnie said, smoothing her hands down her slimmer frame. "I started eating cleaner, meditating, reading spiritual books—under Dahlia's guidance and with the benefits of the mineral spring, I began feeling like a brand new person."

Julia glanced around, noticing the absence of Lisa.

Did the new Minnie not care about her daughter?

Doctor Helena leaned forward, pushing her glasses up her nose and said, "And now, the possibilities are endless. People will come from all over to experience these healing springs."

Chloe snorted, glancing over her phone. "If *you* say so, right?"

Helena's jaw clenched, and, like Ian before her, she removed her napkin and excused herself with a bow of her head. Chloe set her phone on the table, the camera facing her. She angled her body just so, snapping selfie after selfie, relishing the disharmony she had stirred.

With a taut smile, Dahlia gathered her things. "I'm afraid I must be going too. Enjoy the rest of your evening, and I'm sure Luca will be out with the main course soon."

As Dahlia disappeared inside, Minnie scurried after her, and Chloe wandered off to find better lighting. Julia met Barker's gaze, pondering the odd tension that had erupted. She set down her spoon, her appetite vanished.

"I'm just going to say it…" Julia said. "What on earth was all that about?"

Barker nodded. "It seems like there's some lingering tension between the guests and Chloe. I know she arrived with us, but it's obvious they all know each other."

"No surprise Chloe is at the centre of it all," Dot huffed. "And Minnie seems like she's been *lobotomised* since our last visit. I don't like this 'brand new Minnie' one bit."

"And healthy or not," Ethel said, letting the tomato liquid fall off her spoon, "Luca could have at least heated this up."

"Speaking of Luca," Jessie said. "I saw him and Chloe talking in the square earlier. Sounded like she was blackmailing him about something, so I think you're right, Dad. They all know each other from somewhere else."

"And that's not all," Percy said. "Chloe slapped you."

"*Tried* to," Jessie corrected. "She wasn't quick enough for me. I'm more interested in this story around the water. Smells fishy to me."

"Literally," Dot said after a sniff of her glass. "Must be the sulphur."

Julia turned to Sue and said, "You were a nurse. What do you make of all this talk about the healing minerals? Sounds a little far-fetched."

Sue tilted her head. "It's not *too* far off from the fluids we use in the hospital for dehydrated patients. Minerals like magnesium, potassium, and sodium... they're great at doing what they do, but most sports drinks have similar things these days."

"All this conflict has given me an idea for a scene," Barker said as he leaned across the table and plucked Olivia from her highchair. "I think it's time for some writing on the balcony. Julia?"

Julia hesitated, tempted to dig deeper into the odd tensions around the table. Even if they were forced to spend time under the same roof as Dahlia and her strange cohort, their holiday was what they made it. Julia intended to relax, not snoop. And she had promised to help him get unstuck with his book.

Promising they'd meet again for breakfast in the morning, they all went their separate ways, and Julia, Barker, and Olivia retreated to their stark white room.

Julia pushed aside her unease as they settled on the balcony with glasses of sweet sangria poured from plastic bottles bought from the local shop. She tried to listen to Barker reel off details about the cold case of the body found in the field behind the café—hundreds of miles away in Peridale and the plot of his next book—but she was far too distracted.

After that strange dinner where they'd barely eaten a thing, Julia couldn't shake the feeling that things were on the verge of erupting at La Casa, like the burst pipe in the basement.

Dot awoke with a rumbling stomach in the early hours. She couldn't remember the last time she'd woken from hunger. And then she could, and she was once again whisked back to the villa somewhere off in the grassy hills. She almost woke Percy to see if he felt the same, but tucked up tight under the sheets, he slept like a baby who hadn't noticed their thin mattress was only inches off the floor.

She rummaged through her hand luggage and found the broken biscuits she'd stashed away from their flight. Not even the ones with a little chocolate on them... typical. Still, she took them out to the balcony and scoffed them down, crumbs and all. Aside from a distant thumping from a bar still open somewhere, the valley stood still.

Almost peaceful, but she couldn't stop searching for the place. It was somewhere off to the right, high up off a winding road. She was sure of it. She didn't know what difference it made, but she squinted into the distance until the music stopped thumping and her stomach started rumbling again. She left Percy tucked up in bed, and her knuckles hovered over Ethel's connecting door, but there was no use spoiling anyone else's sleep. Resolute that she'd bring them back something of whatever she found, she snuck out.

Alone and hungry, Dot crept through the quiet hotel, her slippers shuffling across the tiled floor. Outside Julia and Barker's room, she heard Barker's familiar snoring —the man sawed logs in his sleep. At Jessie's door, the muted sounds of a movie or show played. The lucky girl must have a TV in her room.

Behind the front desk, she pushed through the swinging door into the kitchen. A light beamed from the open fridge and Dot paused.

"Ethel?" she called. "Did you beat me to it?"

But it wasn't Ethel raiding the fridge—it was Minnie, spoon in hand, as she ate from a large tub of Greek yoghurt. She looked up like a guilty cat caught with the cream, lips ringed with white.

"Oh, Dorothy, I..." she mumbled through a mouthful. "I was craving something sweet."

Dot noticed she'd also helped herself to a pile of fruit —cherry stones, apple cores, and melon rinds cluttered the stainless-steel counter. Minnie tried to laugh it off, but Dot could see the stress in the pinch of her eyes and mouth.

"You always had a sweet tooth," Dot said.

"Old habits die hard. I thought this was one I'd beaten."

"In the name of *wellness*?"

"You don't have to say it like *that*."

"And you don't have to pretend to be into all that stuff in front of me," Dot said, moving to sit beside Minnie at the central island. "If your brother were still alive, we'd still be sisters-in-law, wouldn't we? We go too far back for charades. What's going on here?"

Minnie's smile faltered and for a moment, vulnerability shone through the cracks.

"I'm not pretending," she insisted. "I am trying to better my life after... after everything. I don't have to remind you what happened." She shook her head, shame clouding her eyes. "Last time you were here... I was so stupid to fall for Rodger's act. I thought he was sweet. I thought he was helping me, and he organised your kidnapping to force me to sell this place to him. And he stabbed my Lisa too, and..."

Minnie jumped up, moving to rummage through the pantry.

"Even with him behind bars, I still feel so scared. Like I'll never..." she trailed off as she parted a row of tinned chopped tomatoes. "Dahlia's way of life has helped me. It quieted down the noise... gave me something to focus on... I was having the most terrible nightmares..."

Dot paused, taking in Minnie's words. She hadn't realised Minnie was also still struggling with the aftermath of that horrific time.

"You're not the only one who has nightmares," Dot admitted. "I wanted to stay at home this morning. Almost didn't get on that plane. Coming back here... it's brought it all up again."

"But you're the tough one, Dorothy. You always were. Few could have survived what you did."

"I don't know about that." Dot gave a rueful laugh. "But I suppose we survived, didn't we? And so did you. And Lisa too."

She wanted to ask after her niece, but Minnie had found a bar of dark cooking chocolate in the pantry and returned to the island with an excited grin. Her hands shook as she unwrapped it.

"I haven't had chocolate since... well, since Dahlia arrived. A little square won't hurt, will it?"

Dot took the chocolate and broke off a few rows, handing pieces back. The dark, bitter taste was a far cry from milk chocolate, but it was better than nothing. Even in her own state of anxiety, Dot could see Minnie had been affected by events here. Neither had ever alluded to any lingering side effects in their letters—it was easier to pretend they'd moved on.

"We should go for a mineral bath!" Minnie said.

"It's four in the morning..."

"Who cares?" Minnie whisked Dot off the stool. "It's my hotel, isn't it? You must try it, Dorothy."

"But my swimming costume is in my room."

"You won't need it. It'll just be us two. I promise those waters make everything better. You'll see."

Relenting, Dot allowed herself to be led from the kitchen. Still nibbling on the chocolate, Dot followed Minnie down the spiral staircase into the cool cellar. Her slippers padded on the stone steps as they descended into the dim underground room.

"Sorry it's dark down here," Minnie said over her shoulder. "Before the flood, this was used for storing old furniture from previous renovations. Dahlia had everything cleared out to make way for the future. No use dwelling on the past."

"It is stark," Dot remarked. "Not as lively as I remember La Casa."

"Oh, I'm quite used to it now," Minnie replied in a

breathy tone that made her sound like Dahlia. "Decluttering your surroundings frees up your mind. Makes room to focus on more important things."

Dot frowned. There were some rather important things—and people—missing that concerned her more than the excessive spring cleaning.

"Speaking of which," Dot ventured, "Where's your Lisa? I haven't seen her since we arrived, and you clam up every time she's mentioned."

"Do I?" Minnie's gaze slid away. "Oh, you know Lisa. Always busy. She never knows when to slow down. I believe she's working at a bar in the town square."

"You believe? When we left you, she was sticking around to help you run this place?"

"We agreed it would be best if Lisa... moved on from the hotel," Minnie said. "Sometimes you have to let go of negative influences in order to move forward. That's what Dahlia says."

Dot bristled at the implication. "Letting go of negative influences? Surely that doesn't mean your own daughter?"

But Minnie was already moving ahead.

"You're going to *love* this," Minnie insisted, her tone a shade too bright. "You'll feel like a *new* woman."

Dot bit her tongue, making a mental note to get to the bottom of the Lisa situation later. For now, she allowed Minnie to steer her towards the baths. As Minnie prattled on about the benefits—echoing Dahlia's well-rehearsed dinner sales pitch—Dot noticed they weren't the only ones down there for a late-night soak.

"Occupado," she said.

"The baths are rather irresistible, even at this late hour," Minnie said, swapping her kaftan for a robe as she squinted into the darkness. "Hope you don't mind if we join you?"

Only silence answered. Dot felt a prickle of unease across her shoulders.

"Let's have a little more light, shall we?" Minnie said, reaching for a switch on the wall. Several overhead bulbs flickered on, illuminating the far bath with the rising steam.

"Oh no..." Minnie whimpered. "Are you okay?"

Dot gasped, hands flying to her mouth. A woman lay motionless in the water, face down, blonde hair splayed out around her head. An empty vodka bottle jutted from a pile of crumpled clothes left on the floor—she was far from okay.

Plunging into the steaming bath, Dot and Minnie turned the woman over, and glassy blue eyes stared back at them.

There was no doubt about it.

It was Miss One Million Followers.

And she was dead.

6

Jessie jolted awake face down on her bed, with Donnie Darko playing on her laptop and the job offer from Johnny shining on her phone. She'd fallen asleep trying to distract herself, wishing Johnny had waited until next week to email so she could think about it on solid ground.

Being plucked from home, she didn't know what to do.

She could talk to Julia and Barker about it, but they'd encourage her to do what she felt was right. She didn't know what felt right, and the one person she wanted to talk to about it, Veronica, was in Peridale. She could call her, but even for her always-on-the-clock editor, it was far too early.

Closing her laptop, she wandered out to the balcony and looked out over the hills as the first light of dawn painted the sky with hues of peach and lilac. She was reminded of her time spent travelling and how she always loved this time of day the most—new possibilities in a new place.

She missed that part.

Seeing the village green every morning from her flat above the post office got old. Would it be so bad travelling for work? The guilt about leaving *The Post* kicked in, and she shook her head, looking for a distraction out in the valley. She found one closer, down on the patio. There were two people talking who she didn't recognise.

She leaned over the railing to get a better look, wondering if more wellness influencers had arrived late. Both were women, and one was in a black uniform. The uniformed woman had a tight bun, while the one in a white blouse had wild, bushy hair with sun-kissed highlights. Their body language was tense as they talked in hushed voices. Jessie couldn't make it out, but even being in a different country, she could always spot the police from a mile away.

Jessie changed from her pyjamas into a baggy vest and denim shorts and left her hotel room, careful to close her door. She heard Barker snoring behind his door as she tiptoed past.

She crept downstairs to find the hotel transformed into a bustling crime scene. Police officers and forensic officers swarmed the lobby and dining area. The bushy-haired woman Jessie had spotted on the patio was now addressing a group of black-clad officers in rapid Spanish. Jessie spoke little Spanish, but didn't need a language degree to understand 'suicidio.'

Glancing around, Jessie noticed Dot, Ethel, and Percy huddled in the corner of the dining room. Jessie considered joining them, but movement outside the front doors caught her eye—Chef Luca, pacing on the terracotta tiles, gesturing with both hands as he spoke to someone out of sight. A lit cigarette dangled from his lips.

Jessie's journalistic instincts kicked in, reminded of Veronica's advice to never let her guard down when a story was unfolding. She tiptoed towards the front doors, but with minimal furniture to conceal her, she knelt by the marble sculpture, pretending to tie her shoe.

Jessie leaned in closer, straining to hear Luca's hushed words.

"This looks terrible," Luca muttered, dragging on his cigarette. "And now the police are searching my kitchen? They must think I did this."

"It's just a precaution, Luca," said the soothing tones of Dahlia. "No one is jumping to murder just yet. She seemed drunk... maybe she fell asleep and drowned?"

Jessie's heart skipped a beat.

Who were they talking about?

Who had drowned?

"You do not understand," Luca continued, ignoring Dahlia's reassurance. "After what happened in Bali, this is going to look even worse for me. I need to get out of here. Get ahead of this."

Bali? Jessie's mind raced, struggling to piece together what Luca could be referencing. She had heard nothing about Bali until now, but she put a pin in it.

"Chloe is dead, which means the Bali incident is under wraps," Dahlia replied, each word as slow as Jessie would talk to Olivia. "It will only make you look more suspicious if you flee now. Unless... you have something to hide?"

Jessie detected an edge in Dahlia's tone on that last question. Luca seemed shocked, sputtering something in Italian before shaking his head and stamping out his cigarette. Without another word to Dahlia, he turned and headed back inside the hotel. Jessie froze when Luca's eyes went straight to her. His stare narrowed, and for a moment, she thought he might confront her. But he turned and strode towards the stairs up to the rooms.

Jessie leapt to her feet and rushed after him into the lobby.

"Chef Valenti?"

Luca kept walking, his pace quickening.

"I need to ask you about what you were arguing with Chloe about yesterday," she called. "I saw you with her in the square."

Luca halted in his tracks. He wheeled around to face her, his dark-lashed stare narrowing to black slits.

"What do you know?"

"It sounded like Chloe was trying to blackmail you. Anything to do with what happened in Bali, by any chance?"

"You know nothing about Bali. That woman, she thought she could threaten me? *Me*? I have done *nothing* wrong." He jabbed a finger towards Jessie. "Do not believe her lies. She was trying to ruin me for her amusement. Spreading nonsense about my food, insulting my work. She was poison." His chest heaved with anger. Then he leaned in close to Jessie and lowered his voice. "I am not the only one she has been blackmailing. You want to know the truth? Talk to the doctor."

With that, he turned and stormed away down the hall. Jessie watched him go, her mind racing. Blackmail? The doctor? What was going on here? Footsteps behind Jessie made her turn. Dahlia entered the lobby, pale and shaken in a black floor-length linen dress.

"What happened?" Jessie asked. "Is it true about Chloe?"

Dahlia nodded, her eyes welling up with tears.

"I'm afraid so. She's dead. Drowned in the mineral baths last night."

"Damn," Jessie murmured. "Suicide?"

"It's seeming that way. Or an accident—"

"*Accident*?" Dot scoffed, appearing beside them with Percy and Ethel, all decked out in summer brights. "You could have cut the tension at dinner last night with a wooden spoon. What happened to Chloe was no accident."

"Now, Dot," Percy cautioned, "we shouldn't jump to conclusions."

"The police will handle this," Dahlia added, clasping her hands. "I need to find Minnie. As you will understand, she's quite distressed. Excuse me."

Dot watched Dahlia leave with pinched lips and a tight stare; the death seemed to have shaken away her fear about being here long enough for the Dot Jessie knew and loved to come back.

"Thoughts?" Jessie asked.

"Mark my words, dear, this was no accident," Dot said. "Minnie and I found her in the baths. Face down with a bottle of empty vodka beside her. She might have been an unbearable twit, but I don't think she was an idiot. Even if she was drunk... she wouldn't have drowned, and she was far too vain to take her own life."

Ethel looped her arm through Jessie's. "Come on before the police lock this place down and none of us can leave. I'm famished for breakfast, and the café should be open by now."

As she walked out into the piercing Savega sun, Jessie had murder on her mind.

Julia paused outside her hotel room door, clutching the handle of Olivia's pram in disbelief as Dahlia—collecting towels in a laundry hamper—recounted the shocking events that had unfolded that morning.

"I still can't believe it," Dahlia said, hushed. "Your gran finding Chloe like that in the baths... it's just awful."

Julia nodded, thinking back to the tense atmosphere at dinner the previous night. Chloe had rubbed so many people the wrong way, herself included. But for her life to end so tragically... Julia shuddered.

"The police don't seem to think it's suspicious,"

Dahlia continued. "They think she had too much to drink, fell asleep in the bath, and slipped under the water. I know she took sleeping pills from time to time. Maybe they interacted. The detective isn't treating the hotel like a crime scene. There's no rush to collect evidence or take statements."

Julia furrowed her brow. If foul play was involved, crucial evidence could already be compromised.

"I wanted to check on Minnie, but she's inconsolable right now," Dahlia said, nodding towards the hamper filled with towels. "I'm trying to keep the hotel running during all this. Any towels for the wash?"

"Not yet," Julia said, concerned about more pressing matters at hand. "Did you know Chloe well?"

"We'd crossed paths at various retreats and launches over the years." Dahlia rested a finger under nose. "She was far too young to die like this."

"I'm sorry. This must be very difficult for you."

Dahlia composed herself with a deep breath. "I should let you get back to your family. Don't let this spoil your holiday. I'll manage things here and update you if anything changes."

Julia nodded, though an uneasy feeling still lingered.

"Drinking and sleeping pills?" she echoed. "That sounds like a dangerous combination."

Across the corridor, a door opened, and Ian emerged, dressed in bright tie-dye athletic gear.

"Couldn't help but overhear, but did you say Chloe has been drinking?" he pointed out. "Being 'sober' is a huge part of her online persona. How has she made a fool of herself this time?"

A lump rose in Julia's throat.

"Chloe is... dead," Dahlia said, looking at the floor. "Drowned in the mineral baths."

"Oh," Ian said, and nothing more came.

"Listen, I don't like to speak ill of the dead," Dahlia said, her tone dropping to a gossipy whisper that would have suited the café more than the stark white corridor of the wellness retreat. "Chloe confided in me once that the only reason she was sober now was because she'd been quite the party girl in her youth. I suppose recent stresses could have pushed her back into old habits?"

Ian grumbled low in his throat. "I suppose. Chloe claimed *a lot* of things, didn't she?"

"What are you hinting at?" Julia asked, intrigued by his cryptic tone. She thought back to Ian's abrupt exit from the dinner table. "There was tension between you. What happened?"

Ian's jaw tightened before he took a slow and measured inhale through his nostrils. "Let's just say Chloe had a habit of trying to ruin reputations without evidence. We've *all* experienced it. The girl was troubled."

"And no longer here to defend herself," Dahlia said, raising a hand. "This was nothing more than a tragic accident, but I'm sure the police will want to speak with you, Ian. Anything for the hamper?"

Ian left his bedroom door open and made his way downstairs, and after scooping up Ian's laundry, Dahlia continued down the corridor. Pulling Olivia's pram back into the room, Barker emerged from the shower.

"That was a quick walk," he said, towel-drying his hair. "I've just had a brilliant idea for a scene. Maybe this water *is* magical after all. I was thinking for the second chapter of Act Two, the killer could—"

"Your book may have to wait, love," Julia interrupted as Barker dripped onto her open-toe sandals. "I didn't get any further than the corridor. There's an actual scene unfolding here."

"Another melodramatic *Eastenders* scene like last night's dinner?"

"More like *Death in Paradise*," Julia said, leaning in. "Chloe Saunders is dead."

Minnie paced around her apartment on the top floor, and all Dot could do was watch. The last time Dot had been here, the walls had been plastered with photos of Minnie rubbing shoulders with celebrities and dignitaries.

The pictures were now in an album, but Dot was relieved to see Minnie's flair hadn't been suppressed across the whole hotel—the décor was just as Dot remembered, with warm red walls, ornate wooden furniture, and splashes of colour from textured fabrics.

An assault on the senses, and a welcome one at that.

And Minnie was out of white and back in one of her

oversized leopard-print kaftans. Back in her old look, her weight loss was even more drastic.

"It's happening *again*, Dorothy!" Minnie cried. "I should have let the flood wash this place away when I had the chance. La Casa is cursed."

"Now, Minnie, we know nothing for certain yet." She clasped Minnie's hands to stop her frantic movements. "Try to take some deep breaths. What was it Dahlia taught you about meditation?"

"Deep breathing won't help me now. What if this is *him*? What if Rodger escaped prison and has come for his revenge?"

"I doubt that's the case," Dot said, unsure of what to say. "Percy?"

"Right, love." Percy tapped a finger to his chin before saying, "If Rodger wanted to get revenge, he'd have drowned *you* and not that girl?"

Dot shot him a look as Minnie wailed and collapsed into a chair. In the nick of time, Ethel breezed in with a shopping bag.

"Got the goods," she announced, pulling out a bottle of sangria.

Minnie shuffled from her chair and produced some crystal glasses from a cupboard, staring at the only picture left on the wall once cluttered with frames. It was a picture of Lisa and Minnie from Lisa's childhood. They were on a beach somewhere, both grinning at the camera. Happier times. Ethel poured her a generous glass, but Minnie only stared at it, not drinking.

"Come sit back down," Dot said, guiding Minnie to

the couch. She took the glass from Minnie's hand and placed it on an ornate side table. "You're not alone. We're here."

Minnie nodded, exhaling as she sank into the cushions. Dorothy sat beside her, patting her hand. Dot thought back to her distraught state in her cottage only the morning before—how the tables had turned.

"Sangria, anyone?"

"I'm not sure now's the time, Ethel," Dot said, and Ethel huffed but didn't argue. An awkward silence descended on the room. "Let's just hope the police are figuring this out. We must try to keep a level head."

"I heard something on my way—"

"Please, Ethel. Not just now. I don't think Minnie can handle any more news."

Ethel clamped her mouth shut, scowling before sipping sangria.

"How about some tea?" Dot asked Minnie. "We have some real tea bags with actual caffeine in our room. Percy, why don't you fetch them?"

"Right you are, dear."

"Dorothy, I overheard the police talking and…"

"Yes, yes, Ethel," she snapped, irritation creeping into her tone—trust Ethel not to restrain herself for five minutes. "What is it?"

"They were speaking in Spanish. I heard them clear as day on my way up here."

"You… you speak *Spanish*?"

"There's much you don't know about me, Dorothy," Ethel said with a delighted grin. "I had rather expensive cable television in the nineties, so while you were stuck with four channels, I had four hundred. I was channel hopping one day and got stuck watching a Telenovela. Fell in love with the drama of it all, so I ordered some tapes that I saw advertised in the paper and learned at home." She walked over, and with a finger under Dot's chin, closed her mouth. "You'll catch flies."

Dot sank back onto the couch, dumbfounded. She caught Percy's eye, and he looked just as flabbergasted by this revelation. Minnie asked something in fluent Spanish, and after a moment's thought, Ethel replied in the same language. The two women conversed while Dot and Percy stared at each other like spare parts.

"Translation?" Dot asked.

"I overheard a police officer telling another officer that they're going to shut the hotel down so they can comb every inch for evidence."

"Evidence of what?" Dot asked.

"The girl drowned, but not *in* the mineral bath," Ethel announced, folding her arms. "She had soapy water in her lungs, so it seems she was drowned in a regular bath and then moved there."

A stunned silence followed this revelation. Minnie let out a strangled cry and reached for the glass of sangria, draining it in one gulp.

This changed everything.

If Chloe had been drowned, then they *were* dealing with something far more sinister than an empty bottle of vodka and a tragic accident.

Dot poured herself a small glass of sangria, taking a

bracing sip. As the tart liquid hit her tongue, she turned and gazed out the window at the distant hills.

That reckoning would have to wait.

Right now, her family needed her.

And Minnie was family.

Dot set her glass down with a clearing of her throat.

"We *will* sort this out," she declared, meeting Minnie's frightened eyes. "I promise you, we won't rest until we find out who did this to that girl."

Minnie sniffed, dabbing at her eyes with a leopard print sleeve. Dot felt a rush of tenderness for Minnie, this dramatic, colourful woman whom she'd only seen a handful of times over the past several decades. But they were family, and Albert would have wanted Dot to look after his sister.

Come what may, Dot would find the answers.

Right after she finished her sangria.

7

Julia and Barker returned to their hotel room, exhausted after a long day of questioning by the police. As soon as the door closed behind them, Barker sat on the edge of the bed, rubbing his temples.

"Not the start to the holiday I was expecting," he said.

"So much for relaxing fun under the sun." Julia laughed half-heartedly. "I suppose we could stay out of things. Pretend it's not happening... sunbathe... go on boat trips... all the things we planned."

"Come on, Julia. A woman died under suspicious circumstances at *your* great-aunt's hotel. You can't just ignore it." Barker raised an eyebrow. "I know you won't ignore it."

She wished she hadn't spent all day thinking about it.
Wondering.
Speculating.

Piecing together scraps.

But she couldn't stop her mind from doing what it does. Her curiosity was well and truly piqued.

"You're right," she admitted, pulling Olivia's pyjamas out of the drawers to get her ready for bed. "I want to sort this out. But I don't want to worry the family any more than necessary. They all deserve a break."

"You think they'll be able to relax with everything that's going on?"

"Sue and Neil seem to have had a relaxing day."

"And Jessie and your gran and her gang haven't sat still for a moment, and—"

"Good point," Julia said. "I'm going to start with Dahlia. She's been open with me so far, so hopefully she'll share more details that could help."

Barker agreed with a nod. "And Ian is across the hall. You might get him to open up about what happened between him and Chloe before they came here. Could be important."

A knock at the door made them both jump. Julia opened it to find Jessie standing there, shifting her feet.

"Have you been questioned too?" Jessie asked.

"We just got back from the station. We were discussing the peculiar events around here. I think…"

"Of course you are," Jessie cut in with a roll of her eyes, striding into the room. "And so am I. That chef gives me the creeps. I'm going to see what I can get out of him."

Before Julia could close the door, Dot hurried down the hallway and bombed inside.

"Don't think you're having all the fun without me," she said. "These walls are paper thin." Pursing her lips, she glared at Barker—she must have been kept up by his snoring. "I'll speak to Doctor Helena. I already have a foot in the door with her. Any advice, Barker Brown PI?"

Barker considered his response as he placed Olivia in her cot by the window. After a moment, he turned with folded arms, rocking back on his heels.

"Pin down everyone's whereabouts early this morning and find out their relationships with Chloe," he said. "A lot seems to have happened before everyone arrived at La Casa. I wouldn't be surprised if the answer to what's happening here lies in the past. Unravel the past, unravel the motives. But with Ian, Luca, Dahlia, and Helena, you've got a lot of—"

"Minnie too," Jessie said. "She's been acting too strange not to be a suspect."

"That's preposterous!" Dot shook her head. "No, I won't have it. Minnie would never hurt a fly."

But Julia interjected, understanding Jessie's reasoning. Julia might not have known her great-aunt too well, but she knew she wasn't acting like herself. She wasn't sure Minnie would turn to murder, but stranger things had happened.

"We should try to confirm her alibi," Julia said, resting a hand on her gran's shoulder. "At least until we know the full picture. Just to be thorough... to rule her out."

Dot still looked sceptical, but she didn't argue further.

"Only to rule her out," Dot confirmed, pulling on the door handle. "But mark my words, Minnie didn't murder that girl. I've known Minnie since she was knee high to a grasshopper. She's no killer."

Dot yanked open the door to find the bushy-haired detective standing in the corridor, fist raised as though she'd been about to knock, a slight tilt of the head suggesting she was evaluating the scenario within the room before her.

"Buenas noches," she greeted, stepping inside just enough to maintain personal space yet close enough to engage. "I hope I'm not intruding, but it seemed a suitable moment to introduce myself." She produced a business card with a flick of her wrist. "I'm Detective Catalina Ramirez, the lead on the Saunders case."

"We were discussing dinner plans," Dot said, a little too quick and loud. "Nothing strange is going on."

"Right." The detective smiled. "We're all going to be seeing a lot more of each other, so I wanted to introduce myself."

"Any leads, Detective?" Barker asked, a note of professional courtesy in his voice.

"I'm afraid I can't share that information," she said, her expression giving away nothing. Her gaze swept the room once more, a silent assessment of their collective state.

"He's a detective as well," Dot announced. "Sort of. Used to be."

Ramirez offered a tight, confused smile at Dot before turning her attention to Julia.

"We believe this was no accident, so I'd like to speak with you all if you have a moment."

"Now see here," Dot said, extending a finger, "my family had nothing to do with this. We're innocent. Minnie too. *Innocent*."

"Please, I know that," Ramirez assured, fanning her hands. "But I believe you all witnessed some tensions between Saunders and the other guests prior to her death. Anything you can share would be very helpful for my investigation."

Ramirez pulled a compact notepad from her jacket and flipped it open to an unused page, directing her gaze towards Julia. Their paths had crossed in the station's corridor, where Ramirez had admired Julia's dress—a seemingly minor gesture—but she was familiar to the detective now, and it seemed she was looking at her to take the lead.

"You're right, Detective," Julia said, taking a step closer. "There've been strange undercurrents here since we arrived. Chloe was rather dismissive towards... well, everyone. The chef, Luca, spilled soup on her and she lost her temper."

"And Luca insinuated Chloe had done something to Ian," Jessie added. "And I saw Luca and Chloe arguing in the plaza earlier."

"And how did the others appear to regard Miss Saunders?" Ramirez inquired, her tone devoid of leading inflection.

"Dahlia tried to smooth things over," Julia said, "but I could tell she was annoyed by Chloe's behaviour, but she was the most patient with her. Ian and Helena both walked out soon after Chloe arrived."

"And I heard them talking about Chloe when I was looking for Minnie yesterday," Dot said, wagging her finger. "I didn't realise it at the time, but they must have been talking about Chloe. They said they couldn't believe Dahlia invited Chloe. According to them, Chloe wrote something, and I'm not sure what."

"Anything else?"

Julia looked from Jessie to Dot, but they both shrugged.

"Your observations are invaluable," Ramirez said once the impromptu debriefing concluded, closing her notebook with a soft snap that punctuated the end of their exchange. "Should anything else come to mind that might be of relevance, please do not hesitate to reach out. Since you're all guests here, just... pay attention."

"We'll try," Julia said, tapping the card on her palm. "Thank you, Detective."

Ramirez gave a brisk nod and excused herself. As soon as she was out the door, Julia closed it behind her and turned to the rest of them. Despite the guilt tripping her heartbeat, a heady determination flamed in her chest.

"So," Julia said, exhaling as she looked at the card, "let's see what we can find out for the detective. We start tomorrow."

8

Julia soaked in the warm morning sun, seated on the front patio of Café Rosado in Savega's plaza. The bright rays caused a rainbow to dance in the burbling fountain, where her daughter Olivia chased plump white pigeons with her cousins. Sue and Neil watched the children from a nearby bench while feeding more birds, their laughter ringing out across the cobbled plaza.

She sipped the rich coffee she'd ordered instead of her usual tea. The aroma had been irresistible when Barker ordered his, though she had emergency peppermint and liquorice tea bags stashed in her handbag. Her husband sat immersed in his manuscript next to her, nibbling on toast rubbed with tomato and drizzled with green olive oil.

Despite insisting last night that they investigate first thing, Julia hadn't been able to resist a slow start to the day. Savega moved at a relaxed pace, so different from the brisk morning rush at her own café back in Peridale. The tables here were tiny, just big enough for a coffee cup or two, not the generous surfaces for towering cream teas and triple-layer cakes her customers expected. Instead of clotted cream and jam, little clay dishes held olive oil, fleur de sel, and crushed tomatoes. And the menu was scribbled in colourful chalk, not the neat laminated pages that were wiped down after each use at her place.

Yet the hushed gossip drifting from the table of older Spanish women next to her would have fit right in at home. Their glances towards the side street leading to Minnie's hotel confirmed they were whispering about the shocking death of the drowned influencer. Some things were universal—murder and gossip went together like Savega and sunshine.

She finished the last sweet, flaky bite of her Miguelito pastry, filled with rich custard cream. As she dabbed the crumbs from her lips, Olivia's bubbly laugh rang out, causing the gossiping women to pause and smile. Julia's heart swelled at the sight of her daughter's pure joy as she chased the pigeons.

For a moment, all seemed right in the world.

Sue and Neil returned to the table with the kids in tow. Olivia scrambled onto Julia's lap, her cheeks flushed pink. Neil had a pamphlet advertising local properties for sale. He flipped through photos of whitewashed villas and ocean views, pointing them out to Sue.

"Some of these are quite affordable," he said.

"I know, it's unbelievable," Sue said, picking up her

abandoned coffee. "And just *look* at this place—no one's in a rush here. Even when it gets busy, there's still a relaxed vibe."

"Peridale's known for being a high-flying metropolis," Barker said with a dry smile.

"I know, I know. But even on the quiet days, the old ladies always seem to scurry about like there's a fire even when nothing's happening." Sue took a deep breath, gazing around the sunny plaza. "I can actually *breathe*. After everything we've been through in Peridale these past few years, doesn't the thought of getting out ever cross your mind?"

Julia froze, surprised. Was Sue suggesting... moving here? She'd known Sue's 'one-year break from nursing to work at the café' had just been a sabbatical, and that was ending—was this her next step?

"Moving abroad isn't easy," Barker said, setting his manuscript down. "Especially with young kids."

Julia squeezed his hand, still processing Sue's unexpected words. Was a move really on her sister's mind? She fiddled with her empty coffee cup, unsure of how to respond.

Neil set down the pamphlet, and said, "I know it seems sudden, but think about it. The cost of living here is more affordable. We could get a lovely villa near the beach for a *fraction* of what our home cost back in Peridale."

"And the twins are starting school in September. It would be the perfect time for the kids to transition if we were going to do this."

Julia glanced at her nieces, still giggling as they tossed seeds at the birds. She had to admit the idea of them growing up in this idyllic seaside town painted an appealing picture.

Her gaze drifted down the cobbled side street to Minnie's hotel. She could make out Detective Ramirez conferring with her aunt near the front entrance. A police cordon still surrounded the entrance.

She shivered, the idyllic charm of Savega pierced by the reality that a woman had died here under suspicious circumstances. Julia realised Sue and Neil's eyes were still fixed on the postcard-perfect scene around them, not noticing the police presence down the lane.

Barker squeezed her knee under the table, and before she could dwell further, a burst of yellow tie-dye entered the square, interrupting her thoughts. Ian Fletcher sauntered towards the central fountain, his loose linen shirt and pants rippling in the warm breeze. Reaching the fountain's edge, he folded himself into a cross-legged seat atop the stone.

Ian tilted his face up towards the beaming Spanish sun as the water erupted behind him. He closed his eyes and exhaled in a slow, measured breath, as if releasing all the concerns of the world. His shoulders relaxed while his hands rested on his knees, palms upturned. After a moment, the tense lines on his brow softened into tranquillity.

Julia hesitated, watching Ian's silent meditation. She was reluctant to disturb his peaceful state, especially after the upheaval of recent events. Yet she knew this could be a prime opportunity to glean his perspective on the 'accident' at La Casa.

Glancing again at Sue and Neil's brochure-focused bubble, Julia decided there was no better time than now for an informal chat. She stood, brushing the crumbs from her green maxi dress, and approached the sun-soaked fountain.

She sat down on the sun-warmed stone edge, crossing her legs to mirror Ian's meditative pose. She closed her eyes and tipped her face towards the brilliant sunlight, feeling its radiant heat soak into her skin.

They sat in contemplative silence for a moment, the bubbling burble of water behind them mingling with the muted hubbub of the plaza. Then Olivia's voice rang out—"*Mummy!*"—making them both chuckle.

"She seems like a sweet child," Ian commented, eyes still closed. "Happy."

"She is."

Ian's lips lifted into a half-smile deep in his beard.

"The blissful ignorance of youth. You couldn't even begin to explain to her what was happening at La Casa."

"That's probably for the best."

"Wise." At the mention of recent events, he shifted a little on the fountain's edge. "Chloe was closer to your young daughter's age than my own. Funny how fast they can turn from innocent cherubs to..." He trailed off, leaving the obvious unsaid.

"Chloe was anything but innocent," Julia responded. "But what happened to her was tragic and unnecessary.

The police are saying she was drowned somewhere else and moved."

He shifted again.

"Yes, I heard that."

"Did you know her long?"

"We moved in the same circles," he replied after a pause. "The wellness space is vast, but everyone seems to know everyone, especially those with many followers."

"Chloe had over a million. She mentioned it."

"Yes, that sounds like something Chloe would do. I have around one hundred thousand," he said. "I'm happy with my lot. I make enough to get by so I can live life on my terms."

He explained how he made a living through online meditating seminars and in-person workshops around the world, thanks to social media.

"But it's a double-edged sword," he mused. "I watched the spotlight taint Chloe. I met her when she was young enough to have that naïve excitement that children have. I watched it die as her followers and wealth increased." He uncrossed his legs and stood, joints cracking. "After she wrote that book, she rocketed up in the ranks, but that's exactly what she wanted."

"What book was that?" Julia asked.

"*How I Survived a Serial Killer... and Thrived* by Chloe Saunders," Ian said, following it with a heavy exhale. "Yes, I know. Quite the shocking title, but it was a bestseller. Though I suppose they all are these days."

"She survived a serial killer?" Julia's eyes widened. "Which one?"

"She kept their identity anonymous. Claimed she didn't want to give them the free press." He shrugged, looking out to the ocean far off in the distance. "There were people who thought she made the whole thing up, but by the time those rumours started, she'd gained all she wanted from it, so what did it matter?"

"She *faked* escaping a murderer?"

"Ironic, I know. I always assumed she didn't disclose their name because she didn't want to be sued." He met Julia's gaze with a soft smile. "If you want to know more about the book, talk to Dahlia. She read the thing cover to cover, so she knows more than I do."

Ian turned to leave, but Julia had another nagging question.

"Yesterday in the hotel corridor, you mentioned Chloe tried to ruin your reputation. What did you mean by that?"

He stared off to the shimmering water, considering for a moment whether to reply, then said, "Chloe's large following was a powerful force to be reckoned with. She could sell them whatever she wanted, get them to believe anything she could think up... she used that power to humiliate me when I still trusted her."

"Humiliate you how?"

"I... I'd rather not talk about it right now," he said, running his fingers over his moustache. "She got what she wanted out of it. That's what she did. It's almost a shame she's dead. I imagine the morbid sensationalism of her passing has rocketed her book back up the charts."

With a brief bow, he descended the steep blue and white tiled steps towards the distant ocean and beach. For a moment, Julia stayed where she was going over what he'd told her. He'd said so little, dodged a lot, and yet he'd dropped a bombshell she hadn't been expecting.

"*How I Survived a Serial Killer... and Thrived*," Julia repeated aloud as she typed the book title into her Amazon app.

The paperback and hardback versions had sold out, with only the eBook available to purchase. Regardless, an orange 'BEST SELLER' badge shone under a new subheading: 'The Shocking Prelude to the Wellness Influencer's Tragic Murder.'

Morbid sensationalism indeed, Julia thought with a shudder.

Dot hovered in the doorway to the hotel's kitchen, peering around the corner as Doctor Helena Ford arranged a photoshoot atop the central island. The stainless-steel surfaces reflected the bright artificial lights overhead, glinting off the array of pill bottles Helena had lined up in regimented rows. Each container seemed to contain a different concoction of questionable potions.

"Not like you to be shy, Dorothy," Ethel whispered from behind. "Let's see what she's up to."

"I'm being *covert*, Ethel. We're not all bulls in china shops like you."

"If I'm a bull, you're an old cow."

With a nudge from Ethel, Dot pushed through the swinging doors into the kitchen. She cleared her throat and smiled her an apology as Helena's head whipped around, snapping a picture of the floor instead of her makeshift set-up.

"I'm terribly sorry," Dot said, feigning her best 'little old lady' voice. "I didn't mean to interrupt. I was just hoping to grab some fruit from the fridge."

Helena's shoulders tensed as she shielded the display with her body.

"Help yourself," Helena said. "I need to get on with my work, though."

"How interesting." Dot gestured at the pills. "Some sort of photoshoot?"

Helena nodded, regaining her composure. "I know the timing isn't perfect, but this was always supposed to be a working holiday for me. I should have stacked the content yesterday, but with everything going on..."

Stacked the content? Must have been an industry term, and Dot didn't care to find out. She was interested in the bottles though. They were so bright and eye-catching, and she couldn't help but pluck out a turquoise one.

"That's my patented 'Brain Boost' formula," Helena explained, pulling another bottle from a box under the counter to replace it in the photoshoot. "A proprietary blend of omega-3s, ginkgo biloba, and lutein to support cognitive function."

"It's quite... vibrant looking."

"The colours make them pop on social media," Helena explained. "Plus, it'll help them stand out on shop shelves. I'm sure they'll be stocked somewhere any day now. The coral one is my anti-aging formula."

"Anti-aging, you say?" Ethel twisted the bottle in the light. "How many years will this shave off?"

"It's scientifically formulated with antioxidants and peptides to reduce wrinkles and boost collagen production."

"Hmm," Ethel grumbled. "And the third one?"

"That's my hair, skin, and nails formula." Helena held it up. "Biotin, vitamin E, zinc... everything you need for beauty from within."

"But do they work?" Dot pursed her lips. "Seems suspicious to me, all these coloured pills claiming to be magic cures."

Helena bristled, taking the bottles back and clutching them to her chest.

"I assure you—I have researched and tested these formulations. I would never sell anything that wasn't backed by hard science. They're *luxury* items."

"No offense intended," Dot said. "It's just, in my day, good health came from simple things like eating your vegetables and fresh air, not popping pills."

Sighing, Helena set the containers down.

"I understand your scepticism, and I admit the

supplement industry has issues with false claims. But I am committed to creating high-quality, research-based formulas that provide real benefits." She selected two coral bottles from the box and extended them. "Why don't you try them for yourself, free of charge, and then decide? Consider it my gift to you for your open-mindedness."

"Can't say no to a freebie," Ethel said. "How much do you flog these for?"

"They retail for £49.99."

"Crikey," Ethel cried. "They'd better work for that price."

"Money-back guarantee."

Dot eyed the offering, making no move to accept it.

"Please, I insist. This is a simple gesture of goodwill, no strings attached."

"That's very kind of you." Dot held up a hand. "But I wouldn't want to mix anything new in without asking my doctor first."

"I *am* a doctor." Helena pursed her lips, retracting the sample. Dot couldn't help but notice the woman's jaw tighten as her smile returned. "But of course. I understand. The offer stands if you change your mind."

Dot regarded the doctor as she busied herself rearranging the pill bottles into a new formation, avoiding eye contact.

"Like I said, that's very kind," Dot said, but she wasn't there for small talk about Helena's overpriced snake oil. "Where were you in the early hours this morning, Doctor Ford?"

Helena froze, fumbling with a turquoise container before regaining her grip. She let out an uneasy laugh.

"You're not suggesting I had something to do with Chloe's death?"

"I'm not *suggesting* anything," Dot said, hands folded over her floral print dress. "Merely asking a simple question."

Setting down the bottle with a clink, Helena turned to face her.

"Well, since you asked, I was fast asleep in my room, of course. Sleep is very important to me. I never stay awake past midnight."

"Can you prove that?" Ethel asked

"Why on earth would *I* want to harm Chloe? I'm a doctor, for goodness' sake. I help people. I don't go around committing murder."

"So, you can't prove it?"

"No, I cannot. I was alone."

"You did seem rather perturbed with Chloe at dinner last night," Ethel pointed out. "You stormed off after she said something about your claims about the mineral water."

"I didn't *storm* off. I left calmly." Helena waved a manicured hand. "Please, I've dealt with far worse than Chloe's childish pot-stirring. She enjoyed getting a reaction out of people, that's all it was. If you hadn't noticed, she rubbed *everyone* the wrong way, yourselves included."

"Then why was she invited here, if she had such friction with yourself and others?" Dot said.

"Her social media following was invaluable for publicity. An endorsement from Chloe would have guaranteed this place booked solid for months. Dahlia understood that, even if the rest of us found her insufferable."

Dot observed Helena as the doctor busied herself arranging bottles. The tension in the room was electric, like the heavy stillness before a thunderstorm —and Dot had another bolt of lightning up her floral sleeve.

Clearing her throat, Dot said, "I overheard part of your conversation with Ian yesterday before you showed us down to the cellar. Something about being surprised Chloe was invited after—what was it you said?—'After what she wrote.'"

Helena's shoulders tensed, her movements stilling. When she turned around, her face was composed.

"Yes, I was referring to that scandalous book Chloe put out last year."

"What book?" Ethel asked.

"A true crime book, of sorts. Chloe claimed she had nearly been a victim of a notorious serial killer and proceeded to... *embellish* a rather sensational account of her 'near death' experience."

"A *serial* killer?" Ethel's eyes widened. "My word."

"And I take it the details of this book ruffled some feathers?"

"That's putting it lightly," Helena huffed. "It was beyond distasteful. Dredging up such horrors just to make a quick coin and get attention."

"But was it true?" Ethel pressed. "Did she really almost get done in by some madman?"

"Who knows? She had a penchant for creative liberties, shall we say? Her photographs were edited beyond recognition, and she'd promote products she never actually used. With Chloe, the line between fact and fiction was razor thin."

"Did her account of events contradict the official story?" Dot asked. "Who was this murderer?"

"I really shouldn't say any more." Helena pursed her lips. "Chloe made a lot of unsubstantiated claims, and it's impossible to know where the truth ended and the fabrication began. I don't want to spread rumours about such a sensitive matter. If you're that interested, read the book."

"I think I might have to," Dot said, and sensing the doctor's evasiveness about the topic, she switched gears. "Since we're here, I also wanted to ask about the mineral water you've been endorsing. Chloe seemed to cast doubt on your claims last night."

"I will *not* have my work called into question. Those water samples were tested, the results reviewed by multiple experts."

"Chloe didn't seem so sure," Ethel said.

"Absolute *nonsense*!" Helena forced a laugh as she lay plastic palm leaves atop a pink sheet of cardboard before arranging the bottles in a pyramid. "I oversaw the analysis myself in an accredited laboratory. The mineral content and unique properties of that water are one hundred percent *real*."

Dot regarded the bottles lined up on the counter as Helena busied herself with her camera equipment. The doctor certainly talked a convincing game about the legitimacy of her products, but something still seemed off.

Doctor Helena Ford was far too defensive.

Before Dot could inquire further, Dahlia swept into the kitchen, her heels clicking on the tile.

"How are the product shots coming along?" Dahlia asked, glancing at her watch. "We're on a tight timeline to get these over to the editor for their launch on the app."

"I'm just finishing up now. I've been distracted."

Dahlia's gaze narrowed on Dot and Ethel.

"What are you two doing in here? This is a closed photoshoot."

"We were just having a chat with the good doctor here about her miracle supplements," Ethel piped up. "And I thought we were honoured guests."

"Of course." Dahlia pushed forward an icy smile. "You'll have to excuse the intrusion, Helena. I'm sure our *honoured* guests are simply curious about our resident wellness expert."

"It's no trouble. I was happy to answer their questions."

Dot and Ethel exchanged raised eyebrows.

"Yes, well, I'm afraid you'll have to cut your little demonstration short," Dahlia said, tapping her watch. "We need those photos edited and submitted within the hour if we're going to meet upload deadlines for the launch."

"Bit last minute, isn't it?" Ethel said.

"They were supposed to be shot yesterday, but things have taken an unfortunate turn."

"And these are going to be launched on your..." Dot clicked her fingers. "What was it called? Bellissimo app?"

"*Blisselle*," Dahlia corrected, looking pleased with herself. "But you are correct. I'm featuring Doctor Ford's product line. Her luxury vitamin formulations will be available for direct purchase exclusively through my platform, and they're sure to be a hit. But only with finished pictures to post..."

Dot watched as Helena arranged a few final pill bottles, the bright colours reflecting in the sleek steel surfaces of the kitchen. With quick, efficient movements, she took a series of photos from different angles, checking each shot on a small preview screen.

"I think that should do it," Helena muttered, more to herself than Dot or Ethel. She tapped away on her phone, presumably sending the images to Dahlia. After a few moments, she set the phone down with a definitive click against the countertop. "Right, all set. I think that's everything."

"Excellent. I'll review and send them off straight away. Thank you for working so quickly. I know it was short notice."

"Of course." Helena gave a polite smile that didn't quite reach her eyes. "I'm excited for our partnership to begin."

"I know your products will be our biggest seller. They really do pop."

Helena flushed at the compliment and said, "I hope so."

"They will, no doubt about it." Dahlia checked her watch again. "Now, if you'll excuse me, I must run. A million little fires to put out before we open the doors to this place. Minnie is still in a state of shock, and the police have turned this place upside down in their search for evidence. So much to put right."

She turned on her heels and marched towards the exit in a blur of white linen. At the doorway, she paused and cast a pointed look at Dot and Ethel.

"Ladies, I trust you can show yourselves out? Guests, honoured or not, shouldn't be back here."

The instruction was polite yet firm. With a swish of blonde hair, Dahlia disappeared down the hallway, and after packing up her makeshift photo studio, the doctor followed her out.

Dot watched as Ethel pocketed two of the coral-coloured anti-aging supplement bottles as the door swung shut.

"Stealing, Ethel? That's low, even for you."

"I'm taking the one you didn't want."

"And the other?"

"They're worth almost *fifty* quid." Ethel hovered over the box before stuffing another bottle into her pocket. "All the packing labels on the box are in Chinese. I bet she had them made in the thousands for pennies."

"So, you speak Chinese *and* Spanish?"

"Wouldn't that be something?"

"Ethel..."

"It looks like the writing on the menu of the Lucky Star takeaway on Mulberry Lane back home, that's all. Almost wish I could read it just to see the look on your face." Ethel grinned over her shoulder as another bottle went into her bursting pockets. She ripped off the cardboard flap with the shipping label. "Can find out where she has them made. See if they're all she's saying. I wonder if these really do work?"

Before Dot could object, Ethel had twisted open a bottle and tapped two coral pills into her palm. Without hesitation, she popped them into her mouth and swallowed them dry.

"Ethel! You don't know what's in those. They could be anything."

"Anything that keeps me spry is fine by me," Ethel said with a wink. "Doctor said they're specially formulated. *Luxury*. I'm sure they're as harmless as she claims."

"Helena also claimed that smelly mineral water could practically regrow limbs and have an eighty-year-old doing backflips from just one sip. I don't trust her quack remedies one bit."

"Oh, don't be such a fuddy-duddy all your life. Where's your sense of adventure? We grew up in the experimenting sixties, didn't we?"

"Something tells me we grew up in *different* sixties."

"Well, too late now anyway. Pills are down the hatch." She patted her stomach. "You know... I'm feeling younger already. I can feel my wrinkles smoothing out in real time."

Despite her disapproval, Dot couldn't help but let out an exasperated chuckle.

"You're impossible, you know that? I hope you don't sprout any unseemly side effects."

"Only youthful vitality, my dear," Ethel proclaimed with a dramatic flourish of her hands. "I'll be tap-dancing out of bed tomorrow morning."

The sound of approaching footsteps cut their laughter short. Jessie appeared in the kitchen doorway, out of breath.

"Have you seen Chef Luca around? I've been trying to track him down all morning."

Dot shook her head.

"Damn. I think he might have done a runner. What's all this?"

"Helena's magic potions," Dot said. "Turns out the mineral baths aren't the only miracles here at La Casa."

"You're looking for Luca, you say?" Dahlia's voice carried in from the lobby as she swept by with a natural bristle broom. "I saw him heading into town earlier. Something about looking for some work at one of the local restaurants."

"Work?" Jessie said. "Isn't he a world-famous award-winning chef? Weird."

Dahlia continued her sweeping before Jessie hurried off through the lobby in search of more information on the missing chef.

"I'll be running around like her in no time," Ethel

said, dropping into a slow lunge. "A handful of those pills and I'll be joining the Olympic team."

"You'll get a gold medal for being the biggest fool."

"Silver," she said. "You'll be getting gold."

"I'm not the one taking sweets from strangers, am I?" Dot looped her arm through Ethel's, her cardigan rattling from all the stolen bottles. "Let's get back and check on Percy before he burns to a crisp napping on the patio. Doctor Helena Ford has given us plenty to think about."

9

Jessie's sandals slapped against the cobblestones as she hurried from one restaurant to the next, scanning patios and ducking her head through open doorways in search of Luca. She had combed through the entire main plaza, checking every restaurant, bar, and café. No luck. As she caught her breath beneath the stone archway above the stairway leading towards the beach, Jessie wondered if Luca had already left.

Wiping sweat from her brow, Jessie stepped back into the plaza's relentless morning sun, ready to give up her search for the temperamental chef. She turned towards the shaded side street that would lead her back to the hotel when raised voices caught her attention. Italian curses, unmistakably Luca's voice. Jessie hurried towards the commotion, spotting Luca outside a small restaurant tucked into a corner, red-faced, as he shouted at a man in an apron.

"*Stronzo!*" Luca yelled, jabbing a finger. "You would be *lucky* to have me! My food is exquisite, perfecto!"

The man held up his hands, replying in rapid Spanish, too quick for Jessie to grasp. Luca spat on the restaurant's doorstep.

"Idiota. You will regret turning me away when I am famous across the world!"

With that, he stormed off down a narrow set of stairs that descended towards the beach. Jessie darted after him, calling his name, but Luca didn't turn. He shoved through the crowds packing the stairs, nothing more than a black shirt and slick dark hair bobbing ahead of Jessie.

Reaching the bottom, Jessie hurried out onto the beach promenade. The crowds here were thicker, tourists and locals milling about the beachfront shops and restaurants. Keeping her eyes locked on Luca's retreating, Jessie pushed through sun-kissed bodies and around selfie sticks.

"Luca, wait!" she called again, but her voice was lost in the din of chatter and music.

He slipped down a side street just as she caught up, the crowd momentarily blocking her path. When Jessie broke free, Luca had vanished. She stood panting, scanning the area. The side street was much quieter, with only a few people browsing the little shops tucked beneath the whitewashed apartments. No sign of the chef.

She sighed, about to turn back. Then she caught a whiff of cigarette smoke further down the street.

Hurrying towards it, she spotted Luca in a shaded alcove, lighting up a cigarette with shaking hands. His shoulders were slumped, but his eyes still blazed with anger.

"Luca," Jessie said gently, not wanting to startle him as she approached. "I just want to talk."

He tensed, taking a long drag of his cigarette as he eyed her with suspicion.

"You are the girl from the hotel."

"I was hoping to ask you a few questions if you have a moment."

Exhaling smoke, Luca shook his head.

"I have nothing to say. The police, they already spoke to me for hours."

"I know, but..." Jessie took a step closer, keeping her voice low and calm. "I got the sense you were holding something back. Maybe you don't want to tell the police, but you can trust me."

"Trust? I cannot trust anyone in this town." He took another drag, glancing towards the street. "Now, if you'll excuse me..."

As he tossed his cigarette aside and made to leave, Jessie moved to block his path. Luca's glare would have made a lesser person shrink away, but Jessie stood her ground.

"If you've got nothing to hide, why are you running away?"

Luca crossed his arms. "I am not running from anything. But I am done being accused when I have done nothing wrong."

"I'm not accusing you. But a woman *is* dead, and if you know anything that could help…"

She let the sentence hang, holding Luca's gaze. For a long moment they stood in a tense silence, just the distant sounds of the beach filtering into the alley. He turned and let the crowd swallow him up.

He moved swiftly despite his stocky build, fuelled by anger and desperation. Jessie called his name, trying to get him to stop, but he ignored her.

They emerged onto the wide promenade lining the beach. The crowds here were sparser, soaked in sunlight and sea air. Luca shoved through oblivious tourists, heading for the shore. Jessie kept pace, darting around selfies and bursting beach bags. She had to jog to match Luca's determined stride across the hot sand.

He made for a jagged outcrop of rocks jutting up near the tide line. Finding one flat enough to perch on, he sat and stared out at the glittering sea. Jessie approached with slower steps, catching her breath. Luca's shoulders were slumped, but his eyes still held that simmering fury.

"I won't give up, you know," Jessie said, stopping a few feet away. Luca didn't acknowledge her. "Now that I've got your scent, I'll keep following until you tell me what really happened between you and Chloe."

Luca's jaw clenched, and Jessie edged closer along the rocks.

"Want to walk for a bit? I always find the ocean calming." When Luca didn't respond, Jessie slipped off her sandals. The sand was pleasantly warm between her toes. "I used to hate the sand. Couldn't stand the feeling of it, but I realised you just have to give into it. Let yourself sink in. Nothing you can't wash away later."

Luca dug a crumpled pack of cigarettes from his pocket. He stuck one between his lips, then offered the pack to Jessie. She shook her head.

"I lived with this one foster mum who smoked like a chimney," she said, wiggling her toes deeper. "Never opened the windows in the car either, just told me not to breathe. Never liked the idea since."

Luca arched a brow but said nothing. He lit his cigarette and sucked in a long drag. They stayed in silence for a minute, nothing but the hiss of foam and crying gulls.

"Why are you so interested in this?" Luca asked, smoke streaming from his nostrils. "It is none of your business."

"I'm a journalist back home. Still new to it, but I smell a story on you. A story the police don't know."

"I'm not talking to the press."

"Off the record," she said. "I don't think *The Peridale Post* will have much interest in this one."

"Still, you are wasting your time. If they don't find answers, they'll try to pin it on whoever looks most obvious."

"Only if we let them," Jessie pressed. "If there's more to it, you have to speak up."

Grinding the cigarette into the rock, Luca turned to her.

"And what will that accomplish, hm? You think they will take the word of the cook?"

"The truth matters. No matter who tells it."

Luca's dark eyes searched her face. Jessie tried to radiate trustworthiness, sensing his walls cracking. With a heavy sigh, Luca turned back towards the sea.

"I should have known she would cause problems," he muttered. "Chloe... she was a viper."

"I got that impression."

Staring at the horizon, Luca shook his head.

"She made threats against me."

"I got that impression too. Threats about what?"

Luca hesitated, wrestling with something internally. He opened his mouth to speak just as a police siren wailed nearby. They both turned to watch as a police car cruised along the promenade, and right past them. It continued down towards the marina.

"Come on," she said, stepping closer to the water. "Walk with me."

The warm water lapped over her feet as Luca hopped off the rock. He took his time to unlace his shoes before pulling them off. His socks came off next before he rolled up the cuffs of his trousers into neat rolls. Stuffing his socks in his shoes, he placed them on the rock and trailed after Jessie into the water.

They weaved around laughing children building lopsided sandcastles, toddlers squealing as gentle waves splashed their legs. Parents lounged on towels nearby, slathered in sunscreen as they kept half an eye on their kids. Jessie smiled at a little girl zigzagging after a colourful kite, her ponytail bouncing with each step. Neither of them spoke for a while—it seemed they both needed the calming moment.

"I grew up near a beach in Italy," Luca said in a soft voice. "My grandmother—Nonna—was strict. Read the Bible from morning till night, wouldn't go to bed without kissing her picture of the Pope. Thought fun was a waste of time. Saw no beauty in nature beyond being the Lord's creation."

"That must've sucked," she said. "Having the ocean right there but never getting to enjoy it."

Luca exhaled, gazing out at the glittering waves.

"I would stare out of my window at the other children playing in the sand. But if I asked Nonna, she would lecture me about idle hands and temptation."

"No wonder you're so high-strung. Your nonna sucked the joy right out of you."

Luca shot her an amused look.

"I wouldn't say that. But I had to learn to... enjoy myself in secret." The corner of his mouth quirked up. "I got very good at sneaking out."

Jessie smiled. She could imagine a young Luca sneaking out of his window late at night, running down to the beach to feel the sand between his toes.

"Well, you definitely figured out how to have fun eventually," Jessie pointed out. "I mean, you're a world-famous chef."

Luca gave a noncommittal grunt.

"Come on, take a little credit," Jessie elbowed him.

"You made it out of your gran's place and really made something of yourself."

"Perhaps." Luca's mouth twitched. "My Nonna, she would not approve of my lifestyle now, I think."

"No wild parties on the yacht with models?"

Luca let out a surprised bark of laughter.

"No, no. I am still... quite boring, compared to most chefs."

"Somehow, I doubt that."

They shared a smile. She was chipping away at his prickly exterior. But they still hadn't got to the heart of things.

She pulled out her phone as she walked, navigating to Luca's Instagram page. It was dotted with glossy food photos and shots of him cooking shirtless, flashing the camera a smouldering look. Luca made a noise that was somewhere between a grumble and an embarrassed mumble.

"I wanted none of that," he admitted after a moment. "The shirtless photos, the fake lifestyle." Luca shook his head, kicking up sand with each step. "That private jet? A set. And that tropical island? Photoshop. It gets attention, but it means nothing. Doesn't pay as much as people think."

Jessie nodded as she scrolled through image after image, each portraying Luca and his life in an aspirational light. Through the screen, the shirtless chef had the perfect life—the same man in front of her had sadness in his eyes that his digital smouldering concealed.

Luca seemed uncomfortable with his online persona being scrutinised in front of him, so she slipped her phone away and changed the subject.

"It must've driven you mad seeing Chloe's gigantic following?"

Luca scooped a pebble from the sand and skimmed it across the waves. It bounced three times before disappearing beneath the surface with a plop.

"I met her last summer." He dropped his head, forcing out a single laugh. "I was an idiota. Got swept up in her... charms."

"You and Chloe were involved?"

"We had some... dates," Luca muttered. "I was taken in by her beauty, her confidence." He scooped another pebble, squeezing it in his fist. "I did not see the wicked woman beneath."

Tossing the pebble hard, he sent it bouncing six times before it vanished into the blue. Jessie waited, sensing there was more he wanted to get off his chest.

"One night, there was a big dinner. All the influencers staying at the resort, some very strict vegans among them. Most of them were." He wiped a hand over his mouth. "I was distracted that day. I'd ended things. We were arguing. My mind was not as focused as it should have been. She was distracting me with petty prodding, trying to get a rise out of me."

He quietened, staring out at the horizon. Jessie stepped closer.

"What happened, Luca?"

"I made a mistake with the dishes." His jaw

clenched. "I cooked everything in butter. *Real* butter. Lots of real butter."

"Yikes."

He gave a shameful nod.

"By the time I realised, it was too late. The damage was done. They were eating, so I just... let them. I expected someone to say something, but nobody noticed. They loved it. Ate every bite."

"But it was just a mistake," Jessie pointed out. "Could've happened to anyone."

"Perhaps." Luca leaned his head back, staring up at the cloudless sky. "But *she* saw me do it."

"Chloe?"

"She was in the kitchen and watched me make the mistake. She said nothing."

A chilly feeling crept over Jessie. She could guess where this was going.

"She said she would keep it a secret. But it was all a ploy to sink her fangs deeper into me."

Jessie felt a swell of sympathy for Luca. She could picture Chloe letting him make that mistake, watching silently with calculating eyes. Waiting for the perfect moment to use it against him.

"She wanted leverage over you," Jessie said. "A way to control you?"

"Yes. She was obsessed, always wanting my attention." Luca sniffed, kicking the sand. "I had nothing to give her. No money, no influence, but she enjoyed having power over people. I have worked so hard for my reputation as a chef. One mistake, and she tried to ruin me. I should have known better than to get close to someone like her. She only cared about her image, would step on anyone to climb higher. If she exposed me online, it would make her look better. Get her more clicks." Sighing, Luca scooped up another pebble. He turned it over in his fingers before sending it skipping across the waves. "I just wanted her to go away."

Jessie studied Luca's face, seeing the hurt and bitterness etched in his expression. How much had he wanted her to go away?

"Where were you that night, Luca?" she asked, standing still in the wet sand.

He shrugged, pulling out a fresh cigarette to tuck behind his ear.

"In the plaza. Drinking. Trying to clear my head after that disastrous dinner."

"Can anyone confirm seeing you there?"

"There were people around. But I kept my head down. Just wanted to be alone." He gestured inland. "There are dozens of men who look like me in this town. I doubt anyone paid attention."

His alibi was shaky at best. But somehow, she believed he was telling the truth. Or at least, part of it.

"Why were you trying to get work at that restaurant earlier?" she asked. "I thought your career was going well."

Scooping up a shell, Luca turned it over in his fingers.

"I am done with that world. The influencers, the celebrities." He made a spitting noise. "It is all fake. A constant struggle for attention and fame." Tossing the shell into the surf, he gritted his jaw. "I just wanted to cook. Dahlia convinced me I needed an online presence. Said she would make me the 'face' of her *Blisselle* cooking content." He yanked the cigarette from behind his ear and lit it, taking an angry drag. "But only once I reached one hundred thousand followers. I stalled at fifty-two thousand, and I am tired of playing these games. It's so dull to me."

"It does sound dull," she agreed.

"Then you understand," Luca said, looking back the way they had walked. "You're a good listener. I need to go." His gaze grew distant, pondering something. "I went back to my room in the early hours, and I heard shouting coming from the room next to mine."

Jessie perked up. That had to be a clue.

"Whose room was it?"

"Helena's. I am almost certain I heard Chloe's voice in the argument. I'm not sure of the time, but it was several hours past midnight."

With that, he turned and strode off back down the beach towards his shoes waiting on the rock. Jessie watched him go, her mind spinning. Helena had seemed cagey when she'd left the kitchen after Dot and Ethel's questioning earlier. And she'd stormed out of that tense dinner right after Chloe insulted her...

Jessie watched Luca's retreating figure until it blended with the blur of tourists and locals on the promenade. A part of her itched to follow him, to dig deeper into the tangled threads of Chloe's death, but her

Sangria and Secrets

feet remained planted in the warm sand as the waves splashed at her ankles.

She glanced back at the looming silhouette of Savega, debating whether she should return to the hotel and share what she'd learned. She needed a moment alone to breathe—to think.

Instead, she chose the comfort of the beach. The sea breeze caressed her face as she sat down, hugging her knees close. She hadn't realised how much she'd missed this—the rhythmic lull of the ocean, the simplicity of nature that demanded nothing.

Digging her toes into the cool layer of wet sand beneath the surface heat, she let out a sigh. She pulled out her phone again and saw there was another text from Johnny Watson waiting for her.

JOHNNY

Have you seen my email? Given it any thought? No rush, but I need an answer by the end of the week.

Another fork in the road.

Her thumb hovered over the keyboard as she considered how to reply. The email offered adventure, new horizons—a life beyond Peridale's familiar lanes and never-ending countryside. She started typing a response to Johnny, then stopped, erasing the words one by one until only a blinking cursor remained on the screen. Was she ready to uproot again? To step onto another plane and leave behind everything that had become so dear?

Jessie stood up and brushed sand from her legs. She slipped her phone back into her pocket—Johnny would have to wait longer for his answer.

Right now, there were truths waiting to be unearthed at La Casa—she understood what she'd overheard between Chloe and Luca that afternoon in the plaza. Whether that meant Luca was innocent, she couldn't say, but he'd just pointed a giant finger right at their resident doctor.

10

Garlic and herbs lingered on Julia's fingers as she wiped the pizza grease from her mouth. None of them had been in the mood for the quinoa salad and spirulina smoothies that Dahlia tried passing off as dinner. A takeaway pizza had hit the spot much better, even if it didn't exactly fit with La Casa's new health-conscious ethos.

Now, with full bellies, Julia, Jessie, and Dot were huddled around one of the patio tables by the sparkling pool as the last of the evening light faded over the hills.

Julia leaned forward, lowering her voice and said, "So, let's go over everything we learned today. I spoke with Ian."

"Are his lips as loose as his joints?" Jessie asked, popping the last crust into her mouth. "I saw him sitting with his leg behind his head earlier."

"Strange man," Dot remarked.

"He shared a little," Julia said. "He told me about Chloe's serial killer book and how it seems fabricated."

"Helena backed that up too," Dot agreed with a disapproving shake of her head. "That girl had no shame."

"And it's currently selling like hotcakes," Julia said. "What about you, Gran? You spoke with the doctor. Learn anything useful there?"

Dot leaned back in her chair, fiddling with the pearl necklace at her throat as she recalled the conversation.

"Doctor Ford. Yes, well... I got a little out of her either. She was taking some glamour shots for her supplement line when I popped in. Didn't seem very keen on chatting."

"No surprise there," Jessie said. "She wouldn't want to slip up if she's hiding something."

"Right you are. But she said she was asleep before midnight when I asked about her whereabouts that night. Said she went straight to bed after dinner." Dot paused, her eyes narrowing. "But that doesn't line up with what Luca told you, does it, Jessie?"

"No, it doesn't. He told me he heard Chloe's voice coming from Helena's room. At least a few hours after midnight."

"Helena was very insistent she was always asleep before midnight," Dot said. "What a liar. This isn't looking good for the doctor, if you ask me."

"Maybe Chloe knew something about the water that we don't," Julia suggested. "Blackmail wasn't beneath her. We should monitor..."

Julia let her voice carry away on the breeze as hurried footsteps approached from behind. She turned to see Barker rushing towards them, a brown paper bag clutched tight to his chest.

"I've got it," he said, setting the bag down on the table. "Took some smooth talking, but I got a copy of Chloe's memoir from the airport bookshop. Fresh stock they were saving for the weekend."

"You found her book?" Julia asked in surprise. "That was fast work, Barker."

"There's a catch," he said. "It's in Spanish."

Dot picked up the book, flipping through the pages.

"Well, that's no good. We'll need someone to translate..." Her eyes lit up. "Ethel reads Spanish. She can help."

"If she's awake," Jessie pointed out. "She was fast asleep when I passed earlier. Was putting Barker to shame with her snoring."

"I don't snore," Barker said. "Do I?"

"Yes," the three of them answered.

"I hope it isn't those vitamins," Dot said, her fingers worrying her pearls. "We really don't know what's in them."

"I'm sure she just needed an early night," Julia said, considering their options. "Why don't you take the book to Minnie? I'm sure she could read it. Might help shed light on what Chloe was up to."

"Good idea." Dot pushed out her chair along the patio, scooping up the book. "That's if she doesn't bite my head off. She hasn't been the friendliest since Chloe died."

"We still need to figure out her alibi," Jessie reminded her. "Rule her out."

Dot waved a dismissive hand before she hurried through the dining room with the book in hand. Julia hoped the memoir contained clues—Chloe's secrets had to be the key to unlocking this case.

The creaky wooden stairs echoed under Dot's sensible shoes as she ascended to the top floor of La Casa. Her heart pounded in her chest, not from the exertion, but from the weight of uncertainty pressing down on her. She clutched Chloe's Spanish memoir tighter to her chest, as if the book could shield her from what she might uncover. The soft glow of a lamp filtered through the gaps in Minnie's door.

It was late, but Dot had a mission.

Dot raised her hand to knock when she heard a voice —Minnie's voice—fraught with anxiety. It seeped through the cracks of the door, sending a shiver down Dot's spine.

"It's me," Minnie whispered, her words heavy with distress. "I need your help. I'm in real trouble this time."

Dot froze, her knuckles mere inches from the door.

"I don't know what to do," Minnie continued, her voice cracking with despair. "I don't think I can get out of this one. I've done something really, *really* stupid..."

Dot recoiled, gasping as if she'd been struck. Her mind raced to catch up with the implications of Minnie's confession. Her heart pounded in sync with the seconds ticking away on her wristwatch.

She had promised Minnie that she would help solve Chloe's death. But what if Jessie's pestering had a point? What if Minnie *was* the culprit? What if the woman she had vowed to help was behind Chloe's demise?

With one last glance at Minnie's door, she turned and made her way back down the creaky stairs, Chloe's book clutched tight to her chest. She hoped she'd heard wrong.

Had Minnie...

Could she have...?

The questions buzzed like hornets in Dot's head, each one more distressing than the last.

"Percy," she said, interrupting his newspaper reading in bed. "We have a problem. It's Minnie... she's done something 'really, really stupid.'"

Jessie scrolled through the curated lives of strangers, blinded by the light of her phone screen, with the pulsing bass of distant music drifting through the warm night air. She glanced at the clock. Almost midnight. The night was still young for the locals who danced in the cobbled streets below. Not for her family though. They'd be tucked up in their cool, crisp sheets, lulled to sleep by the gentle whirr of the ceiling fan.

All except her.

Sleep evaded Jessie as she lay awake, her thoughts churning. She couldn't shake the nagging feeling that Luca had told her half-truths.

Sighing, she clicked over to the chef's profile. His feed depicted a handsome, carefree man grinning over sizzling pans and clinking glasses. Luca, the celebrity chef, living his best life, had no troubles in sight. Swiping left, she landed on Chloe's page. A kaleidoscope of perfect images flooded her screen: Chloe lounging on pristine beaches, sipping green juice amidst lush jungle, standing on mountain peaks with arms outstretched, her blonde hair billowing like a supermodel.

The comments told a different story of the woman who almost slapped Jessie in the street. Hundreds of strangers grieved the tragic loss of this young woman they'd never met, calling her inspirational, life-changing, a beacon of light in a dark world. Rose emojis bloomed beside declarations of grief, and paragraphs spilled with hollow words from people who knew only the Chloe she wanted them to see.

Jessie had witnessed only a glimpse of the real Chloe, but it was enough to grate against the polished veneer of her online persona. Still, she'd only been twenty-two, the same age Jessie would turn in a few short months.

How different their lives had been. One life devoted to cultivating the perfect image, the other spent carving a space in a small community. Chloe chasing fame and fortune across continents, Jessie finding meaning in the fishbowl of her village.

Yet despite their contrasting paths, fate had led them both to the quiet village of Savega, to Aunt Minnie's hotel on that pivotal night—the night when Chloe's curated life came to a brutal end.

And even that had been staged.

She clicked on a link that took her to Chloe's personal website, a glossy online hub of wellness articles, product endorsements, and nestled among it all, an in-depth interview titled 'Chloe Saunders: Behind the Brand.' She scanned the text, the words blurring together as her eyes darted down the page. A section about Chloe's childhood caught her attention, describing how she was orphaned at a young age and brought up in a string of foster homes.

The story struck a chord within Jessie. She'd known that world, the desperate longing for love that danced just out of reach. Could Chloe have been seeking the love she never got through the virtual embrace of her followers?

Jessie felt an odd kinship with Chloe, a strange connection born from shared experiences and parallel lives. But then she remembered Chloe's track record for deceit and manipulation. Could this be another lie? Fabricating an orphaned childhood seemed unthinkable, but then again, so did inventing a near-death experience with a serial killer.

She navigated to the book section of Chloe's website. There it was—*How I Survived a Serial Killer... and Thrived*.

A black and white, unsmiling picture of Chloe stared back at her, dead-eyed from behind the title. She scanned the comments section beneath it':

Inspirational!'

'A testament to survival'

'Brave and moving'

And the accolades rolled in like waves crashing against a shore. She scrolled to the blurb and read:

You know me for my no-flinching wellness truths, but not this. I've stared into the eyes of a killer—and lived to tell the tale. A man who shall remain nameless nearly claimed me as his next victim. My story isn't just survival—it's a raw showdown with death itself. In this searing exposé, I take you inside the mind of a killer and my desperate fight to escape his grasp. Every secret, every pulse-pounding moment, I reveal how I turned prey into power. Dare to dive into my darkest hours and discover the truth that nearly cost me everything. This is my life. My truth. My escape.

Jessie frowned at the screen, uncomfortable with what she was reading. According to those who knew her behind the scenes, it was all a lie, yet it all felt so real to the people who followed her.

The buzz of her phone interrupted her. Glancing down, she saw a text from Dante lighting up the screen.

Tapping to open it, she saw he had sent her a screenshot of an article with the words 'Popular Wellness Influencer Murdered in Savega...' visible in the preview.

> DANTE
>
> This is where you're staying???

She hesitated, caught between the impulse to reply and the desire to maintain the fragile peace of the night.

She still hadn't told him what was going on. Any of it. But it was too heavy to share over a late-night text.

With a sigh, she put her phone down, opting for silence. She would deal with Dante's questions in the morning. After all, it was late.

But restlessness gnawed at her as she lay in the dark, her thoughts spinning like a whirlwind. In one swift motion, she threw back the cool sheets and swung her legs over the side of the bed. She tugged on her Doc Martens, the leather cool against her skin. Decision made, she grabbed her phone and strode out into the night, letting the pounding music reel her in.

As a journalist, she knew she shouldn't have had a bias, but after their conversation on the beach, she hoped she could find an alibi for Luca.

11

Julia and Sue stood side by side in the hotel kitchen the next morning, their hands dusted with flour as they rolled out pastry on the stainless-steel counter. It had only been a few days since they'd baked in the café, but with an ocean between them and home, it might as well have been a lifetime.

"I know it's a big change, but Neil and I have been thinking about it for a while," Sue said, cutting circles from the golden pastry with a fluted cutter. "During all that mess with James and our house and the library last year, we talked about moving away a lot. Running away, more like."

"You never mentioned it."

"I didn't want to alarm you," she said, shrugging as her cutter hesitated over the pastry. "It was just pillow talk. A daft idea we shelved in case we needed an escape. But everything worked out for the best, didn't it?"

It had, yet Sue still wanted to move away. Julia wanted to be the supportive older sister, but the idea of her sister moving abroad felt like a request for a pound of flesh.

"Could open a little shop," Sue suggested when Julia couldn't think of what to add. "Or a little B&B with a view to die for. I could be the Evelyn of Savega, though now that I've said it, I think Minnie has that title under wraps."

"I could see you doing wonderfully with a B&B." She crimped the edges of the filled pies, hesitating. "I... I'd miss you at the café. It wouldn't be the same without you."

"I'd miss it too. Truth be told, some of my happiest memories from the past year are in that café," Sue said, staring off into the distance. She snapped back, pushing the next pie casing to Julia. "But you know I'd only be a phone call away. And I'll come back to visit. Flights are cheap. Practically the same price as getting a train these days."

Julia nodded, but it wasn't the same. After the twins were born, they'd drifted apart somewhat, and they'd only been a short walk away from each other. Julia understood more when Olivia came along. Being on a baby's ever-changing schedule had been a challenge, to say the least, so she couldn't imagine multiplying it by two. But since Sue had swapped her nurse's scrubs for the café's apron, they were the closest they'd been in years. It had made Julia realise how much she'd missed her sister.

Before Julia could articulate her feelings, Dahlia strode into the kitchen, her heels clicking on the tile. She stopped short at the sight of them.

"What are you doing?" she asked. "I was just about to prep for lunch."

"Baking," Sue answered, not beating around the bush, "in *our* great-aunt's kitchen."

"We found a sack of cooking apples in the pantry," Julia said, a tad more apologetically. "If you were saving them for something, I'll replace them—"

Dahlia's expression softened.

"No, it's fine. I'm sorry, I... I'm a bit on edge today."

"Any developments?" Julia inquired.

"I'm afraid the police are still clueless, and now Minnie's locked herself in her room." She sighed, massaging her temples. "Please, finish your baking. I have some admin to attend to. We should postpone the launch, but with the media coverage of... well, you know... bookings are pouring in."

More of that morbid sensationalism.

Dahlia hesitated before turning to leave, and Julia could have let her rush off to her tasks, but she wasn't the easiest woman to pin down. She flitted about like a hyperactive robot with fresh batteries. Julia pulled out a stool before hurrying to the oven.

"A five-minute break won't hurt anyone," Julia said, ducking out of the way of the steam as the scent of caramelised sugar and sweet hot apples filled the air. "It doesn't get fresher than this."

Dahlia paused again before sitting down. Sue busied

herself with the washing up while Julia cut the mini pies in half—designed to be one per person, but Dahlia didn't seem like a dessert person.

"It's been years since I've had real sugar," she said, eyeing the plate as if it might detonate. "I shouldn't... but..." She forked a modest amount into her mouth, closing her eyes as she chewed, relishing the taste with a flutter of her eyelids. "Wow. This is delicious. Is there real butter in this?"

Julia shook her head.

"We had to make do with what was available."

"But how did you achieve such a flaky pastry?"

"Julia's a wizard in the kitchen," Sue called over her shoulder from the sink.

"Vegan butter has improved remarkably," Julia said, shrugging, though she welcomed the praise. "I adapted my mum's old recipe. The trick is to use ice water in the dough, then let it rest in the fridge for an hour, and... *ta-da*."

"Ta-da, indeed," Dahlia murmured, taking a larger bite. "You know, this would be a hit on *Blisselle*. We should chat sometime. I'm always on the lookout for new contributors for the app. How many followers do you have?"

"Oh, I..."

"One hundred and twenty-three for the café's account," Sue interjected. "I've been urging her to take social media more seriously for years."

But Dahlia's eyes sparkled.

"One hundred and twenty-three thousand is

impressive. We must talk—"

"Not *thousand*," Julia clarified. "Just one hundred and twenty-three."

"Oh." Dahlia laughed, choking on her pie. "How... quaint."

The atmosphere in the kitchen shifted. Despite Dahlia's patronising tone, Julia remained undaunted. She preferred genuine interactions to online engagements. Steeling herself, Julia steered the conversation towards more pressing matters.

"I heard about Chloe's book."

"Oh, dear," Dahlia said, pushing aside her half-eaten pie. "Quite the sensational title, isn't it?"

"A sensational read, I presume?"

"I couldn't say."

"You haven't read it?"

"I skimmed over it."

"Ian mentioned you'd read it," Julia said, piercing her own pie to let out the steam. "He was quite specific, suggesting I ask you about it. Claimed you read it from cover to cover."

Dahlia's smile waned. She nodded, taking another bite before replying.

"I'm not sure why he'd think that. He might have seen me flicking through it and assumed too much. If I wanted a book of concocted tales of scandalous murder, I'd choose an Agatha Christie."

"You're certain she concocted it?"

Dahlia exhaled and nodded again.

"Chloe confided as much in me, and she seemed

rather pleased with herself for the ruse. It brought her fame, and..."

"And?"

Dahlia licked the crumbs from her lips.

"It put a target on her back. I told her she was playing a dangerous game, but she wasn't one to listen."

"Do you think someone murdered her because of the book?"

"How am I supposed to know the reason for her murder?" Dahlia narrowed her eyes at Julia. "All I know is, the more famous she became, the more impulsive her actions became with those around her. She had little regard for consequences. She thought she was protected. Above it."

"So, what are you saying?" Sue inquired, drying her hands on a tea towel.

"What I'm saying is... now that I've had time to process it, I'm not surprised someone exacted their revenge on her. Her currency was scandal, and she knew how to exploit those around her to give herself a boost. Like Ian, for example..." Dahlia didn't finish her sentence. "I've said too much."

"You haven't said enough," Sue said. "Like Ian...?"

"Is this about Chloe humiliating him?" Julia asked. "He said that he trusted Chloe, and she used her fame to humiliate him in some way."

"That's an *edited* version of what really happened," Dahlia said, her voice hardening. "Search for Ian's live stream from July 24th last year. It's still online. You'll see what I mean for yourself." She dusted off her hands. "I'll start lunch later. Thank you for the apple pie. It really was delicious. Make sure you clean up after yourselves."

"We always do," Sue said, saluting. "We're professionals."

The echo of Dahlia's departing heels was replaced by the rhythmic thump of Sue's knife as she diced apples for their next batch of pies. Julia, cradling a cup of tea, watched her sister's hands move with the ease.

"Notice how her 'oh we must have a conversation' act dropped when she found out how many followers you had?" Sue said, breaking the comfortable silence. She tossed the apple pieces into a bowl and reached for another fruit. "How shallow can you get? And her *Blisselle* app is a right rip-off."

"You've used it?"

"Didn't realise it was the same app when she first mentioned it, but I subscribed right after the twins were born. Thought it might help me lose some baby weight, but it was all rubbish. Unhealthy diets and ridiculous exercise routines. Cost me an arm and a leg too."

"Perhaps she's changed since then?" she offered, though she had her own reservations about Dahlia.

Sue shrugged, dumping a handful of brown sugar into the bowl of apples.

"With the way she's been carrying on hyping up the miracle water in the basement? Doubtful. I think she's full of hot air."

Julia sighed. She had to admit, Sue had a point. Perhaps she was being too charitable in her judgment of Dahlia. A moment of silence fell between them as Julia considered her sister's words. She opened her mouth to change the subject back to Sue's fantasy plans to leave Peridale when Sue pulled off the black apron they'd found in the pantry.

"I should get going," she said, glancing at the clock on the wall. "Neil and the twins will be waiting for me. We're going on a boat trip today."

Julia hid her disappointment with a smile. She'd hoped to spend more time with Sue, to talk about her decision, but now wasn't the time to bring up such heavy topics.

"You can come with us? The boat trip could be fun. Get the sea breeze through your hair instead of more of this murder madness."

Julia hesitated, glancing towards the door where Dahlia had exited earlier. She still had questions about Chloe's book and Dahlia's involvement in it all. A boat trip, though tempting, wouldn't help her find the answers.

"I think I'll stay here," she said. "There's still a lot I need to do."

Sue gave her a knowing look, but didn't press further.

"Alright," she said, rinsing off the cutting board. "Just don't work too hard, okay? We are on holiday."

Jessie found a near-empty rock bar tucked away in a shaded corner of the plaza. She slid onto a barstool, the metal cool against her thighs, and ordered an espresso martini. The bittersweet coffee liqueur and vodka concoction reminded her of late nights at Richie's Bar back home.

She scanned the near-empty place, bathed in afternoon light filtering through stained glass hanging in the windows. Behind the bar, a bartender with long black hair worked with efficient motions, slicing lemons and shaking cocktails. As she set a fresh napkin on the counter next to Jessie, recognition sparked in the woman's eyes. She gave Jessie a lingering, knowing look before moving down to the far end of the bar.

Jessie studied the bartender's strong jawline and the tattoo curling up her forearm as she wiped down the already-clean counter. She swiped through the photos on her phone from her last trip until she found the one she wanted. Lisa. Minnie's daughter, her hair dyed black over her natural chestnut. She looked so different, but there was no mistaking those dark eyes—they looked just like Minnie's.

Jessie's phone vibrated with an incoming call, 'Dante' flashing across the screen. She should have smiled at seeing his face, but she only felt guilt—she still hadn't replied to his text message from late last night. She let the call ring out, and the stone of guilt weighing her down turned into a brick.

The murder.

The job offer.

Them.

They had so much to talk about, but she wasn't sure

she could face it now. She searched the dark bar for a distraction and found it when she noticed two familiar faces hunched up in a dark booth by the jukebox. The doctor and the chef. Helena and Luca were engaged in what appeared to be a tense discussion. Helena crossed her arms while Luca gestured in frustration.

Jessie had spent several hours the previous night visiting bars with pictures of Luca from his Instagram. She hadn't found anyone who could confirm his alibi. Yet, here he was, sitting with the very person he had accused.

Tucking her phone away, Jessie downed the last of her drink, the coffee jolt giving her fresh energy to pursue this new lead. Weaving her way through the tables, she moved closer while keeping her eyes averted from the arguing pair. She stood at the jukebox and flicked through the rock songs while straining to make out their hushed conversation.

Out of the corner of her eye, Helena unfolded her arms and pulled something from her coat. Jessie stole a glance as Helena slid a slim envelope across the table to Luca. He glanced around before tucking it into the inside pocket of his jacket.

"That should be more than enough to get you started somewhere new," Helena said in a low voice. "Maybe it's time to go back to Italy. You have that house there. Get away from all this."

"Where did you get this money?"

"Is it so hard to believe I had it saved up?"

"Yes. Where?"

"You *know* where," she said in a firm, low voice. "The fewer questions you ask, the better. Go. Tonight."

"I can't."

"You were ready to leave yesterday."

"And then I thought about how it would look."

"And how will it look when the police dig more into your history with Chloe? Have you told them you were engaged?"

Luca shook his head in silence, and Jessie couldn't help but sigh. She'd been right about her hunch—he'd only told her half of the truth. A little more serious than the few 'dates' he'd suggested. She fished a euro coin out of her pocket, having found the perfect song.

"Luca, I'm trying to help you," Helena whispered. "That money is a gift. Stay offline, lie low, and let all this blow over."

Luca stewed in the silence, spinning a beer mat between his fingers.

"If you end up behind bars, you'll lose everything," she urged. "Please, take the money and go. I know things didn't work out between us, but..." Helena's hand hovered over his chest before she withdrew it. "I'll always care about you, Luca."

Jessie held her breath. He'd been engaged to Chloe and been involved with the doctor too? How much more hadn't he told her during their walk on the beach?

"Okay," Luca said. "I'll go. Tomorrow."

"*Tonight*," she said as Luca stood. "One more thing. I saw that nosey girl following you yesterday. Did you tell her anything?"

Unless Dot or Julia had got to him, Helena was talking about Jessie. Finger hovering over the music selection button, she shifted more out of view.

"Nothing important."

"Good. Keep it that way. The last thing we need is her sticking her nose in. You know she's a journalist? And Minnie said her mum is some sort of super-sleuth. They keep asking questions." Helena exhaled as Jessie jabbed the button. "Go."

"I owe you."

"You don't," Helena said. "I hope we see each other again on the other side of this."

Luca left the bar as 'Born to Run' by Bruce Springsteen filled the quiet space, and Helena didn't linger either. Leaning against the jukebox, Jessie watched the doctor hurry out and tried to make sense of what she'd just heard. There had been a flicker of romantic tension between them, so why had Luca pointed the finger at Helena back on the beach?

Before she could dwell on it too much, she pulled out her phone, facing her own romantic tension. She considered calling Dante back, but opted for a text message instead.

Sangria and Secrets

JESSIE

Hey. Sorry, lost my phone in the hotel. It's been crazy here. That article you sent was about here. It's a long story, but some bratty influencer was drowned in a bath. The police are handling it. I'm fine, don't worry. Hope Veronica isn't working you too hard.

Miss you

She pressed the second message and hit the rubbish bin icon.

Message deleted

Dot and Percy had staked their claim on a corner table of the dining room, its surface a battleground of poker chips and dog-eared playing cards. The sun slid from the sky, its golden rays streaming through the half-closed blinds, casting a warm glow on the game at hand. Dot, a dab hand at poker, couldn't focus on her cards.

"Are you alright?" Percy asked, eyeing her over the rim of his round specs. "It's not like you to lose three games in a row. You don't have to let me win."

"I'm not," she replied, attempting to force her attention back to the game. "I'm warming up. The next game is mine."

"Right you are, my love."

Ethel sat at the next table, absorbed in the Spanish

copy of Chloe's book, her reading glasses perched on the tip of her nose.

"'I found myself trapped,'" she read aloud, "'my only escape being through a narrow window. I knew I had to get out… to fight for my life… I smashed the glass with my elbow, cutting myself to smithereens, but I had to try. Not just for me, or my family, but for you, too… my beloved followers.'" She snorted, shaking her head as she turned to the next page. "What a load of drivel!"

Dot and Percy shared a look. They'd escaped their villa prison through a window too, though Percy had used a lamp rather than his elbow to smash the window after they'd pried the bars off from the crumbling stone.

Dot tossed her cards down in frustration.

"I'm sorry, Percy. I just can't focus. I can't stop thinking about what I heard outside Minnie's door last night. She sounded so distraught, so guilty."

Ethel glanced up from her book. "You're letting your imagination run wild, as per usual. The only way to know for sure is to ask her outright."

"But what if she did it and admits it?"

"Isn't a confession what we're looking for?" Ethel arched a brow. "I'd like to enjoy at least a few days of this holiday without a murderer lurking about the place."

Dot shook her head. Not that simple. She wanted to help Minnie, not condemn her.

She drifted back through the years to her youth with her first husband, Albert. She remembered the day Minnie had announced she was leaving Peridale to pursue fame and fortune as an actress. It had been over a Sunday roast at the dining room table in the cottage Dot still lived in.

"What's wrong with a simple life?" Albert had said, after dropping his knife and fork. "Get yourself a proper job and put your feet back on the ground. The odds are stacked against you, Wilhelmina."

But Minnie couldn't be deterred, and off she went with her suitcase only a few weeks later. Dot wished her well and rooted for her success from afar; she wished she had the courage to follow her own secret acting ambitions. Dot had met Albert—a humble plumber—while working as the coat-check girl in a theatre, but she'd pushed those dreams aside to start a family. Albert never got over his sister's departure, and despite accompanying her to the train station to wave her off, he couldn't bring himself to wish her luck.

Over the years, Dot kept up with Minnie through letters and cards. Minnie would write pages upon pages of her stories from brushing shoulders with the rich and famous, but, as Albert had forewarned, the odds were against her.

An acting career never materialised.

Albert passed away, and Minnie never moved back to Peridale. She'd only returned to the village once for Albert's funeral, and she didn't stay the night. Dot regretted not welcoming Minnie back with open arms and insisting she stay all those years ago. Perhaps if she had, they wouldn't be in this current predicament. If Dot remembered correctly, Minnie had been on her second of four marriages by then and was about to sail off on a cruise.

Percy's gentle touch on her hand brought her back to the present moment.

"Maybe there's another way we can sort this out?" he suggested in his soft way. "What about Minnie's daughter? Lisa might be able to provide some insight without putting Minnie on the spot."

"Minnie mentioned Lisa worked at a bar here in town," Dot remembered aloud. "I don't like the idea of going behind Minnie's back, though."

"Minnie is hardly being upfront with you," Ethel said, snapping the book shut. "It sounds to me like Percy is suggesting a night on the town, and I'm all for it."

A night-time visit to the local bars was not an activity Dot would have ever envisioned for herself. But desperate times called for desperate measures.

"I suppose it wouldn't hurt to talk to Lisa," Dot agreed.

"Then it's settled," Ethel said, springing to her feet. "Get your glad rags on. It's been far too many years since I've had a proper night out."

Despite her reservations, excitement bubbled up in Dot. Ethel's enthusiasm was infectious, and they needed answers. Given Minnie's evasiveness whenever Lisa came up, she might hold the key to unravelling La Casa's mysteries.

12

After the day swept her away, Julia tried to recall the date Dahlia had mentioned for the live stream—the one where Chloe had embarrassed Ian. She needed to watch that video herself to grasp the context of their quarrel.

Leaving Barker to prepare Olivia for bed, Julia proceeded down the corridor to Sue's room and knocked, but there was no answer. She was about to knock again when she remembered their boat trip. Wondering whether to ask Dahlia once more, Julia realised she had another route—seeking the truth from Ian.

With Ian's room just across the corridor, Julia decided to approach the source. She knocked, and he welcomed her inside. Soft meditation music played, and a lit incense stick perfumed the air with a sweet, earthy scent.

Ian's room mirrored Julia's in its sparse and

minimalist design, but he boasted a few additional comforts. A grander balcony, a lounge area with chic cream sofas, and the centrepiece—a massive stone bath in the centre of the room, which captivated Julia.

Her mind conjured disturbing images: Chloe struggling in the shimmering foam, her pleas for help stifled by the water. The soapy froth the police had described filled her lungs with every shout, sealing her tragic end beneath the surface.

"Tea?" Ian asked, breaking Julia from her haunting thoughts. "I have camomile, peppermint, or one of my personal favourites—peppermint and liquorice."

Julia's smile returned. "I've heard of it, and I'd love a cup."

"Perfect," Ian responded, his expression brightening. He moved to a small kitchenette and began making the tea. Instead of guiding Julia to the sofa, he cast a finger at a plush cushion on the floor. "Please, take a seat."

Julia hesitated before settling onto the cushion. It was an unconventional seating choice, yet it had an inviting aspect.

As Ian busied himself with the tea, Julia noted his occasional glance at the clock—the sole item on the pale walls.

"Do you have somewhere to be?"

"I'll be going live on social media in twenty minutes, but I'm happy to spend this time with you." He smiled at her. "You should never pass up the opportunity to pause and share a cup of tea."

"As a café owner, I'm inclined to agree."

"A café?" His face lit up. "How lovely. My grandmother used to run a little tearoom in Yorkshire. Tiny place, but she'd make everything herself by hand. I try not to eat refined produce, but if you put a slice of her homemade carrot cake in front of me, I'm not sure I could turn it down."

"What's life without a little sweetness now and then?" she said, eager to rewind the conversation now that she'd found some common ground. "Do you go live online often?"

"Every night. It's something I've been doing for a while now. I invite people to stop and reflect on their day with me. It's a great way for me to feel connected." She smelled the familiar minty sweet aroma of her favourite tea as it filled the room—it always put Julia at ease. "I resisted social media for the longest time, but I appreciate it as a fascinating resource that can keep us all connected. Do you use it much?"

"I feel plenty connected in my café," she said, lifting her cup in a toast. "To connections."

As Ian mirrored the toast and their cups clinked together in the quiet, Julia made her own connection—since he'd brought up the live streams, it was the perfect time to ask him about what Dahlia had revealed.

"When we spoke at the fountain, you mentioned Chloe tried to embarrass you online," Julia started, putting her cup on the polished stone floor. "I spoke to Dahlia this morning, and she mentioned something happened between you and Chloe during one of your live streams?"

Ian's soft smile dropped, his gaze averting hers. He sipped his tea without answering.

"I hope you don't mind me asking. It's just, with everything that's happened, I'm still trying to understand the dynamics between everyone here."

Ian nodded. "No, that's understandable. I didn't mean to withhold information from you, and to be honest, it wasn't one of my finer moments." He sighed. "What happened during that livestream is my biggest regret."

"Do you mind telling me what happened?"

"Chloe and I have had a somewhat tumultuous relationship over the past year," he said. "We've collaborated on various projects and events, but we often didn't see eye to eye. I disagreed with her ethics regarding how she used her influence. Wellness is a lifestyle you inhabit, but for some, it's a marketing opportunity. Chloe, for want of a better word, was a fraud." He sipped his tea. "She didn't practice what she preached, and she preached *a lot*. And her preaching would shape-shift depending on who was paying her the most to sell their products. I prefer to be more selective."

He set his tea down on the small table between them.

"During one of our influencer trips to Bali, I tried to have this conversation with Chloe in a mature and respectful manner. I wanted her to reflect on her decisions for the sake of the people who looked up to her."

"Something tells me that didn't go down well?"

"Not at all." He exhaled, closing his eyes for a moment. "She took the advice as a personal attack, and in that moment, I saw myself through her eyes. An enemy who needed to be destroyed, and she didn't wait long." He opened his eyes and stared off at the crescent moon high above the valley. "That night, during one of my live streams by the pool, Chloe hijacked the comments section, accusing me of... unsavoury business practices, let's say. She made claims about my retreats being scams. Said that I preyed on vulnerable people. Which, of course, couldn't be further from the truth." His jaw tensed. "She was mere feet away on a sun lounger off camera, typing out her comments with a wicked grin. I knew I had to do something. Just her name alone in the comments was enough to have people believing her."

"What did you do?"

Ian reached for his phone on the table, his fingers scrolling through his gallery until he found the video he was looking for. He turned the screen towards Julia, pressing play on a live stream from months ago.

Julia watched as a relaxed Ian appeared on screen, sitting by a pool, palm trees swaying in the background against an ink-black sky. He spoke to his followers about mindfulness, the serenity in his voice like a calming lullaby. However, the tranquillity shattered when a familiar name, Chloe Saunders, popped up in the comments section. Her comments were harsh and accusatory, painting Ian as a charlatan, exploiting vulnerable individuals.

Ian tried to maintain his calm demeanour in the video, but there was a noticeable strain in his voice as he attempted to address Chloe's accusations. Julia watched with a furrowed brow as the Ian in the video had enough of Chloe's cruel comments flooding his live stream. He picked up the phone and walked over to where Chloe lounged nearby, relaxing by the pool without a care in the world.

"What do you think you're doing?" Ian demanded, his usual composure replaced by frustration as he held his phone screen out towards Chloe.

Chloe glanced at it over her sunglasses.

"Oh, just chatting with your followers. They're so interested in learning more about you and your programmes." Her tone dripped with mock innocence. "Don't you think the people deserve full transparency?"

"You know what you're doing. You can't start a hate campaign against me because you feel like it."

"*Campaign?*" Chloe repeated with an exaggerated gasp. "It's the truth."

Ian put the phone down in the video. The camera pointed up at the swaying palm trees and a splash erupted off camera. The peace of the Balinese poolside shattered with that sound, and the video ended, leaving Julia with an unsettling cliffhanger.

The Ian next to her ran a hand through his long beard.

"She flung herself into the pool right after that. I didn't understand what was happening at first. I thought it was an accident."

Ian scrolled through his phone once more and brought up another video taken a week later. The stark contrast couldn't be more pronounced. There was Chloe in a sparse VIP area at a concert, whipping her hair around and dancing with a bottle of something in her hand as a DJ played loud club music on the stage.

"You can see she's fine," Ian continued as he paused the video on Chloe's exuberant face, "but for the next month, she only appeared on her social media wearing a neck brace. She told hundreds of thousands of people that *I* pushed her. And she *kept* telling them. And it wasn't true!"

Even though Chloe wasn't there to defend herself, she believed Ian didn't push her—she'd experienced that same twisting of reality when Chloe recorded Julia and Olivia on the plane.

"Chloe fed off the attention chaos brought her," Ian said, locking his phone and placing it on the table next to his tea. "And an injury—especially one caused by a fellow influencer—was a feast for her. If it weren't for her releasing that book, she would have dragged it out for as long as she could. I received months of death threats from her supporters. I lost thousands of followers, brand endorsements disappeared overnight." He looked away from Julia then, out to the balcony as Savega's evening breeze rustled the curtains. "And nothing I said made any difference. People believed *her*."

Julia sat in silence for a moment, allowing Ian's words to settle in the space between them. She had experienced and witnessed how reputations could flip overnight in Peridale with just a few choice words. Dealing with gossip that ripped through a small village was difficult enough. She couldn't imagine what it would be like if the effects were amplified by hundreds of thousands of people online.

"It must have been difficult for you," Julia finally said.

"Difficult is an understatement. I dedicated my life to helping others find peace. To have my name tarnished by someone who saw me as nothing more than a stepping stone to greater fame... it challenged every belief I held dear." Glancing at the clock, he said, "Now, if you'll excuse me, I must prepare for my followers. I don't want to let my tribe down."

Julia finished her tea, placing her cup on the table beside Ian's. The taste of peppermint and liquorice lingered on her tongue, soothing yet tinged with the bitter aftertaste of their conversation.

After pushing herself up off the floor, she moved towards the door, pausing by the stone bath. The image of Chloe drowning sent a shiver down her spine.

"I know how it looks, Julia," Ian said, his voice calm yet firm. "I didn't kill that girl."

Julia turned to look at him, his words echoing in her mind. There was a conviction in his tone that gave her pause. She wanted to believe him, but after witnessing the calm yoga instructor snapping at Chloe in the video —no matter how provoked—she knew appearances could be deceiving.

Julia returned to her hotel room where Barker had

got Olivia off to sleep. Sat on the edge of the bed, he looked up from his phone with a contemplative smile.

"Was just checking in with Katie," he said. "She said she's had hundreds of votes so far, and that people keep asking where you've gone."

"I'll be back before they know it," she said as she sat next to him. She ran her fingers through the back of his hair and he bounced his phone on his knee. "Was there something else?"

"I wanted to ask Katie about that old housekeeper that used to work at the manor," he said. "Thought she might know something about where Katie came from. Katie was in too good a mood. Couldn't bring myself to remind her. Don't suppose you remember?"

"Hilary," Julia said with no need to think about it, picturing the tight-bunned bulging eyed stern housekeeper. "Hilary Boyle. And it's a good idea. She worked at Wellington Manor from before Katie was on the scene."

"Do you know where she moved to when she retired?"

"Some seaside town. Not too sure of the name."

"Might be worth seeing if I can track her down," he said, giving his phone one last pat before turning to Julia. "Did Sue remember that date?"

"I got one better. Spoke with Ian about it."

"And?"

"Chloe did try to destroy his reputation over nothing. He lost his temper with her for a moment, and she ran with it. She brought out the worst in people."

"Think he's behind it?" he asked, massaging her shoulders from behind. "He seems like a chilled-out guy."

Julia wasn't sure.

But she couldn't stop thinking about that bath.

Dot tugged at the hem of her dress, smoothing out imaginary wrinkles as she took in the lively atmosphere of the plaza bar. She felt out of place among the youthful patrons, but Ethel seemed to blend right in. She shimmied through the crowd with ease, drink in hand, giving no care to the bemused glances from the youngsters.

Percy offered Dot a sympathetic smile and guided her to the bar. As they waited to order, Dot's eyes scanned the room. No sign of Lisa yet, though she hadn't expected their quest to be so easy.

Ethel returned to them, cheeks flushed, and shouted over the music, "This brings back memories. Don't you miss dancing all night, Dorothy? I feel so *young!*"

Before Dot could respond, the bartender arrived. Percy ordered drinks for them, having to repeat himself twice to be heard. Dot sipped her gin and tonic, wondering how on earth they were going to find Lisa in this sea of strangers.

"Maybe we should split up, cover more ground," Percy suggested.

Ethel nodded. "I'll take the dance floor. You two check the tables and booths."

As she disappeared again into the swaying crowd, Dot let Percy guide her around the edge of the room. She felt invisible in the dim lighting, forgotten among the youth and music. Each face that passed was unfamiliar. After two laps yielded nothing, Dot sighed in defeat.

"This was a mistake. We're never going to find her."

Percy gave her hand a supportive squeeze.

"Why don't we step outside for some air? Clear our heads."

Dot agreed, and they made their way out to the plaza. The cool night air was a relief after the stuffy heat of the bar. Dot looked up at the stars, finding comfort in their familiarity.

"Maybe we should just go back to the hotel," she said. "I don't know what I was thinking..." Sighing, but not ready to give up, she scanned the plaza. They'd been in all the bars except for the one blasting head-pounding rock music. "Let's make this one quick. I owe you a rematch at cards."

After Ethel joined them, they headed to the rock bar. The man on the door looked at them like they were lost, but he didn't deny them entry. This place was a seething mass of people, all clad in leather and black denim, all gleaming with piercings. The air was heavy with the musky scent of sweat and spilt ale, creating an atmosphere as intense as the music blaring from the speakers. They pushed through the packed place, arriving at the bar. Dot tried to talk to the man behind the bar, but he spoke little English. She attempted to get Ethel to come and translate, but she was too busy dancing with an older gentleman with a mohawk she'd met on the dancefloor.

"Should I fetch her?"

"Let her have her fun," Dot said, reaching into her pocket for the photograph. "I've never seen her like this. She's like a woman unleashed."

Everyone was all smiles in the photo taken on their last day in Savega from their previous visit, despite what they had gone through. Dot pointed to Lisa in the picture, and the man looked before shrugging.

Dot felt like giving up, but then another of the bartenders, a woman, leaned in and said, "That's Lisa? She looks different now. Dyed her hair."

"You know her? Do you know which bar she works in?"

"Here."

Sweet relief.

"Great! Where is she? Tell her that her auntie Dot is here."

"She's not working tonight. Sorry."

Percy cleared his throat. "Do you know where we could find her? Perhaps an address?"

She considered it while pouring a pint, squinting at them both like she didn't trust them.

"Sorry, don't know."

Dot slid the photo back into her purse, defeated.

Another dead end, but at least they knew where Lisa worked.

"We can come back tomorrow," Percy declared, ever the optimist. "Not a wasted trip. How about a little boogie first? Lift the spirits before our rematch?"

Dot swayed to the pounding beat, wishing she could share some of Ethel's wild ways on the dance floor. When a Rolling Stones track played, Percy perked up and extended a hand.

"May I have this dance, my love? I was always partial to the Stones back in the day."

Though her feet ached, Dot couldn't deny his charming smile. She let him guide her into an awkward two-step as they attempted to mimic Ethel's smooth moves with her new rocker friend with the wandering hands, not that Ethel seemed to mind one bit. Percy got into it right away, throwing in silly dance moves straight from the sixties that soon had Dot giggling like a schoolgirl despite herself. He gave an enthusiastic hip shake, eliciting laughter from those around them.

To Dot's surprise, nearby youngsters emulated Percy's goofy style. She felt herself relaxing, caught up in the ridiculousness of it all. Maybe Ethel had been right —they needed to let loose.

As the song wound down, Dot spotted Ethel in a close embrace with her mystery dance partner, their faces inches apart.

"Why don't we give those two some privacy?" Dot suggested.

They bid Ethel goodnight, though she was too lost in

her dancing to acknowledge them. The cool night air was a relief after the club's stifling heat. Percy slipped an arm around Dot's waist as they meandered through the lively plaza. No rush to return just yet.

"Dot?"

She turned at the sound of her name to see a dark-haired young woman approaching them, arms loaded with shopping bags. After a moment's confusion, Dot recognised the familiar eyes.

"*Lisa?*"

The woman with the black hair and eyebrow piercing nodded, shifting the plastic bags in her arms. She seemed surprised to see them, and despite having been looking for Lisa all night, Dot was surprised to see her—in her current guise, at least. She'd been brunette in the picture.

"Not that it's not good to see you, but what are you doing back in Savega?"

"We came for the hotel relaunch."

"Ah." Lisa nodded, eyes darting to the side street leading to the hotel. "Well, it was good to see you."

"Lisa, before you go," she blurted out, "I need to talk to you. We've been looking for you all night. I have some concerns about your mother."

Lisa considered this, then sighed.

"I was just heading home. You can come up for a quick nightcap. It's not far from here."

She headed off without waiting for a response. Exchanging a look, Dot and Percy hurried after Lisa towards a souvenir shop. Finally, they might get some answers.

After climbing a narrow staircase to the flat above the shop, Dot surveyed the cramped space as Lisa boiled the kettle. It was a far cry from the hotel, but it had a cosy, lived-in feel that the hotel now lacked.

"I know it's not much," Lisa called over her shoulder as the kettle boiled, "but the rent is cheap and I get some privacy. That counts for a lot these days. Tea?"

"Please," Dot said. "It's lovely. Reminds me of my great-granddaughter Jessie's flat above the post office back home. Very homely."

"Most of the furniture is from the hotel. I fished it all out of skips when *she* started the refit. Years of our lives, tossed away like rubbish."

"Would 'she' be Dahlia Hartfield?" Dot guessed.

Lisa's lips puckered, and her brow furrowed as she glanced away, the abrupt silence between serving as ample evidence of her disdain. The kettle whistled, and Lisa busied herself with making tea. She handed them floral china cups, her gaze distant.

"Things were getting back to normal after the hotel almost went under the last time you were both here," Lisa explained, tucking her legs up in a soft armchair. "I was running everything on my own before then, so it felt like a big reset. Mum hired some extra staff, so I wasn't running everything on my own. We were getting there, slowly but surely." She stared into her tea, fiddling with her new brow piercing. "Then the pipes in the basement burst and flooded the place. And from that moment, nothing was the same."

Dot leaned forward in her seat, the worn cushion sagging beneath her. Lisa's words hung heavy in the air, mingling with the faint aroma of stale tea and musty furniture. She studied Lisa, taking in the tight lines of her face and the way she toyed with her eyebrow piercing.

"Dahlia took over everything?" Dot asked, her voice soft. She didn't want to push too hard, but she needed to know more.

Lisa gave a bitter laugh. "Like a hurricane. Everything had to change, everything had to be her way." She glanced around the room, as if seeing it for the first time. "Mum and I... we drifted apart, and once again, she picked her latest flavour of the month over me."

"And this time it was Dahlia," Dot finished.

"I should've been relieved it wasn't another man, but at least Mum didn't change herself for them like she did for Dahlia. She said she was bettering herself, but she didn't seem 'better' to me."

Dot watched Lisa as she spoke, noticing the way her hands clenched and unclenched in her lap. There was an anger there, simmering beneath the surface. But there was also pain—a deep-seated hurt that went far beyond any business disagreement; a woman who missed her mother.

"I know I look different too. I think it's some late-in-life return to my teenage years. Stopped caring so much about what people thought about me after the stabbing. Started to live authentically to how I felt. But Mum... I don't recognise her anymore. Inside and out." Lisa let out another laugh. "Parading around like some enlightened guru... it's not who she is. At least before she wore her darkness a little more on her sleeve. I preferred it. It was more honest."

Dot wanted to reach out and comfort Lisa somehow, but she wasn't sure how. She felt out of her depth, navigating unfamiliar waters.

"Is that why you left the hotel?" Dot prompted.

"Mum told me about her plan to market the water as 'healing'. I told her it sounded like a scam. That's when she gave me an ultimatum." Her voice cracked on the last word. "She called me a 'toxic influence' and said I could go or stay and 'join them'."

"And you left."

"I tried to make her see sense that she was getting swept up in another mad scheme. But when that didn't work, I had no choice." She shrugged, a helpless gesture. "What else could I do?"

Dot didn't have an answer for that. She took a slow sip of her tea, the warm liquid offering little comfort. Lisa's story painted a grim picture of Minnie—one that was far removed from the glamorous woman she remembered.

"And now," Lisa continued, "I'm just waiting for Dahlia to get bored and move on. Mum doesn't know the first thing about running a health retreat."

There was still so much she didn't understand about

what was going on with Minnie and this Dahlia woman. But hearing Lisa's perspective made one thing clear—Minnie was slipping back into old, dangerous habits that had already hurt those closest to her. Placing her teacup back on its saucer, Dot met Lisa's eyes.

"I think your mother may be in real trouble this time," she said.

Lisa tensed but remained silent, waiting for Dot to continue.

"I overheard her saying some very worrying things the other night," Dot explained. "That she had done something terrible she couldn't take back. You heard about what happened to the girl in the mineral bath?"

Lisa's face darkened at this, nodding as her fingers curled tighter around her teacup.

"She *needs* you, Lisa," Dot pressed on. "Despite everything, you're still her daughter. Perhaps you can talk some sense into her, make her see what she's got herself into."

Lisa shook her head, a bitter smile touching her lips.

"Don't you think I've tried that already? Many times over the years. But she won't listen. Not to me."

"But if you just came to the hotel and spoke with her..." Dot began.

"I've made my choice, Auntie Dot," Lisa interjected, an edge to her voice. "And she's made hers. Maybe facing the consequences for once is what she needs."

With that, Lisa set down her tea and lifted the hem of her t-shirt. An angry red scar marred her stomach. Dot's hand flew to her mouth.

"A parting gift from the same man who held you two hostage," Lisa said. "I learned I had to put myself first because she wasn't going to."

"I'm so sorry, dear," was all Dot could think to say, her voice thick with emotion.

"Scars fade." She smoothed her shirt back down and gave Dot a weary smile. "Even the ones you can't see. I'm glad to see you two are looking well. Seems you've healed too."

"It's been a long road," Dot admitted. "But yes, we've come through it together."

Dot longed to convince Lisa to reach out to Minnie one more time, but she could see the hurt and determination in the young woman's eyes. Lisa had made her choice, for better or worse. With a heavy heart, Dot decided not to press the issue further tonight.

"Well, I suppose we should let you get some rest," Dot said, rising from the lumpy sofa. Percy followed suit. "Thank you for the tea, dear. And for confiding in us."

Lisa walked them to the door and said, "I'm happy you stopped by, even if I don't have the answers you wanted."

Dot pulled her into a brief but fierce hug.

"You take care of yourself," she whispered.

With a last goodbye, Dot and Percy made their way out into the cool night air. The streets were quieter now, the crowds having thinned. Arm in arm, they strolled back towards the hotel, each lost in their own thoughts.

Their talk with Lisa had illuminated some shadows surrounding Minnie and her puzzling behaviour. One thing was certain—Dahlia Hartfield had Minnie under her sway.

Dot was so lost in thought that she almost didn't register their approach to the hotel entrance until Percy gave her arm a gentle squeeze.

"Look there," he whispered, inclining his head towards the front of the hotel. "Isn't that the doctor?"

Dot followed his gaze to see Doctor Helena Ford slipping out the front door. She pulled Percy into the shadow of a large palm tree before Helena could spot them. Peering around the trunk, they watched as Helena hurried up the front steps, phone pressed to her ear.

"Have you got it?" Helena asked, her voice echoing around the tight side street. "Good." She paused, listening to the response, then set off in the opposite direction of the plaza. "No, I'm on my way. No, I'll walk. It's safer that way."

Before Dorothy could think better of it, she made a split-second decision. Gripping Percy's hand, she pulled him along as she crept after Helena into the shadows.

"Dot, what are you doing?" Percy whispered.

"Following her," Dorothy whispered back. "Something strange is going on here. We said we'd keep an eye on the doctor. Well, *I* said I would."

"What if we're... walking into danger?"

Dot considered if they could be, but she didn't turn back.

"We've lived through worse."

∼

Jessie sat on the edge of the bed in her hotel room, the moonlight streaming in through the open balcony doors. She clutched a postcard she had bought earlier that day in the plaza—a scenic view of the marina. She ran her thumb over the glossy image, her mind churning with indecision.

With a sigh, she pulled out her phone and opened the email from Johnny, reading over his offer for the umpteenth time. A travelling journalism job. It was an amazing opportunity, one she knew she should feel excited about. But all she felt was uncertainty.

She set the phone down and reached for the pen on the nightstand. If she couldn't make sense of her conflicted thoughts alone, maybe putting them down on paper would help clarify things.

To Veronica,

I know this will get back after I do and I might end up yanking it out of the mail before you read it, but I need to get my thoughts out. Johnny offered me a job. A travelling journalism job. Sort of like a travelling reviewer, but with a salary. Great opportunity, right?

Problem is, I don't know what to do. When you (practically) forced me to take the job at the newspaper, you told me it was an opportunity I shouldn't pass up. You were right. All the work we've done. Fighting James and Greg... and everything in between... I'm not the same person I was. If I take this new job, it'll mean leaving the paper and leaving you. Not sure I want to do that. Not sure what I want. But if I take it, I'll become another new me, won't I? Maybe I'm not making sense. It's late and I'm tired and I'm running out of space. If I take the job, you know I wouldn't be here without you, right? Thank you. And if I don't... I want a pay rise.

She set down the pen and stared at the note. The jumble of thoughts now seemed concrete, but no less confusing. With a sigh, she stuffed the postcard into the bedside drawer. She'd decide what to do with it in the morning.

After a knock at the door, she opened it to find a cross-eyed Ethel leaning against the doorframe, lipstick smudged and hair askew.

"Ethel! What are you doing here?" Jessie asked in surprise.

Ethel hiccupped, and slurred, "I seem to have misplaced my room key, and Dot and Percy have wandered off somewhere. Would you be a lamb and help me find a spare?"

"Why don't you come in and rest while I run down to the front desk? I'm sure I can get you a new key."

"You're such a sweetheart," Ethel said, stumbling into the room and collapsing onto the bed.

Jessie hurried down the hall towards the reception, hoping to find a spare key so she could get back. When she arrived, she found the front desk deserted. After glancing around to make sure she was alone, Jessie ducked behind the counter and began rifling through the desk drawers.

"There must be a spare somewhere," she muttered, shuffling through paperwork until she came across a stack of passports. Curious, she thumbed through them, pausing when she came across Ian's. According to his passport, he was sixty, though he looked much younger. Further down, she found Dahlia's passport, which listed her surname as Clayton. Jessie made a mental note of the name change before replacing the passports.

After a few more minutes of searching, she found a key labelled 'master' buried under a pile of brochures.

She paused outside the reception area, the newly gained spare key card for Ethel clutched in her hand. The sound of something heavy hitting the floor by the door made her jump, the plastic key slipping from her grasp and skittering across the tiles.

She bent to retrieve it, frowning as she glanced around the sculpture. There was no one in sight, but she could make out the angular shape of a large suitcase resting near the entrance. It seemed an odd time and place for someone to be arriving with luggage.

Pocketing the key card, she moved towards the discarded bag. As she drew nearer, the scuff of approaching footsteps outside made her freeze. A figure pushed through the front door, the overhead light glinting off a hood pulled up over their head. Jessie's heart thudded as the person strode towards her. She stood paralysed as they halted an arm's length away.

The hood flung back, revealing a familiar face that made Jessie gasp.

"*Dante?*"

Her boyfriend grinned, pleased by her surprise.

"Did you miss me?"

She remained fixed in place, shock rooting her to the spot. This was the last thing she had expected. Dante's smile faltered at her lack of reaction.

"What are you doing here?" she said, her gaze flickering between Dante and his luggage.

"I wanted to see you. Aren't you happy?"

"Of course." She moved back around the reception desk, putting some distance between them. "Just wasn't expecting to see you in Spain out of the blue."

Dante looked wounded by her hesitation.

"Yeah, well, I got worried. Felt like something weird was going on. You've been acting weird since you got here." He took a step towards her. "I just wanted to make sure you're okay."

He wasn't wrong—she had been acting distant, conflicted by the job offer from Johnny. But Dante showing up now, unannounced, at the height of the hotel's turmoil, complicated things.

She sighed, coming out from behind the desk to pull him into a hug.

"I'm fine. You're right, something weird is going on here." She felt some of the tension leave his shoulders as he embraced her.

"Well, I'm here now, so we can figure it out together." Dante smiled down at her, but Jessie couldn't mirror his enthusiasm. As happy as she was to see him, his arrival cast everything into uncertainty once more. "So, are you going to fill me in?"

13

Dot and Percy climbed the steep stone steps carved into the side of the hill, their breathing growing heavier with each upward stride. Dot felt a pleasant chill in the night air as beads of sweat formed on her forehead, but she continued to persevere. She looked back at how far they'd come. From this height, the town was a sea of lights, yellow and white, stretching down to the dark shimmer of the sea. The three-quarter moon hung overhead, lighting their way along the steep hillside. Percy trailed behind, one hand braced against the rock wall for support.

"My love, I think we should turn back," he said between laboured breaths. "We're going to get ourselves into trouble."

But Dot didn't slow her pace, her eyes fixed on the dark silhouette of Helena ahead. The doctor's unwavering confidence suggested a sense of superiority, as if she believed she was untouchable.

"You *heard* what she said, Percy. We said we'd monitor her, and that's what I aim to do."

"Well, I didn't think you meant chasing her up a mountain in the dead of night," Percy said. "Can't we just wait and talk to her tomorrow?"

Dot squinted ahead into the dark. Helena had disappeared, but she couldn't be too far ahead. Turning back to Percy, Dot set her jaw.

"We've come this far. We need to know the truth."

"Lead the way, my love. But much further and these old legs are going to give up."

The steps ended and a winding road stretched before them, following the contour of the hills even higher. In the distance, she could see Helena's shadowy figure hurrying across the road towards the thud of music and the pulse of lights in the trees.

But as Dot went to follow, she froze in the middle of the road. Percy stopped beside her, and he seemed to realise where they were. The winding uphill road, the trees on either side…

"It's here, isn't it?" Percy whispered.

"We've returned," Dot said, wrapping her hand around his. "Only a little further."

Dot continued across the road, Percy by her side. As they broke through the trees, the music pulsed loud enough to vibrate the earth beneath their feet. Lights glowing every colour of the rainbow burned through the trees and into the night sky.

"It looks like some kind of party," Percy said, a little giddy. "An outdoor disco."

"I think the kids call them 'raves'," Dot said, stiffening her neck.

They carried on until Dot could taste sweat in the air. Hundreds of dancing bodies gyrated under frantic laser lights as hidden machines pumped a sea of smoke across the forest floor. A DJ stood on a makeshift stage, blasting the electronic beats while he danced like he'd stuck his finger in a plug socket.

"Makes the rock bar look like a children's nursery," Dot said, clutching Percy's hand tight. "We're not in Kansas anymore, Toto."

Not wanting to draw even more attention from the bemused eyes staring out from the writhing mass, they skirted around the chaotic scene, searching for Helena. But the doctor had vanished among the undulating crowds and disorienting lights. Cries of "Abuela!" and "Viejo!" rose as fingers pointed and laughter echoed in their direction.

"I... I think we've lost her, my dear," Percy exclaimed over the music. "Let's get back before we cause more of a scene."

Dot stood frozen amongst the throbbing mass of dancing youths as the mass moved and somehow swallowed them up. Percy's hand slipped from hers in the disorienting mess of sensory overload.

"Do you *mind*?" Dot cried as someone stomped on her foot. "These shoes are *new*!"

A hand grabbed her hand and pulled her back, and she was soon back on the edge with Percy. They backed away as the disco zombies continued their thrashing.

"*Wait!*" Percy cried, tugging her arm. "Over there... near that big white tent. Isn't that Helena?"

Dot followed his finger through the haze, and she made out Helena's silhouette—she stuck out among the youngsters as much as they. A swaying man accompanied her. She clicked her fingers in front of his face several times. The man handed Helena something, and she slipped it into her pocket. He leaned in, whispered something in her ear, and with that, she turned around. She glanced at the party before heading back towards the road.

"You were right," Percy said. "She's up to something. And there's something else, my love. Just beyond that tent... I think that's the... the..."

She followed his gaze further uphill, where a small, dilapidated villa rose out of the darkness. Vines crawled up its charred walls up to the collapsed ceiling.

Dot felt sick. Maybe it was the music, its relentless pounding vibrating through her bones. Or the cloying smoke wafting around them, thick enough to taste. And the two gin and tonics she'd drank earlier before their mountain trek weren't sitting quite right.

But there it was.

The villa.

Straight out of her nightmares.

Dot swayed, the coloured lights and smoke swirling into a dizzying phantasmagoria. She blinked hard, trying to force the world back into focus. She opened her mouth to speak, but the pounding music took her words away.

"Time to go," he shouted over the noise. "This was a mistake."

Dot managed a weak nod, and she tore her eyes away from the villa. They pushed back through the crowded rave, the reckless dancers banging into them with no care. She kept her eyes down, focusing on each step, trusting Percy to guide them to safety.

When they broke free of the last swaying partygoers, the night air had never tasted sweeter. Dot gulped it down, steadying herself against a tree as her churning stomach settled.

Percy stood close, rubbing her back.

"What was I *thinking*, dragging us all the way out here? I'm sorry, Percy. This night's been a fool's errand."

"Well, we saw Helena up to something odd," he offered.

In her need to uncover the truth, she'd let things go too far, and now it was time to leave. She took her husband's arm and let him guide her back to the road, away from the rave and the looming villa. With each step, she felt the tightness in her chest ease.

Dot felt the vice-like grip on her arm before she saw Helena emerge from the shadows.

"You *followed* me here, didn't you?" Helena hissed, her nails digging into Dot's flesh. "Are you insane?"

"I could ask you the same thing." Dot winced, but she didn't pull away. "My husband and I are just big ravers. Aren't we, Percy?"

"Oh, yes," he said without missing a beat. "Can't get enough of glow sticks and the drum and bass music."

Helena let out a sharp laugh.

"Pull the other one! You're both playing a dangerous game."

"You don't know the first thing about danger," Dot shot back, emboldened by adrenaline mixed with gin and tonic. "We're not the ones who are suspects in a murder case."

In one swift motion, she reached into the pocket of Helena's jacket, snatching out a mysterious envelope. Helena lunged to grab it back, but Dot was quicker, dancing out of reach with the prize in hand.

"Give that back," Helena shouted, swiping at the air.

Dot went to open the envelope, but Helena was faster. She snatched it from Dot's hands and ripped it open in one aggressive motion, sending its contents fluttering to the ground.

"Stupid woman!" Helena cried, dropping to her knees. She scrambled to gather up the scattered papers.

"My Dorothy is anything but stupid."

"Oh, shut up." Helena's head shot up, eyes blazing. "You've made a grave mistake."

Helena scooped up the remaining papers and stuffed them back in the envelope. She turned on her heels and stormed off down the path, gravel crunching under her furious footsteps.

Percy tapped Dot on the shoulder and held up a piece of paper.

"Oh, Percy. You brilliant man."

"Just a little sleight-of-hand magic, my love," he said

with a wink. "Haven't lost my touch. Not sure what to make of it, though."

Dot glanced over the mysterious paper, the contents illuminated by the glow of a nearby streetlight. The columns of data and chemical names meant little to her, but words she'd heard that week jumped out.

"Magnesium, sulphur, zinc..." she read aloud. "The same composition as the so-called healing water at the hotel."

"So, this is proof of the water's properties?" Percy said. "But Helena said she *already* had conclusive results. Why go through the trouble of getting more data, and *here* of all places, and who—"

Sudden shouts and commotion from the rave cut him off. The pulsing music sputtered and cut out, replaced by alarmed cries in Spanish. Dot couldn't understand the words, but the panic in the voices was unmistakable.

"What's happening?" Percy asked. "Sounds like something's gone wrong."

The DJ's voice rang out over the speakers, tense and urgent as he repeated the same phrase again and again in Spanish.

Dot shook her head. "I can't make it out. We need Ethel."

People rushed around near the stage, obscured by the smoke machines. A small crowd gathered around someone on the ground. Cries for "doctor" and "ambulancia" rose above anxious murmurs.

Dot's gaze snapped to the man who had given Helena the envelope only minutes before. He pushed through the crowd, kneeling beside the fallen person. With steady hands, he reached into their mouth and pulled something out of their throat with calm precision, allowing them to gasp for air.

"He must be a doctor too," Percy announced, clicking his fingers together. "Helena's colleague or something? But why meet her way out here?"

"Very suspicious indeed."

Dot folded up the lab report and slipped it into her handbag for safekeeping. In the distance, flashing ambulance lights cut through the darkness, and the crowd scattered in all directions.

"Well, I think we've seen enough excitement for one night, my dear," Percy said, taking Dot's arm. "Let's head back and look over this evidence. This might be the breakthrough we've been hoping for."

Dot nodded, casting one last glance back at the chaotic scene behind them. The ambulance doors slammed shut, and the vehicle sped off down the winding road, lights flashing.

As Dot and Percy descended the stone steps leading back to town, her mind raced over the implications of Helena's secretive meeting. With the new lab results in hand, it seemed they were one step closer to unravelling the truth.

But Helena's cryptic warning still echoed in Dot's mind... "You've made a grave mistake."

What exactly was the doctor hiding? And how far would she go to keep it hidden? Dot quickened her pace as an ominous feeling settled in her gut. She wouldn't let Helena intimidate her. Not when she was so close to answers.

14

*J*ulia cupped her morning coffee in the dining room, letting the warmth seep into her palms as she listened to Dot recount the strange events of the previous night. She had to admit, Dot and Percy's late-night escapades following Doctor Helena raised more questions than it answered.

"You're saying Helena met this man at some kind of rave, and he gave her these lab results matching the mineral content of the water?" Julia asked in a hushed voice, leaning in closer across the table.

Dot nodded, her expression grim. "It's mighty suspicious if you ask me. Why go to all that trouble to get new results when she claimed she already had proof?"

"Maybe she lost the original documents?" Jessie suggested, though it didn't sound like she quite believed that theory herself.

"Or maybe she had no *legitimate* results in the first place," Julia said.

She glanced over at the paper again, reading the list of minerals and compounds. It seemed similar to what Dahlia and Helena had been claiming about the healing spring waters. Too similar to be a coincidence.

What had Minnie got herself wrapped up in?

Julia glanced up from her coffee as her sister slid into the seat beside her.

"Morning," Sue said, stifling a yawn. "Neil's taken the kids to some museum, but I'm still feeling seasick from that boat trip yesterday. Was someone else up being sick last night? I could have sworn I heard retching down the hall."

"That'll have been Ethel," Dot said, rolling her eyes. "Seems she had the wildest night out of us. I do not know how she got back into her room because I found her key card in my handbag this morning."

"Magic," Jessie said.

"Speaking of magic," Sue said, pouring herself a cup of coffee from the French press, "I saw that note you slipped under my door last night, Gran."

"And?" Dot leaned in. "Did you?"

"I did." Sue took her first slurp of coffee. "I popped into my old nursing group chat to ask if anyone knew about a Doctor Helena Ford."

Julia leaned in, intrigued. She had suspected there was more to Helena's story than the polished, enlightened persona she portrayed, even before her gran's late-night rave stalking.

"Go on," she urged.

"One of my old colleagues, Mary, came up trumps. Her sister is a doctor, and she is best friends with a surgeon who once dated Helena," Sue explained, glancing around the dining room—they were alone except for Ian, who hadn't opened his eyes from his meditating in the corner since Julia had turned up. "According to Mary, Helena isn't who she claims to be."

"I *knew* it!" Dot said, slapping the table. "I bet she's not an actual doctor."

"You're not far off, Gran. She *was* a doctor, but she had her medical license stripped last spring."

"Stripped?" Jessie said, choking on her orange juice. "You're kidding? What did she do? Kill someone?"

"Again, not far off." Sue leaned in even closer. "Helena was working as a GP in London. Busy surgery with tons of patients. The type of place where things slip through the cracks, and according to Mary, Helena was convincing her patients for *years* to go without traditional medicine. She had one patient with a heart condition, and she was prescribing her natural remedies. Pills made from garlic and green tea. One step up from magic beans."

Julia watched as the faces around the table mirrored her own shock. The revelation of Helena's past hit them like a bucket of icy water, washing away any lingering doubt about the doctor's credentials.

"She was found out when that patient had a heart attack and her son reported Helena when he found the pills in her bedside drawer," Sue said. "Helena denied it, but people who worked with her gave statements confirming Helena's patients seldom left her office with prescriptions. Whole thing went unnoticed, and then they swept it under the rug."

"I *knew* she was a con-artist!" Dot declared, staring at Sue in disbelief. "And to think, she's out there peddling 'luxury' vitamins for a rip-off price. Codswallop!"

"That tracks with what I've found online," Jessie said, scrolling through her phone. "Helena's social media presence only started this summer, so that wouldn't have been too long after she lost her license. Seems influencer fame was her back-up plan."

A chill prickled up the hairs on Julia's neck. She thought back to Helena's confident assertions about the healing properties of the water during that first dinner. She'd sounded so confident about the claims and the science backing it up.

"There's something else," Jessie said, leaning in and lowering her voice. "Yesterday afternoon, I saw Helena giving Luca an envelope stuffed with money. She was pushing him to make a run for it. Has anyone seen him since?"

Julia shook her head, as did the others.

"It seemed like they had some kind of romantic history," Jessie added. "And she mentioned that Luca and Chloe were once engaged. He told me they had a history, but he left that part off."

Dot leaned back in her chair, letting out a low whistle she said, "They're all a bunch of liars."

"I wonder if Dahlia knows about any of this," Julia

thought aloud. "There's a chance this charlatan doctor has duped her."

"Or she's *in* on it," Dot stated, stamping her finger down. "She's happy to promote this 'doctor' on her app, so you'd *assume* she's done her own research? And how can Helena have the cheek to start such a company without being a proper doctor?"

Sue cleared her throat. "They consider most supplements as foodstuffs and not medicine. Any of us could start a vitamin business. It wouldn't surprise me if she's buying pre-tested vitamins in bulk and slapping her logo onto the bottle."

"*Ah*!" Dot perked up at that, pulling out a scrap of cardboard. "Ripped this off one of her stock boxes. Ethel said it's Chinese. Do you think we could trace this back to the manufacturer?"

"It's worth a shot." Jessie took the label, squinting at the small print. "I'll look into it."

"We can't let Minnie go ahead with this relaunch," Julia said. "Not if the benefits of the water are backed by Helena's dodgy claims."

Dot nodded in agreement. "Speaking of which, has anyone seen Minnie today?"

Julia shook her head, as did Jessie and Sue. She had been wondering about her aunt's whereabouts herself.

"I think I'll go check on her," Dot said, pushing herself up from the table. "Given that we've already found one body, I'd like to see Minnie *alive* with my own eyes."

With a curt nod, Dot left the dining room. Julia

watched her grandmother go, worried for Minnie. Her great-aunt was headstrong and stubborn, yet she was too quick to trust people like Doctor Helena Ford.

"We need a plan," Julia thought aloud, turning back to Jessie and Sue.

"I say you confront Helena," Sue said. "If she denies it, I'll have Mary gather some evidence. She said she thinks she can get her sister to find a copy of the reports."

Julia nodded, her mind racing with plausible scenarios. She knew they had to watch their steps; they couldn't afford to make any missteps.

"Good idea," Julia said, "but I think I should talk to Dahlia first. She seems the closest to Helena. If Helena has duped her, we need to let her know."

"And what if she knows Helena's a fraud and doesn't care?" Sue said. "I didn't warm to her after how she spoke to us in the kitchen when we were baking."

Julia considered this, but she wasn't sure.

"Dahlia has a lot to lose," Julia said, finishing her coffee. "She wouldn't jeopardise her reputation for someone with such a questionable past, would she?"

"You'd hope not," Sue agreed. "I still had *Blisselle* downloaded, and there's even more whacky stuff on there than what I remembered. Candles that can improve your mood, jewellery with cleansing stones, bath salts to reset your chakras... she's one step away from selling magic beans too."

"Speaking of beans," Jessie said, looking up from her phone. "I've found the factory. Those vitamins are *far* from magical luxury. I've found pages upon pages of reviews. Pretty scathing stuff about the quality of their products, and several people mentioned the factory has been fined multiple times for not following health and safety standards."

Jessie slid her phone across the table and Julia's stomach knotted as she read through the reviews. If this was the factory producing Helena's vitamins, then they were far from the 'luxury brand' she'd claimed.

"These reviews go back years," Julia pointed out. "Why would Helena use them?"

"They're cheap," Jessie said. "Prices start at pennies per pill."

Julia nodded as she took in the mounting evidence against Helena. It wasn't conclusive, not by a long shot, but it painted a disturbing picture. Helena, the so-called doctor and wellness expert, was an impostor, exploiting the trust of others for her own gain.

"If Chloe found out about all of this," Julia said, pushing her chair out, "Chloe might have threatened to expose her. Just like she tried to do with Ian after their live stream clash."

"And Luca's vegan food slip-up," Jessie said. "Luca suggested I talk to Helena. I just haven't had a chance yet. It's looking like Helena had every reason to want Chloe silenced."

"For as awful as she was, Chloe deserves justice for her death." Julia folded the scientific paper and slipped it into her pocket. "If Helena is behind the girl's death, we've found a gigantic thread to pull on."

Sue left to go in search of Neil and the kids, and as Julia watched her go, she spotted Detective Ramirez near the front desk with Dahlia. For a moment, she considered approaching to share their mounting suspicions about Helena.

But they needed more definitive proof before taking it to the authorities. And there were still too many unknowns surrounding Dahlia's involvement.

"Before we split up, have you got a moment?" Jessie asked, nibbling at her bottom lip. "Something happened last night."

"What is it?"

"It's nothing bad, don't worry," Jessie insisted, though the crease between her brows suggested otherwise. "Dante showed up at the hotel late last night."

"Dante's here?" Julia asked in surprise.

"Veronica let him take a few days off to come and check on me. He said he was worried about me because I wasn't keeping him up to speed with what was going on here."

"That was... spontaneous of him," Julia said, trying to gauge Jessie's reaction—she didn't seem over the moon about it. "You were upset when he cancelled, but I'm getting the feeling you'd rather he wasn't here?"

"It's not that. It's nice to have him here, but..." she trailed off, avoiding Julia's gaze. "There's something else. Johnny emailed me."

"Johnny?" Julia's face lit up at the mention of her old school friend. "How's he doing? I haven't heard from him in a few months."

"It wasn't a social email." With a heavy sigh, Jessie met her eyes again. "He's... offered me a *job*. A travelling job reviewing hotels and restaurants and all that kind of stuff... it would mean living and working on the road... it would mean leaving Peridale, and I don't know what to do, Mum."

Dot sighed as she looked at Minnie, still curled up in bed despite it being almost noon. The drawn curtains cast the room in gloom, matching Minnie's defeated mood.

"Let's get some light in here," Dot announced, walking over to the windows. She pulled back the heavy drapes, allowing bright sunlight to flood the room.

"Close them, please!" Minnie groaned and pulled a pillow over her head. "My head is pounding."

Dot hesitated, then drew the curtains halfway to allow some light in while shielding Minnie's eyes. She perched on the edge of the bed and placed a hand on Minnie's shoulder.

"I know things seem bleak, but staying in this darkened room all day won't help matters. You need to get up, get dressed, and face this challenge head-on, as you always have."

"I don't have the strength." Minnie peeked out from under the pillow, her eyes bloodshot and mascara smudged. "Everything is such a mess. This whole endeavour has been a disaster from the start."

Dot glanced over at the array of vitamin bottles on Minnie's nightstand. The labels boasted of increased energy, mental clarity, and inner calm. Yet they didn't seem to have the desired effect.

"Are you taking *all* of these?" Dot asked.

"They help."

Dot pursed her lips. She wanted to express her concerns about Helena and her sullied reputation, but she knew she had to watch her words. The last thing Minnie needed right now was to feel attacked.

"You know I only want what's best for you," Dot began. "I can't help but worry that perhaps those supplements aren't from the most... reputable source. Ease up on them for a few days. See if that helps you feel more yourself?"

"They *help*," Minnie repeated, as her eyes flashed with sudden anger. "These vitamins are helping me be my best self, just like the minerals. In fact, I'd bet the *only* reason I feel like this is because I haven't had the energy to take my usual baths." She gave a convinced nod. "Unless you have something *positive* to say, leave me be. I won't have another *toxic* influence trying to interfere with my progress."

Dot stared at Minnie, anger rising in her chest at her dismissive words.

"Just like Lisa, you mean?" Dot said, unable to restrain herself.

Minnie rolled over to face the window. "Lisa *abandoned* me in my hour of need. Dahlia has been more of a daughter to me than Lisa ever was."

Minnie's callous words shocked Dot to the core.

"You don't mean that."

"I do."

Dot took a deep breath, steadying herself. She had to make Minnie understand the damage she was doing.

"Take a long, hard look in the mirror, Minnie," she warned. "You're a woman in her seventies, not some petulant child who can't get her own way. I spoke with Lisa. She has a *very* different version of events."

"Then she's lying."

"You're calling your daughter a liar now? Frankly, I'm more inclined to believe *her*," Dot said, and though Minnie's shoulders tense, she continued. "You almost lost your daughter for real once. Stabbed by a man *you* invited into your life. Aren't you worried that history might be repeating itself?"

Minnie said nothing, staring out the window.

"You have *nothing* to say to that?"

She snuggled further under the covers.

"Fine." Dot sighed. "I'll leave you to wallow."

Dot walked to the door, casting one last worried glance at Minnie's unmoving form before leaving the gloom-filled room. If that's how she wanted to spend the day, she could suit herself, but Dot would not lie around doing nothing. Something had to be done, and if Minnie refused to face the problem head-on, Dot would only have to try harder.

Back at their adjoining rooms, Dot was less surprised to find Ethel still curled up in bed. The curtains cloaked the room in shadow.

"*Up!*" she commanded, clapping her hands as she marched to rip open the curtains. Ethel groaned and shielded her eyes as bright sunlight flooded in. "We've got work to do. This mess will *not* sort itself out."

"Do pipe down, Dorothy. I'm terribly unwell."

"Hungover, more like," Dot said, ripping back the covers. "Self-inflicted. I don't care if your head's pounding to the beat of the Rolling Stones. *Up!*"

"What's the emergency?"

"A girl is dead, a murderer is still out there, and…" Dot trailed off, remembering the point at which she'd separated from Ethel the night before. "Last night, while you were dancing the night away, Percy and I followed Helena into the wilderness and came back with concrete evidence that she's a complete charlatan. I was right to suspect those vitamins."

"Are you sure?" Ethel pulled herself up with a groan. "I felt rather young last night. Haven't been able to dance like that in—"

"*Centuries?*" Dot cut in. "And that'll have been the gin and the disco lights, and they're doing little to help you bounce back from this hangover, are they?"

"Fair point." Ethel clapped her tongue against the roof of her mouth and looked around the room. Being the good friend that she was, Dot reached out and grabbed the glass of water off the bedside table for her. "Thanks. Jessie must have put that there. Oh, I hope I didn't embarrass myself last night."

"Aren't you *always* embarrassing yourself, dear?" Dot bit back her smile, slapping Ethel's legs. "Get a shake on.

We need to dig up more dirt on Helena, and I think having a poke around her room might be a good place to start. We'll need to figure out a way to get into there."

At that, a slow smile spread across Ethel's face and she said, "Well, it just so happens my embarrassing escapades last night proved rather useful." She patted her hand around on the bedside until she came across a plastic card. "Lost my key somewhere in the plaza. Only got into my room because Jessie found this behind the reception desk. It's the *master* key card."

Dot couldn't help but grin. This was the stroke of luck they needed. She unclipped her handbag and retrieved Ethel's card from within a bag of Werther's Originals, and placed it on the bedside.

"You left it on the bar in the first pub we checked," she said. "What was that fella's name we left you with last night, anyway?"

"No idea," Ethel said, groaning as she rose to her unsteady feet. "Didn't want to ruin the fun. So, which room is Helena staying in?"

"Not sure, but Jessie mentioned that Luca heard Chloe shouting in Helena's room, so it's one room on either side of his."

"And which room is Luca staying in?"

"*Ah*. Good question." Dot held the shiny key up to the light. "But since this opens up *all* the doors, there's only one way to find out."

15

Julia sank into the wicker chair on the balcony while a warm breeze tousled her hair, immersing herself in Barker's latest chapter draft. She recognised the fictional village as Peridale, picturing the sloping hills scattered with grazing sheep, the forest embracing the church, and the cosy café facing the village green.

It transported her back home, a bittersweet ache rising in her chest. She missed the familiar faces, the gentle rhythm of days spent baking and brewing tea and coffee. It seemed as though they had been away for weeks.

"That bad, huh?"

Julia smiled her support as Barker peered over his notebook.

"No, it's great. I just..."

How could she explain it? The creeping fear that

when they returned to Peridale, things would never be the same. Sue and Neil's sudden desire to start again abroad, Jessie's tempting job offer—everyone's paths were shifting, diverging from the comfortable one they'd left behind.

The prospect of managing the café alone while she found replacements filled her with dread, but that was nothing compared to the thought of not being able to see her sister and daughter most days of the week. Sue had drifted before and Jessie had travelled, but both of these things hadn't felt so permanent.

"It *is* the book, isn't it?" Barker pulled off his reading glasses and rubbed at his eyes. "Go on. You can say it. I know it needs some work."

"No, it's..."

A knock at the door pulled Julia from her thoughts. Handing the pages back, she walked past Olivia sprawled out on the bed having an afternoon nap. She opened the door to find Dahlia holding out a stack of fresh, fluffy towels.

"Need a bedding change?" Dahlia asked, peering around Julia at the dozing toddler. "Ah. I can come back later. The little angel is out like a light."

"I think the heat is getting to her."

"I'll give you these," she said, handing over the towels. "Any more for the wash?"

As Julia collected the used towels from the room, Dahlia waited by the door. After not being able to find her earlier, Julia had assumed she'd have to wait until dinnertime to question Dahlia, but now she had Dahlia on her doorstep.

"Just these," Julia said, handing over two damp towels. "Before you rush off, I was hoping to talk to you about something."

"Go ahead."

"It's rather sensitive."

"Ah, I see." Dahlia nodded her understanding as she scanned the hallway. "Well, you're in luck. I was just about to take my afternoon break. Grab your costume. We'll head down to the mineral baths and have a nice soak while we chat."

Julia tensed. The scene of the staged drowning? She forced a smile, trying not to let her discomfort show.

"Sounds perfect. I'll meet you there in five."

Back inside the room, Julia explained where she was going to a puzzled Barker before rummaging for her swimsuit. She had hoped to avoid the eerie basement after the shocking scene her gran had described, but she couldn't pass up the opportunity to speak with Dahlia.

After making her way through the hotel, Julia descended the stone steps, the echo of dripping water replacing the cicadas' hum. Dahlia waited by the largest bath, billowing steam rising like mist. Though empty of water and any sign of Chloe, Julia couldn't help envisioning the influencer's limp body floating beneath the surface of the bath at the end. She shuddered.

"Everything alright?" Dahlia asked, slipping into the steaming water in her white one-piece.

Julia nodded, sliding in beside her and said, "Yes, sorry. It's just... a little strange being down here after what happened."

"I understand. It was tragic what happened to that poor girl. Such a troubled soul from what I knew of her."

They sat in silence for a moment, the sulphur-scented steam enveloping them. Julia shifted in the warm mineral water, unsure how to broach the sensitive subject. Across from her, Dahlia leaned back against the smooth stone edge of the bath, eyes closed, as if soaking in the calming atmosphere.

When Dahlia spoke, her voice was soft, almost mournful. "She had a tough life, you know. I think that's why I always tried to be patient with her."

"Tough how?" Julia asked

"Chloe grew up without a family." Dahlia let out a slow sigh, her eyes still closed. "Bounced around different family members her entire childhood. She had to be a tough cookie to survive." Opening her eyes, Dahlia gave Julia a sad smile. "I'd hoped with the right guidance, she would grow out of her more reckless behaviours. Stop making such poor decisions, but isn't that the point of being young? You make mistakes, maybe burn some bridges, but you find your way in the end."

"I wish she'd had the chance to get there," Julia said.

Dahlia agreed with a solemn nod. After a moment, she added, "I saw a lot of myself in her. I grew up without a supportive family. I was close to my brother, but he went away." She dipped almost all the way under, only her face poking out of the water. "After that, I was on my own. I didn't feel like I'd found a family until I found the wellness community. I thought if we embraced Chloe, she'd soften."

"I'm sorry to hear that," Julia said. "We adopted our eldest daughter when she was a teenager. She had her thorny edges when she was younger. She's grown up so much." Smiling, she sunk a little lower into the water, thinking of their earlier conversation about Johnny's email. "She's *still* growing... still finding her way."

"She seems like a sweet girl," Dahlia said. "You've done well. I thought I could be a mentor like that for Chloe. Stop her thriving on online drama and shock value so much, but she was savvy. Knew how to generate press for herself in this new digital age where there's no line between fiction and fact. Why should she want to stop something that was benefiting her so much?"

"She liked to stir the sauce," Julia began, her tone careful and neutral. "Even with people within the community who wanted to embrace her. Ian... Luca..."

"She did. It was unfortunate, to say the least."

They stewed in the steamy silence for a moment.

"Did she ever try to do it to you?"

"No. I guess I was one of the lucky ones."

"I heard Chloe was engaged to Luca?" Julia asked.

"That was brief." Dahlia gave a small shrug, her gaze drifting to the end bath. "He proposed to her soon after they met, and she agreed. There was a huge online announcement—all since scrubbed—but they clashed too much. Luca called it off after only a few weeks."

"And Ian?" Julia asked, her heart pounding as she ticked the questions off—she was saving the biggest for last. "I saw the live stream you told me to look at. Ian had a different version of the story Chloe put out there. It looked like Chloe jumped into the pool herself."

Dahlia was quiet for a moment, her eyes shutting again as she bobbed in the water. The silence dragged out for an uncomfortable amount of time before her eyes opened.

"I found that strange too," Dahlia admitted, "but what I found stranger was Ian's total lack of a defence. He didn't make a *single* post about it, he just let the hate flow his way." She sighed. "Behind closed doors, Ian said Chloe staged the push, which I *wanted* to believe. However, I checked the hotel's security footage, just to be sure."

Julia's heart dropped to the pit of her stomach.

"And?"

"I saw it with my own eyes," Dahlia said, her gaze locked on Julia's. "Ian *pushed* Chloe into that pool. It was like a switch flipped. He grabbed her, threw her in, and then watched her flounder in the water. For all of her posing by the pool, she wasn't the strongest swimmer."

Julia felt sick. She'd believed that part of Ian's story without question. She thought about the bath in his room as she peered down the row to where the drowning had been staged. Disturbing images flashed in her mind's eye again, and this time, Chloe was slung over Ian's shoulder. She blinked them away—she needed more proof.

"I confronted him about it," Dahlia continued, her voice hardening. "He blew up at me. His temper is closer to the surface than he lets on. He meditates to keep it under control, but he's a long way from being as enlightened as he presents. If he hadn't begged to come on this trip, I wouldn't have invited him. None of us are perfect, but I can't tolerate liars."

Julia took a deep breath, trying to process what she'd just heard.

"Ian *begged* to be invited?"

"He wanted to resolve things with Chloe. I suspected he wanted to have his picture taken with her. Chloe's endorsement would have helped his online redemption arc, but he never got the chance."

Julia wondered if drowning Chloe counted as a resolution.

But as shocking as all of this information was, she hadn't come to talk about Ian, and she didn't know how long Dahlia's break would last.

"And Helena?" Julia asked, forcing her voice to steady.

Dahlia swivelled her gaze towards her, the lines on her forehead deepening into a near-scowl.

"What about Helena?" Dahlia said, and it sounded like she was forcing her wobbly voice to steady too.

"Did Chloe ever seem like she wanted to expose anything about Helena?"

Dahlia considered this for a moment and said, "Not

that I ever witnessed. They had their disagreements over the water's benefits, but nothing that seemed malicious."

Nodding, Julia moved on. "And do *you* believe the claims about the healing properties?"

"With my whole heart," Dahlia said without hesitation. "I would never promote something I wasn't convinced of myself."

"How can you be so sure?" Julia pressed, sitting up in the water. "Have you seen solid scientific proof?"

"I've spoken with the experts Helena consulted for the analysis." Dahlia gave her a patient smile. "She showed me their credentials and testing methods herself."

"Experts recommended *by* Helena? What if those experts turn out to be fraudulent? Or they are genuine experts, but making exaggerated claims?"

"You have *quite* the imagination, Julia. What is it you said you did for a living?"

"I run a little café."

"Well, I can assure you, these are respected scientists Helena has worked with for years. Their claims are sound. You stick to the baking and we'll stick to the science."

"Are *you* sure?" Julia persisted. "Couldn't someone sway them to embellish results if compensated?"

Dahlia's smile faded, her eyes narrowing to slits—Julia had pushed too hard and hit a nerve.

"That's *quite* an accusation. I can't imagine Helena, or her colleagues, would ever engage in such unethical practices."

"You must have known her for a long time if you're so trusting of her?"

"Let's see... we first met last summer in Bali," Dahlia said with a confidence that suggested weeks *was* a long time—perhaps an eternity in the world of influencers. "Helena was new to the wellness scene, but she had some exciting ideas. We hit it off right away and became close friends." She smiled, closing her eyes for a moment. "We were here at La Casa together on holiday when we first discussed going into business together. That ended up being the same weekend the pipes burst. Minnie was lucky Helena was here with me. She was the one who picked up on the sulphur and suggested the water might be more special than it seemed."

Dahlia spoke with such certainty that Julia knew she had to be careful about what she said next. If Dahlia thought Helena was her close friend, it would not be easy to convince her—she wished she had the scientific paper with her. Taking a steadying breath, she decided it was time to reveal what she knew.

"Dahlia... did you know Helena is a disqualified doctor?"

"Oh, come on, Julia! This has gone *too* far."

"It's true. She was struck off last spring for giving bad medical advice to patients. She convinced a woman to stop taking her medication, and she died."

"That *cannot* be true! Helena has multiple advanced degrees." A laugh strained in Dahlia's throat. "Her credentials are *impeccable*. Who's your source?"

"I'm afraid it's true," Julia said. "My sister is a

registered nurse and did some digging with her old colleagues. She's sure she can get the evidence if that's what it'll take, but I trust my sister."

"And *I* trust Helena!"

"Who you've known for less than a year?"

Dahlia's smile faded as she processed this new information. For the first time, Julia saw a flicker of doubt cross the placid woman's face.

"She would have told me," Dahlia muttered, shaking her head. "She's my friend."

But she lacked her earlier conviction, and Julia could see the seeds of suspicion taking root. Dahlia shook her head, sinking deeper into the steaming mineral bath.

"My gran saw Helena meet someone at a party late last night. She took some papers from him that had the same mineral levels and compounds listed as—"

"I won't entertain any more *accusations* against my friend without her present." She stood up, water cascading down her swimsuit. "Let's go speak to Helena and get this sorted. We'll go to her room right now."

Julia hesitated, but she had little choice. She climbed out of the bath and followed Dahlia upstairs, wrapping herself in a towel against the cool hallway air. Dahlia charged ahead, water dripping behind her. This wasn't how Julia had expected their conversation to go, and as much as she knew she should try to deescalate the situation, she was curious to see how the interaction between Helena and Dahlia would go.

Climbing the stairs, Detective Ramirez came up behind them in a rush, paying them no attention. Julia and Dahlia turned, watching as she charged past them and along the hallway. Moments later, a paramedic crew rushed past, equipment clattering and echoing off the hotel's grand walls.

"What's happened?" Julia called, but her question went unanswered.

Dahlia sped up, striding down the hallway towards an open door. Julia trailed after her, fear weighing her steps.

Inside, Dot and Ethel huddled together, their faces pale in the harsh beams of the afternoon light burning through the windows. They were peering at the bed with wide eyes, their hands clasped together.

Laid out on the crisp white sheets was Helena. Her eyes were closed, and her face had lost every drop of colour. Colourful vitamin bottles surrounded her—the same ones she'd been promoting. The paramedics' voices were loud and urgent as they tried to rouse Helena. Dot turned to them with a grim shake of her head.

"You're too late," Dot said, her voice thick like syrup. "From the looks of it, I'd say she's been dead all night."

Dahlia staggered at the news, reaching out to steady herself against the door frame. She stared at Helena's lifeless body, her face a mask of shock and disbelief.

"No..." Dahlia choked out. "But... *how*?"

"Looks like an overdose," Ethel said over the clamour of the paramedics. "Guilty conscience."

Julia glanced at Dahlia, expecting her to protest, but

she didn't object. Her blank gaze locked on Helena's still form.

A tense silence filled the room, broken only by the soft murmurings of the paramedics as they confirmed what everyone knew.

Helena was gone.

16

Jessie and Dante walked hand-in-hand back to the hotel after enjoying a seaside lunch together. The sun-drenched cobblestone streets were bustling with tourists and locals, a lively backdrop to their stroll.

"That paella was good, but it could've used a bit more saffron," Dante remarked as they sauntered along. "And the seafood was just a touch overcooked."

"Maybe I missed something?" she said. "I thought it was top-notch."

"I'm not saying it was *bad*." Dante grinned, giving her hand a playful swing. "Just a few minor tweaks could have elevated it. You must not have my refined taste buds."

"Apparently not."

Jessie leaned into him, glad they could joke and banter. After the shock of his sudden arrival, his presence was starting to feel comfortable and familiar again. Still, she knew she had to tell him about the job offer from Johnny soon. She hadn't found the right moment.

The morning's confession to Julia lingered in her mind like the fishy aftertaste of the paella. Her mum had listened, her expression morphing from disbelief to a strained sort of encouragement.

"Follow your heart, Jessie," Julia had said, though the same concern that knotted Jessie's stomach tinged her eyes.

But hearts were fickle, and hers was a confusing compass spinning in every direction.

She squeezed Dante's hand tighter.

"You're quiet today," he pointed out. "Can never shut you up back home."

"Just thinking about everything going on. It's a lot, isn't it?" she said, wondering if she should open up—she didn't want to throw in a grenade just yet. "Tell me more about this paella, master chef. What would you have done differently?"

They entered the plaza as she tuned back into Dante, and he had comments on everything from the ingredients to how the dish was served, remarking on the ambiance of the restaurant and the serving staff as well.

"You sound like a professional food critic," she said.

"My first job at the *Riverswick Chronicle* was reviewing local food joints. I figured out I had to write about *something*, so I started paying attention to *everything*." He shrugged. "Maybe I'm being too harsh."

"No, you sound like a pro. I don't know the first thing about food outside of baking at the café."

There was still so much to learn about Dante, even though they'd been dating since last autumn. She dropped his hand and stuffed hers into her pockets as they turned the corner onto the street leading back to the hotel.

They strolled back to the hotel, basking in the warm sun. Dante pulled the pamphlet he'd picked up from the rack at the restaurant from his pocket, flipping through the glossy pages.

"There's so much to see here," he said. "We should visit the marina tomorrow—says here they have fresh seafood markets and street performers." He rattled off more ideas, pausing on a page showing a grand museum. "And we could do a boat trip to the island on our last day. Looks like there're cliffs for diving if you fancy it?"

She only half-listened, looking at the road ahead rather than the pamphlet. As the hotel came into view, she froze. Police cars lined the street, lights flashing.

"Looks like there's been a development."

Before Dante could respond, she jogged down the side street.

"Best not to wade in," he called after her.

But Jessie's journalistic instincts propelled her forward. She approached two officers talking by their squad car.

"What's going on here?"

The officers exchanged amused glances.

"Police business, lady. Please, step back."

"I'm a guest at this hotel," she insisted. "My family is in there. If something has happened, I have a right to know."

When they remained silent, she scanned the scene until she saw bushy blonde highlights. She waved to the detective, and Ramirez squinted back with a flicker of recognition. She wrapped up her conversation and walked over to the blue and white police tape.

"Please tell me you're here to give the place another sweep?" Jessie asked.

Detective Ramirez sighed. "I'm afraid not. We found Doctor Helena Ford dead in her room. Apparent suicide. No note, but circumstances suggest she may have felt guilt over the death of Miss Saunders."

"Helena's dead?" Jessie repeated, almost to herself. "What else do you know?"

"That's all for now. Please, let my team do our work."

The detective headed back inside, and Jessie ducked under the police tape before the officers outside could stop her. She walked into the dining room, Dante trailing behind her.

Jessie's mind raced as she paced between the tables. The tables in the deserted dining room were set for lunch, with white linens and polished silver glinting in the afternoon sun.

Suicide?

No, her instincts told her that wasn't it.

Helena had been too self-assured, too cunning.

"This is another murder," Jessie said to Dante as he watched her. "It has to be."

"You spent most of our lunch talking about how guilty you thought Helena was. Guilt eating her away makes sense."

Jessie shook her head. "But it doesn't *feel* right. Someone staged Chloe's murder to look like an accident. She was drowned somewhere else and moved."

"How do you know that?"

"Soap residue in her lungs," Jessie explained. "Whoever did it threw an empty bottle of vodka in with her to make it look like she'd drowned her sorrows and then… drowned herself."

"Transported? How?"

"Not sure. Is it important?"

"Well, if someone carried her, there'd be a trail if she was dripping wet." He glanced around the room. "Depending on which way they came, there'll be soap residue everywhere. Couldn't they just follow the trail to wherever it leads?"

"If that was the case, I'm sure they'd have found that. I can't think about that right now. I need to find out as much as I can about this fresh crime scene. The killer was sloppy once already." She met Dante's gaze. "If this was staged, I bet they've left more unintentional breadcrumbs."

Dante flapped the pamphlet and said, "No chance of a normal holiday?"

"That boat sailed for me days ago." Guilt itched in

Jessie's chest. She touched his arm. "Go off on your sightseeing adventures."

Dante considered her for a moment but said, "I'd rather help. Could be good work experience, right? Though I don't have your detective chops. You're like a bloodhound."

"Just paying attention."

But Dante was right.

It would be good work experience.

For whichever route her journalism career took.

With Percy keeping watch in the corridor, Dot stepped into Helena's hotel room, the memory of finding the doctor's lifeless body still vivid in her mind. Though the police had since moved her, the space still bore the heavy imprint of tragedy—and the bed the imprint of her body.

She scanned the rumpled sheets and scattered vitamin bottles, trying to glean any details the police may have overlooked. But she didn't know what she was looking for. She looked at Ethel, lingering in the doorway, subdued.

"Why don't you sit this one out?" Dot suggested. "I won't be long."

Ethel screwed her face up in protest but seemed to think better of it.

"Maybe a bit of fresh air first. This hangover still has its claws in me." She shuddered. "The flashbacks from the bar last night aren't helping. I think I took a ride on a mechanical bull at one point. Explains my lower back." She twisted her middle with her hands on her hips. "The devil must have got hold of me in that rock bar."

"I thought it was the vitamins?"

Ethel gave the bed a wide berth and dragged open the sliding doors to the balcony before stepping through the fluttering curtains into the fresh air.

Dot turned as footsteps came up behind her. She expected to see the police, but Jessie and her handsome boyfriend, Dante, strolled in.

"I should have known you'd be in here already," Jessie said as she stared at the indent on the bed. "What happened?"

"We wanted to have a poke around her room for more evidence to back up that scientific paper. That's when we found her sprawled out on the bed. Quite the shock."

"Did you see anything that might point to it being a staged crime scene?"

Dot thought for a moment, then walked over near the bathroom and pointed at the floor.

"There was a smashed plant pot here. Police have cleared it away." She crouched down, examining the spot. "There's still some soil."

"Could have happened at any moment?" Dante suggested.

"Could've been a struggle?" Jessie said instead. "Maybe someone came in, grabbed Helena from the bathroom, and dragged her to the bed?"

"Smashing the pot on the way." Dot nodded along, using the chest of drawers to pull herself back to her feet. "It's possible. Though I'd expect more of a mess if there was a true fight. And why not clear up the mess they left behind?"

"Maybe they got distracted?" Jessie said. "Or interrupted?"

"Hard to know for sure what happened. But it doesn't feel right, that's for certain."

Dot stepped into the bathroom, scanning the cream tiled space for any signs of a struggle. At first glance, everything appeared to be in order—towels folded, soaps in place, surfaces wiped clean. She lingered near the doorway, picturing the sequence of events. If someone had accosted Helena here, there would be some evidence left behind in the perpetrator's haste.

Jessie entered behind her, phone at the ready to document any clues. Within seconds, she gestured to the shower curtain.

"Look at this," she said, holding up the liner. The last few hooks had popped off, leaving the curtain sagging in the corner. It was subtle, but the detail a killer in a hurry might overlook.

"Great catch!"

Dot imagined Helena by the sink next to the edge of the shower curtain, startled by an intruder entering from behind. Grabbing the curtain in panic as she was pulled away, hard enough to dislodge the cheap metal hooks. Not hard enough to save her life. Dot turned and mimicked the motion, seizing the curtain and dragging it as she stumbled backwards through the bathroom door.

Her fingers scraped along the doorframe, catching on the wood grain. Dot examined the spot, finding a faint but visible scratch mark where her hand had been.

"Another clue," Jessie said, holding up her phone.

"Could be coincidence." Dante shifted in the bedroom, glancing between the women. "This feels like enough to go on. Maybe we should head out?"

"Chicken?" Dot asked, but she was undeterred, consumed by the emerging picture of what had transpired. She surveyed the bathroom again. "Someone wanted us to think Helena took her own life. But how do you get someone to take pills against their will? That part makes little sense."

"Maybe someone threatened her?" Jessie suggested. "Take the pills or die another way?"

"If faced with that decision, I'd rather just die any other way."

"*Emergency!*" Percy called, head popping around the doorframe. "The police are coming, *post haste*! Looks like they didn't finish processing the scene after all."

"*Ethel?*" Dot hissed out to the balcony. "Time to get a move on."

Beyond the fluttering curtains, Ethel had crouched into a squat, looking at something on the floor. She dabbed a finger at it, then stood up and peered over the edge, rubbing her thumb against her forefinger.

Dot hurried over and pulled Ethel back inside just as Percy's spoon-playing against his knee could be heard distracting the officers down the hall. Bless her husband for always keeping a set in his pocket. She popped her head around the side of the door as the amused officers watched his antics. They snuck out one by one in the opposite direction.

As they hurried from the scene, Dot noticed Ethel still rubbing her fingers together.

"What is it?" Dot asked.

"What does that look like to you?" Ethel said, holding out her grey fingers.

"If I had to put money on it, cigarette ash."

"That's what I thought," Ethel agreed, sniffing her blackened fingertips. "And as much of a hypocrite as our dead doctor friend was, I never once caught a whiff of ciggies on her."

"No, me neither. What are you suggesting?"

"That we have a look under that balcony."

As they slipped downstairs, Dot had an extra spring in her step. Her theories about their prime suspect might have fallen apart, but they would not let the actual killer slip away again.

17

Down in the dining room, Julia tried to console both Dahlia and Minnie. Dahlia hadn't stopped crying all afternoon and Minnie was drinking sangria like it was tap water, blasting melancholic Spanish music on a vinyl player she'd dragged down from her room. It reminded Julia of Minnie's reaction to Dot and Percy's kidnapping, and she'd been at a loss for what to do then.

"Remember your wellness journey," Julia reminded her.

But Minnie poured herself another generous glass of sangria and with a toast, said, "What's the point? La Casa has a dark shadow looming over it and *always* has."

Julia looked to Dahlia, hoping she would talk some sense into Minnie. But Dahlia poured herself a large glass of sangria.

"Maybe Minnie is right," she said, staring into the

bobbing fruit. "You can't run away from your shadows forever."

Julia sat between the two despondent women as the vinyl spun its mournful Spanish ballads. She eyed the half-empty bottle—she couldn't let this continue.

"I know things seem bleak," she began, moving the bottle to the other side of the table, "but we can't give up hope. The truth will come out. We just have to find it."

Minnie sniffled, her blank eyes fixed on the far wall. Her fingers danced along to the music in some spilled sangria on the table like she was drawing with blood.

"You're still so young and naïve, Julia," Minnie said. "Some stains don't wash out, no matter how much you try to scrub."

"Dahlia?" Julia pleaded again.

"I'm sorry, Julia. I'm in double shock." Dahlia sounded as if she'd swallowed shards of glass. "First, finding out Helena wasn't who she *claimed* to be. Then her death. I'll never get closure. *Why* did she lie to me? A tempest has engulfed me, flinging me from one shocking twist to another."

Julia reached across the table and placed her hand on Dahlia's.

"Perhaps she felt it was her last chance? To fake the water results to profit off the hotel, and get close to you to sell her vitamins through your *Blisselle* app?"

"*Fake?*" Minnie wailed, shaking her head with vehement desperation. "They *can't* be. They've helped me so much. *I* am living *proof* that those waters *are* healing."

Dahlia's face softened at Minnie's outburst, and she pried the glass from Minnie's hand.

"You may have had one too many, my friend," Dahlia suggested, sliding the glasses away—she hadn't touched her own. "This will be playing havoc with your mind."

Dahlia's words seemed to resonate with Minnie, who allowed Dahlia to guide her hands away from the jug. She slumped back in her chair, and the harsh lighting revealed every bit of her seventy-something years—the airy Minnie, who had floated into dinner in a white robe claiming to have been cured of life's ills, must have been somewhere else in the hotel.

"I'll help you up to bed," Dahlia offered, extending a hand towards Minnie. "It's best not to jump to conclusions. We don't know the results of the mineral baths are fake yet, only that Helena used less than reputable sources to get the results. I have faith and so should you."

As Minnie allowed herself to be guided away from the table, Julia sat alone with their sangria and the melancholic string music grating in the air. When she couldn't take it anymore, she scratched the needle off the record and looked out onto the patio where Dot, Ethel, and Jessie walked around the pool half-hunched, as if searching for clues. She considered joining them for a moment, but then Detective Ramirez strode into the dining area.

"I heard you wanted to speak with me?" Ramirez asked.

Julia nodded. "I learned some concerning things

about Helena that may shed light on why she took her own life."

The detective's dark eyes sharpened with interest and she said, "Go on."

"Well, it seems Helena was a discredited doctor using the wellness community to rebrand herself," Julia explained. She hesitated for a moment, hating to speak ill of the recently-deceased, but the detective gestured for her to continue. "There's also a possibility Helena falsified the scientific results for the mineral water."

"Savega has many things," Ramirez said in a low, gruff voice, "but magical water is *not* one of them. You believe Chloe Saunders may have discovered the truth about Helena's credentials?"

"It's possible," Julia agreed. "Chloe had a reputation for trying to expose people. If she found out Helena was a fraud…"

Julia let the implication hang in the air. The detective nodded, her intelligent gaze drifting over the beautiful sunset vista surrounding the patio. She watched the hunched trio with a curious squint for a moment before turning to Julia.

"So, when faced with exposure, Helena took her own life rather than face the consequences?" the detective mused. "This gives me some new angles to investigate, but there are other angles that I'm looking into." She scanned the empty dining room and moved in closer, and Julia took a mirroring step. "You seem like a woman who is switched-on. Can you tell me about her dynamics with Dahlia, Luca, and Ian?"

"Dahlia was her business partner, at least regarding the vitamin line and the mineral baths promotion. My daughter Jessie mentioned it sounded like there was something between Helena and Luca at some point, either before or after he was engaged to Chloe. And I'm not sure about her dynamic with Ian. My gran mentioned she saw them talking, so they were at least cordial."

"Thank you. That's very helpful."

Detective Ramirez flipped her pad shut, but she lingered.

"What's on your mind?

"Despite what the scene suggests at first glance, I don't believe this was a suicide." Ramirez exhaled through her nostrils, her expression grave. "First, there's no confession note. Second, there are definite signs of a struggle in the room." She lowered her voice and said, "And third, more sensitively... was there any evidence Helena may have been a... injecting herself?"

"Not that I ever witnessed. I wouldn't have suspected that, given how health conscious she was. Though, I suppose we didn't know her at all. Why do you ask?"

"We found an injection mark on her leg."

"Oh."

"Oh, indeed. Taking all the evidence together, I'm considering this another murder, not a suicide. Once your family has finished being questioned, I suggest you all return home to England."

Julia let the information sink in, feeling the weight of the detective's directive. Two murders in her aunt's hotel, and neither what they first appeared. She shivered despite the warmth of the early evening air.

"We cannot abandon Minnie until this mess is cleaned up," Julia said. "She needs people around her she can trust. She can't run from this, so neither should we." The detective nodded her understanding, though her dark eyes remained troubled before Julia added, "I'll move Olivia to another hotel. My nieces too."

"That's wise," she said. "One last question. Have you seen Ian or Luca today?"

"I've not seen Luca, but I saw Ian meditating in that corner during breakfast, not that he ate anything."

"Call me if you see them," she ordered, taking a step back. "We're looking for them as a matter of urgency."

With that ominous update, the detective departed, her heels clicking across the tiles. Julia watched her go, resolve hardening within her.

"I've *got* it!" Ethel's voice rang out from the patio.

Julia watched as Ethel fished something from the pool with a skimmer. Ever prepared, Dot pulled a pair of tweezers from her handbag and extracted a soggy item pinched in the skimmer's net.

A cigarette butt.

"Luca," Jessie chimed in, stepping closer. "He's always lighting up."

"Care to explain?" Julia asked, stepping out into the sun.

"That balcony right above us belonged to Helena," Ethel explained, pointing the skimmer above her head. "I found ash on the balcony, but no butt, so..." She mimed finishing a cigarette and flicked it. "I knew it had to be down here somewhere. Pass me those tweezers, Dorothy. I'll run after that detective so she can have it tested."

Dot handed over the tweezers with care before Ethel ran back into the hotel. Eyes shielded from the sun, Julia looked at Helena's balcony, imagining Luca standing there, smoking as he stared out at the never-ending view of the valley behind them with Helena's body on the bed behind him.

"Detective Ramirez said Luca is missing," Julia said, forcing her mind into the present.

"Not as missing as she thinks," Dot replied, pulling from her bag a key card marked 'Maestra.' "I know for a fact that Luca is passed out in his room *right now*."

Jessie stared at her in surprise and said, "How do you know that?"

"I'll explain on the way." Dot beckoned for them to follow as she marched towards the reception area. "But we must move fast. All this police noise is bound to wake him up."

Julia followed them upstairs, but she turned off at the first floor. As much as she wanted to question Luca, she still had Ramirez's warning about fleeing at the forefront of her mind. Inside, she was pleased to find Barker packing.

"Already found another hotel around the corner," he explained, scooping Olivia up from the bed. "This isn't suicide, is it?"

"No," Julia said, exhaling. "The murderer is still out

there. We need to stop them, Barker. Before it's too late."

18

Jessie shifted her weight from one foot to the other, peering around the corner at the police milling about outside Luca's room. Their presence made this whole sneaking around business a lot more complicated. She turned back to face Dante, Ethel, and Dot, huddled together against the wall.

"Any ideas how we're going to get in there?" she asked.

"Maybe we should just let this one go?" Dante folded his arms across his chest. "We're not detectives."

"We're journalists, aren't we?" Jessie cocked an eyebrow. "It wasn't *too* long ago you were all up for breaking into Wellington Heights to search a politician's apartment."

"Yeah, and that was a *terrible* idea, if you recall," Dante shot back. "I was trying to act cool because I fancied you. But this..." He gestured towards Luca's room. "This is serious business right under the nose of the local fuzz. We shouldn't be messing around."

Maybe he had a point. Things had escalated since Helena's death, and the last thing she wanted was to put any of them in harm's way.

"Alright," Jessie conceded. "Maybe we should split up."

"Split up?"

She heard the echo of what she'd said.

"As in... why don't you head back to the room for now and wait for me there?" she said, scrambling. "You know what I meant."

Dante sucked his teeth, but he didn't argue further. Hands in his pockets, he slunk off. Jessie turned to Dot, who was watching with a tight smile.

"I could have handled that better, couldn't I?"

"Maybe." Dot waved a dismissive hand. "But you know how men are, dear. Typical to choose a moment like *this* to throw their toys out of the pram." She glanced down the hallway as Dante rounded the corner. "We'll manage fine without him. Now, let's figure out how to sneak past those officers into Luca's room."

"I've got an idea!" Ethel announced.

Before either of them could ask what the idea was, Ethel rushed over to Helena's room next door—where the police were still investigating—and yanked the door shut.

"*Ethel!*" Dot hurried over, Jessie on her heels. "You reckless oaf!"

"Gives us enough time to get into Luca's room," Ethel replied, holding the handle to Helena's room with a firm grip. "Stop your dillydallying and get on with it."

Jessie hovered by the door as Dot brandished the master key card. Her stomach churned with uncertainty. While the others were convinced of Luca's guilt thanks to the cigarette, Jessie had her doubts.

Their beachside conversation replayed in her mind. Luca had seemed genuine when talking about his past with his family and Chloe, even if he hadn't told her the full truth. And the way Helena had tried to pay him off to leave town made him seem more like a scapegoat than a criminal mastermind.

They hurried inside. Even in the dark, Jessie could see they were alone with only the stench of the musky scent of a man to keep them company.

"He was right *there*!" Dot cried, tossing her hand at the bed before flinging open the linen curtains. "The scoundrel's done a runner, and now we know *why* he was lingering around. He was waiting to do away with Helena first."

Jessie scanned the room. The open, empty wardrobe and lack of a suitcase on the luggage rack suggested Luca had fled. But something still didn't sit right with her.

"He was definitely here when you saw him earlier?"

"Out cold on the bed. Didn't so much as stir. We were only in here for a few seconds, mind you. Weren't sure which room belonged to Helena. The first one we checked on the other side had to be Dahlia's, given the patchouli perfume. Then Luca's, then Helena's."

"And you found Helena after seeing him on the bed?"

"Seconds later."

It made little sense to Jessie. If Luca had murdered Helena, he would have fled right after instead of lazing around drunk. And if he'd killed Chloe too, why wait so long to run?

Unless he was innocent.

But if that was true, why disappear now?

While Dot continued her frantic search, a glimmer of white peeking out from under the bed snagged Jessie's attention. She crouched down, the floor cool against her knees as she picked up a small piece of paper. A receipt. Her heart pounded as she scanned the words, but her excitement faded when she realised it was written in Spanish.

Leaving the room, she found Ethel in the hallway, using her body weight to hang back off the handle as the police banged and shouted.

"Let me," Jessie said, swapping places with Ethel and holding the door shut. "Can you translate this?"

Ethel squinted at the receipt, her lips tracing the words.

"Looks like a receipt for a travel ticket," she said after a moment. "For a journey on El Espíritu del Mar."

"What does that mean?"

"The Spirit of the Sea."

"A boat?"

Ethel nodded. "A one-way ticket to Gibraltar from Savega's marina."

Dot joined them in the hallway.

"When?" she asked.

"In thirty minutes," Ethel replied.

Dot looked from Ethel to Jessie, then gave a decisive nod. She stepped forward and took over holding the door.

"We'll only slow you down," she ordered. "*Go.*"

Jessie hesitated for only a second before breaking into a sprint down the corridor. She could hear Dot behind her, offering explanations to the bemused police officers as they escaped from Helena's room.

But Jessie wasn't going to linger. She pounded down the stairs two at a time, ignoring the startled glances from more police officers as she dashed past them. She considered grabbing Dante, but she dismissed the idea just as fast. There was no time for explanations or arguments.

The front doors of La Casa burst open before her, and she barrelled down the side street, gasping for breath as she sprinted towards the marina.

Time was running out, and she couldn't dispel the nagging fear that her greatest asset in solving the mystery was on the verge of sailing away.

Julia stood at the oven, stirring a bubbling pot of vegetable soup while Sue chopped carrots at the counter. Despite the familiar rhythm of cooking together, a tense mood hung in the humid air.

"I can't believe what's happening here," Sue said, her knife hitting the chopping board in a steady rhythm. "We can't escape the chaos for five minutes."

Julia nodded, her eyes fixed on the simmering pot.

"It's certainly been one thing after another since we got here."

"Maybe it's time to get the kids out of here. Go to another hotel down the coast," Sue suggested. "Hate the thought of them being under this roof while there's a two-time murderer on the loose."

"Barker's taken Liv to a small hotel around the corner. There's a room there for you and the kids if you want it."

Sue paused. "And you're staying here?"

"I need to help Minnie get things in order before I go anywhere."

"You can't help yourself, can you?"

"She's family, Sue."

"When it suits her," Sue replied in a brash whisper as she scraped the carrots into the stew. "All these years, and I've only seen her *once*, and this is only your *second* time. She's never come to visit us in Peridale... never invited us to this hotel until things were hitting the fan..."

Julia couldn't argue with that, but the pull to stay was

too strong—Sue hadn't been there the last time the Sangria soured.

"I know," Julia said, smiling at her sister. "But... I am staying."

"Well, there are some pleasant villas to rent near the beach. Not too expensive either. I might see if Neil can negotiate a short term let for us. Get the ball rolling."

Julia paused stirring, eyebrows raised. "Even with everything that's going on, you and Neil are still thinking about moving here?"

"Why not?" Sue countered. "This mess has been stirred up by Dahlia's stuck-up lot coming in. But the town itself is beautiful. It's a dreamland, don't you think?"

A dream turned into a nightmare, more like.

The door swung open, and a woman strode in, her jet-black hair falling across an eyebrow piercing. Julia squinted, and it took her a moment to recognise the woman beneath the gothic makeover.

"*Lisa?*"

Lisa grinned. "Julia. It's been a while."

Julia rushed over and wrapped her arms around Lisa. After what they'd experienced together after Lisa's stabbing, there was an unspoken bond lingering between them in the hug—she'd been wanting to see Lisa since the moment they showed up at the hotel.

"It's so good to see you." Julia turned to her sister. "Sue, you've never met Lisa. She's Minnie's daughter."

"Of course. First cousins, once removed, right?"

"Something like that," Lisa said, accepting a quick

hug from Sue. "No mistaking that you two aren't sisters. Spitting image of each other."

"We are?" Sue glanced at Julia with a wink. "People say we look like our mum."

"Yeah, I used to get that a lot too," Lisa said, less enthused.

"Well, it's lovely to meet you," Sue said, not knowing how to take Lisa's awkwardness—Julia understood it, all too well. "This used to be your domain, didn't it?"

Lisa scanned the kitchen, her smile growing uneasy. She nodded, and Julia remembered this was where Lisa had taken a knife to the midsection.

"I couldn't help but overhear as I came in," Lisa said, leaning against the counter. "Are you thinking of moving here, Sue?"

"It's just something we've been throwing around." Sue took over stirring the soup, her shoulders tensing. "This seems like it would be a great place for the kids to grow up."

Lisa smiled, though her eyes betrayed a flicker of disagreement. Rather than respond, she changed course and said, "I heard about what happened with that doctor. Word travels fast around the plaza."

"Doctor Helena Ford," Julia said. "And we're used to gossip spreading back in Peridale too."

"They're saying it was a suicide?"

Julia nodded. "It looked like that, but the police suspect foul play."

"A staged suicide?"

"The second this week," Sue said, tasting the soup before adding salt.

"This hotel seems to have the worst luck," Lisa said.

"You should come to Peridale if you want to see *real* bad luck. Wellington Manor alone has had more deaths than I've had hot dinners," Sue joked before shaking in more salt. "The soup is almost ready if you're staying? I'd love to pick your brains about Savega."

"Another time, perhaps," Lisa said, her smile straining into a tight line. "I've dropped by to see my mother. Knowing her, she won't be taking this well."

"Not at all," Julia said.

Lisa pulled out her phone, her dark painted nails tapping across the screen.

"You might want to hear this voicemail Mum left me the other night. Your gran came and found me, worried that Mum had made some sort of confession over the phone to someone."

Lisa turned up the volume and pressed play, and Minnie's distressed voice emanated from the phone's small speaker.

"*Lisa, it's me again. I don't know what to do. I don't think I can get out of this one. I've done something really, really stupid...*"

Minnie's voice cracked with despair before giving way to a long pause. Julia thought the message had ended until she heard Minnie sniffle on the other side.

"*I... I never should have let Dahlia convince me to rebrand the hotel like this. I don't know the first thing about wellness retreats,*" Minnie continued. "*You were right. I don't know what I'm doing! Please Lisa, help me fix this mess before it's too late. Please... please..."*

The message ended and Lisa slid her phone back into her pocket with a sigh.

"I didn't hear it until this morning," she said. "I don't wish Mum ill will. I just wish this wasn't the first time I'd heard from her since I left the hotel months ago. Is she up in her room?"

"I was just about to take some soup up to her. She might need it to soak up some of the sangria."

"Ah, so she's off the 'detox' then. Let me." Lisa lifted the tray that Sue had prepared. "We have a lot to catch up on."

She headed out of the kitchen, leaving a heaviness lingering in the air.

Sue set down her knife, shaking her head. "Blimey, she's intense. You don't think she could be behind all this, do you? Ruined the launch to get back at her mum?"

"No." Julia looked to see if her sister was being serious, but she was too busy shaking more salt into the soup. "Lisa is the last person I'd suspect."

"Sometimes those people are the *first* people you *should* suspect." She blew on a spoonful and handed it over. "Tell me if it needs anything."

Julia sipped from the tip of the spoon, the saltiness curling her tongue.

"We'll peel some potatoes to help soak it up," Julia said, crossing the kitchen to the pantry. "Everything can be fixed, even a salty soup."

As Julia got to work peeling potatoes, she hoped Lisa's presence could fix the rift with Minnie and shed some light on the troubling darkness shrouding La Casa.

Jessie sprinted down the sloped street towards the marina, her calves burning and lungs aching for air. Clenching the damp, sweat-soaked receipt in her fist, she raced against the clock. With less than ten minutes to spare, Luca's ferry to Gibraltar was on the brink of departure.

She had to reach the docks before he slipped away for good.

The sun hung high over the glimmering Mediterranean Sea as she made her way onto the marina boardwalk. She scanned the signs listing dock numbers and ship names, searching for El Espíritu del Mar.

"Excuse me?" Jessie panted at the nearest man by a boat. "El Espíritu del Mar?"

"Tourists," he grunted, turning away.

Jessie didn't have time to argue. She staggered down the boardwalk, clutching her ribs as a stitch kicked in.

"El Espíritu del Mar?" she called out. "*Anyone*?"

An old fisherwoman untangling her nets looked up at her frenzied state and pointed Jessie towards the far end. Her footsteps pounded the weathered planks as she ran while seagulls circled and squawked above. Up ahead, the outline of a small passenger ferry came into view. A uniformed crew member stood at the top of the boarding ramp, glancing at his watch.

This had to be it. But was she already too late?

As she slowed to catch her breath, a loud groan rose from a narrow gap between two stacked crates. Peering into the shadows, she spotted a hunched figure slumped on the ground—Luca. He kicked over an empty bottle as he struggled to rise to his feet.

The bellow of the ship's foghorn blasted, startling Luca sideways. He stumbled up from his hiding place, swaying. Jessie reached to grab his arm, hoping to steady the drunken man.

"Luca... what are you doing?"

"Leave me!" He shook free of her grip. "I'm getting out of here. *Arrivederci* Savega! Time to start a new life..."

"You're not going anywhere in this state."

Jessie stepped in front of him as he tried to lurch towards the ferry, but Luca shoved past, intent on his escape. But as he staggered up the ramp, the waiting crewman put up a hand to stop him. After a brief exchange, the crewman shook his head and blocked Luca's passage with his clipboard.

Seeing his opportunity slipping away, Luca screamed up at the sky before he lunged forward. Jessie rushed to intervene, grabbing Luca by both arms this time.

"*Calm down*, Luca! Listen to me..." She pulled him back down the ramp to the safety of the dock. The crewman gave her a nod of thanks before turning to prepare for departure while tourists smirked and gasped from the boat. Still gripping Luca's shoulders, she looked into his bleary, bloodshot eyes. "You need to sober up. I know you're scared, but running away won't solve anything."

Luca stared back at her with a wandering gaze that wouldn't focus. For a moment, she thought he might shove past her again. But his tensed shoulders relaxed as her words seemed to sink in.

In the distance, the last boarding call echoed across the marina, first in Spanish, then in English. The foghorn blared again while the crew hauled in the ramp.

"Let's get you away from the water," she said, hoisting his arm over her shoulders. "There will be other ships, but not today."

Luca nodded, the fight draining from his body. As El Espíritu del Mar motored out of the marina, she guided the broken man back along the boardwalk. Though his drunken state made him unsteady on his feet, he didn't stop scanning the marina, as if expecting the police to emerge from the shadows at any moment.

"Why are you helping me?" he mumbled. "You think I killed Chloe, no?"

Jessie wasn't sure what to believe, but she knew that allowing Luca to flee in his current state wouldn't help solve any mysteries, especially with a recent murder still unresolved.

"Luca, do you know what happened?"

He turned his bloodshot eyes toward her, squinting.

"Helena is dead."

"*Morta?*"

Luca stopped, swaying as he tried to process this

information. Jessie tightened her hold, worried he might collapse into the water.

"You think *I* did this?" Luca barked. "That *I* killed Helena?"

"I'm not accusing you of anything. But it won't look good if you run now."

"They will blame me. This is what they do."

"Not if you're innocent," Jessie countered. "Where did you get the money for the ticket?"

"I... I save it. For emergencies."

Jessie knew this wasn't the full truth, but she let it go for now. There were more pressing questions.

"What about you and Helena? Were you ever more than friends?"

Luca didn't hesitate to shake his head before he lurched away from Jessie. She jumped back as he hurled up his guts over the edge of the boardwalk. Distant shouts carried over the water as boaters yelled their disgust.

"*Scusa*," Luca groaned, still hunched over.

"Come on," she said as she gave his back an awkward pat. "Let's get you back to the hotel."

"No, no, I cannot go there. They will find me, arrest me..."

"No one has to know you're there. You can stay in a new room. I'll sort it out."

Luca wavered, glancing back at the sea. But he nodded and allowed Jessie to guide him onward. As they walked, she couldn't help but see the frightened child inside this broken man. The boy who wasn't allowed to go to the beach. The boy seeking validation, terrified of being blamed for something he may not have done.

"It's going to be okay," she assured him. "We'll figure this out."

Luca said nothing, but his shoulders relaxed as he followed her lead. Step by step, they made their way back towards the hotel and the tough conversations they needed to have.

19

"Isn't it funny how when we get older, the roles of parent and child can reverse," Dot said, tugging the curtains shut as the sun dipped behind the hills.

Lisa sighed, keeping her eyes on Minnie as she dabbed her mother's flushed face with a cool cloth from the edge of the bed.

"That would imply that my mother ever looked after me to begin with," Lisa said, taking her time to refold the cloth. "There was always somewhere better to be—a celebrity party to network, a yacht filled with producers to schmooze, some glittering red carpet opening to stumble her way across."

Regret nibbled at Dot as she watched Lisa tending to Minnie. Even though they were family, she had never been there for her niece.

"I'm sorry, Lisa," Dot said, sitting next to her on the

edge of the bed. "I'm your auntie. I should have been more involved in your life."

Lisa turned to Dot, her expression unreadable.

"It's fine. I know you had your own troubles to deal with after Uncle Albert died."

"That's no excuse," Dot insisted. "Yes, after my Albert died, I shut myself off from everything and everyone for a long time. I got myself stuck in a horrid cycle, and by the time you came along, I had already drifted so far from your mother." Her head moved side to side in quiet refusal. "I never attempted to get to know you or be a real family member to you. As the elder, I'm sorry for that."

"Really, Auntie Dot. It's not your fault." Lisa's shoulders lifted in a subtle noncommittal gesture. "Mum was always so focused on her career and social life. If she'd known you were interested, she might have palmed me off on you." A soft exhale of resignation escaped her lips as she tilted her head at her mother. "It wasn't *all* bad, I suppose. She cared in her own way. When she was home, she'd bring me little gifts from her travels—autographs from famous people she met, swag bags from fancy parties." A faint smile crossed her lips. "If she came home in a good mood, we'd stay up late watching old films eating popcorn."

"She could be quite fun."

"You're right about the cycles," she said. "Mum has been doing the same thing for as long as I can remember. Someone new comes along, changes her life, makes it *better*. But somehow... she always ends up back in the same place... the same mess... *this* mess."

"Oh, I'm sorry, Lisa."

"I shouldn't blame Dahlia for what's happened to this place." Lisa smoothed a crease from the bedsheet as Minnie groaned in her sleep. "Mum *clings* to people. She's always been that way."

Dot bobbed her head in agreement.

"I think your mother does it because she's afraid."

"Afraid?"

"She's afraid of the past haunting her," Dot continued. "Of history repeating itself. Broken marriages... shattered dreams... things she'd rather run away from..."

Dot's eyes drifted to the closed curtains—she'd been so close to that villa and still too scared to face it.

"Your mother surrounds herself with people like Dahlia because it helps her feel safe," Dot continued, taking the cloth from Lisa to dab Minnie's glistening cheeks. "If she hands over control, she won't be to blame when it all goes up in smoke again."

She continued dabbing Minnie's flushed face as she stirred from her sleep.

"Lisa..." Minnie mumbled, her eyes flickering open for a moment as she reached out a trembling hand. "I'm so sorry, love... *so* sorry..."

Lisa leaned forward and took her mother's hand, though her expression remained impassive.

"I'm here, Mum," she assured her. "Try to rest."

Minnie's eyes closed again, and her breathing grew

steady once more. Lisa placed her mother's hand back on the bed.

Dot could see Lisa's emotional distance, even while she cared for her ailing mother. The young woman kept glancing at the clock on the wall, shifting on the bed, eager to finish her duty and get on with her own life. After a few more minutes, Dot set down the cloth and placed a hand on Lisa's shoulder.

"Why don't you go on and get some rest, dear? I can sit with your mum for a while."

"Are you sure?" Lisa looked up, relief relaxing in her eyes. "I know she can be a handful when she gets like this."

"Nothing I haven't handled before," Dot reassured her with a smile. "I think I can manage for one evening."

"I'll come back first thing tomorrow to check on her." She leaned down and placed a quick kiss on Minnie's forehead. "Thank you, Auntie Dot. I know she doesn't make it easy for people to stick around."

Lisa left the two of them alone in the apartment, and Dot sighed as she dabbed Minnie's forehead with the cool cloth. Her mind drifted back to the morning she left for Spain—the morning she'd almost given up on herself. She was back in Peridale, standing in her hallway, Evelyn's tarot card reading bouncing off the walls.

The ten of swords—betrayal, defeat, and hitting rock bottom.

Dot had never believed in any of that mystical tripe, but she'd still assumed something sinister awaited them in Spain. Looking at Minnie now, lying flat out at rock bottom, maybe the card hadn't been for Dot at all, but a message for her to pass along.

"Giving up would be the easy option," Dot said, more to herself than to the sleeping woman. "But I won't give up on you, Minnie. Not until you're back on solid ground again."

Julia headed down the quiet street away from the small hotel above Café Rosado where Barker and Olivia were staying for the night. The evening air had a chill to it compared to the sweltering daytime heat, and the plaza stood still—the dinner rush had ended, and the nightlife had yet to take over.

Up ahead, she noticed a familiar figure emerging from the doorway of the museum just as the attendant was locking up.

Ian Fletcher.

If not for his distinctive beard, she wouldn't have recognised him. A black hoodie hid his face as he walked at a hurried pace. He didn't seem to notice Julia until she crossed into his path.

"Ian! Wait a second."

He turned, looking none too pleased to see her.

"Julia. Hello."

"I'm glad I caught you," she said, out of breath as she approached him. "Did you hear about Helena?"

Ian blinked, his expression unchanged.

"We found her dead in her room this morning."

"Oh." His tone conveyed little emotion. "That's... *unfortunate*."

Julia studied his face, searching for any hint of a reaction. But he remained expressionless, and he didn't ask what anyone would ask when hearing about a death: how did it happen?

"The police think it was murder," she added. "They're questioning all the guests. Detective Ramirez is looking for you."

Ian stuffed his hands deep into the hoodie pockets, glancing over his shoulder down the dark street towards the hotel. Julia crossed her arms tight to herself, less comfortable in his presence this time around. His stoic state now felt aloof and cold.

"Where have you been all day?"

"Here," Ian replied, gesturing at the museum behind them as the lights within switched off one by one. "I needed some time away from that place to clear my head. I've been wandering the exhibits, taking in the culture, losing myself in different worlds." The words came out slow and measured, as if reciting a prepared script. "It was just what I needed."

"And what about last night?" she pressed.

"I'm not doing this whole suspect interview thing again with you." Ian's shoulders tensed in the hoodie. "I don't have the energy."

He turned to set off, but Julia moved to block his path.

"Why are you being so defensive?" she asked. "If you have nothing to hide you—"

"You want the truth?" He ran a hand down his face, shaking his head. "The truth is, I've been in there burying my head in the sand. Hiding."

Julia gulped.

"Hiding from what?"

"The people in my phone," he said, looking around the quiet plaza like they might be waiting for him. "Chloe's death has gained her a lot of media attention. Every story with her name attached is being dredged back up, and mine has been doing the rounds today. And guess who's getting attacked online and in the press? *Me*." He sighed, some of the tension leaving his shoulders. "I wanted *one* day to myself to turn off my phone and turn off my mind. To forget about Chloe and everything else going on at that hotel. Is that too much to ask?"

Julia studied his face and saw the glimmer of genuine frustration. But she thought back to what Dahlia had said about seeing the hotel footage of Ian pushing Chloe into the pool in Bali. She found she felt less sorry for him this time.

"I should get back to my room," he said, breaking the stuffy silence that had grown between them. "I'm going to pack up and move onto California to prepare for my next speaking engagement. I should never have come here."

"You came here hoping to repair things with Chloe,

didn't you?" she tilted her head. "To ask her to post some pictures with you to stop the online hate against you?"

"*Repair* things?" A dry laugh escaped his lips. "No. I didn't know Chloe would be here until I arrived. Dahlia *invited* me, and if anyone needed to repair their relationship with Chloe, it was Dahlia."

Julia was about to ask Ian to elaborate when a police car pulled up alongside them. Detective Ramirez stepped out into the lamp-lit plaza. Julia looked up at the hotel window and saw Barker looking down from their new hotel window. He pulled his phone down from his ear and nodded at Julia.

"Mr Fletcher, you've been a hard man to find," Ramirez said, her obvious exhaustion chewing at the edges of her voice. "I've been looking for you all day."

Ramirez gestured for Ian to get in the car. He complied without a fight, his hood still pulled up over his head.

"Why did Dahlia need to repair her relationship with Chloe?" Julia asked through the window.

"Since she has so much to say about me," he said, turning away to stare in the ocean's direction, "ask Dahlia to tell you about the subject of Chloe's scandalous book..."

20

With Dante in the shower, Jessie snuck to the floor above and knocked on the door of room 204 at the end of the hall.

"Luca? It's me," she called.

She heard shuffling from inside before Luca opened the door just a crack. His eyes were bloodshot, his hair dishevelled. He was shirtless and still smelled like he needed a shower, but he stood steadier on his feet than when she'd left him.

"What do you want?"

"I wanted to see how you're holding up."

Luca sighed and opened the door wider to let her in. The room was one of the smallest she'd seen in the hotel, with an uninteresting view looking out over the built-up street at the front of the hotel. Perfect for hours of sobering self-reflection. Luca collapsed onto the unmade bed while Jessie took the only chair.

"How are you feeling?"

"Like my head is in a vice." He rubbed at his temples. "Remembered why I gave up alcohol. Poison."

"Isn't that the point?" She attempted to laugh, but he didn't join her. "It'll pass. Just need to get some food in you. Have you been drinking water? I put some electrolyte powder in that jug. There are tons of tubs of the stuff in the kitchen. They always do a cracking job when I've had one too many espresso martinis."

"Why are you being nice to me?" He raised a tight smile. "You don't know me. For all you know, I killed those women."

"Did you?"

He shook his head.

"I'm being nice to you because we all need someone to be nice to us in our hour of need, and this is yours." She sifted through everything she knew about Luca, all the questions she had, and the biggest of them all pushed forward. "Why didn't you mention you were engaged to Chloe?"

He sighed, clutching his knees close to his hairy chest.

"It was a mistake."

"Relationships end all the time," she said. "Sometimes you're with someone for a reason, sometimes a season, and sometimes—"

"Sometimes it's not a *genuine* relationship," he interrupted as he sat up a little straighter. "I didn't want to propose to Chloe. I was pressured into it."

With Luca's rising fame as a food influencer, Jessie could imagine the pressure to boost his status by creating a power couple match with an influential partner.

But he didn't say 'the pressure', he said 'pressured'.

"Did someone push you into proposing to Chloe?"

He looked away. "It doesn't matter now."

"Was it Chloe?"

"I said it doesn't matter," he repeated.

Deciding not to push him further on that, she changed the subject.

"What about Helena? You two had a fling at some point. And don't deny it. I saw you together in the plaza."

"Yes, and it was very brief after I ended the engagement with Chloe. I was in an awful place, and Helena was... convenient." He raked a hand through his greasy hair. "But she fell harder than I did. Tried too hard to be everything she thought I wanted in a woman. I didn't feel the same about her."

That aligned with Helena's desperation to give Luca the money to leave town.

"I saw Helena give you that money," she admitted. "She seemed keen for you to get away."

"She was just the messenger," Luca said. "The money wasn't from her. I'm certain it came from Dahlia."

"*Dahlia?*" Jessie asked in surprise. "Why would she want you to leave?"

"It's complicated."

"Complicated how?"

"*Complicated.*"

Another brick wall.

"When's the last time you saw Helena?"

Luca considered his response. "Late last night. I came back to the hotel to pack my things after booking my boat ticket. I went into the kitchen and raided the alcohol. I snuck it into sauces when Dahlia wasn't looking. I saw Helena going into her room late with that yoga guy. I overheard her tell him she needed to talk to him about something important. But I didn't catch what it was about."

"She was with Ian?" she repeated in surprise. "Were they friends?"

"I don't know. They disappeared into her room. That's the last I saw of her."

Ian and Helena meeting late at night, before she ended up dead? It gave her a lot to think about. She decided not to press Luca further until she could check his account.

"Get some rest," she said, standing up from the rickety chair. "I'll bring you some more food later. Try to eat something."

Luca glanced at the fruit bowl she'd brought him earlier with a snarl.

"You know, even after all these years as a vegan, there's only one thing I want in this hungover state."

"What's that?"

"A bacon sandwich."

"You're only human," Jessie said, laughing. "I think

you should stick to the fruit before you do something else you might regret. And no running, you hear me?"

"Sì signora."

Jessie walked back to her room, and all she could think about was what Helena had needed to tell Ian. And why had Dahlia been so eager to get Luca out of Savega that she paid for his ticket? Nothing added up.

In the room, Dante was out of the shower, a towel around his waist, sitting on the bed using her open laptop.

"What are you doing?" she asked.

Dante looked up, tilting the laptop lid down. He'd seen the email—it was written all over his face. She walked over and slapped the laptop shut.

"I... I was looking for a film for us to watch," he said, squinting at her. "I saw the email open from Johnny. I... I read it."

"That was private."

"I know, I'm sorry," he said, and his twisted expression wrung Jessie's gut. "When were you going to tell me?"

She sighed, walking over to the window to stare out into the night.

"When I'd figured out what I'm going to do."

Dante let out a strained laugh. "Seriously? Jess, opportunities like this don't just fall into your lap every day. You *have* to take it."

"It's not that simple—"

"What's there to consider?" he pressed. "A chance to

travel the world doing what you love, getting paid for it? It's perfect. Don't be an idiot!"

"Don't call me an idiot."

"I didn't mean it like that, it's just—"

"It's just not *that* simple," she repeated, pulling her arms tight around herself. "It would mean leaving Peridale. Leaving my family. Leaving *The Post*."

She couldn't bring herself to look back at Dante, not when her heart felt so conflicted.

"I can't believe this," Dante said, shaking his head. "I'd take that job with both hands without even thinking about it. This is what I went to university to study for—a job like this, with a salary like *that*. The chance of a lifetime."

His words twisted the knot in her stomach tighter. She drew in a deep breath before turning to face him again.

"Yeah?" she said. "Well, maybe it's not the chance of *my* lifetime, because that's not how I feel…"

She was on the verge of confessing that a factor in her hesitation was their growing relationship. But hearing how eagerly he would grab such an opportunity made her bite her tongue.

"I'm tired," she said instead. "I need to have an early night."

She busied herself rummaging through her bag for her toiletries, avoiding meeting his tracking gaze.

"Talk to me, Jess," he implored. "I want to understand where your head's at with this. I… I don't get it."

"I told you, it's complicated," she said, her tone sharper than intended. "Remember when you asked me to go travelling with you last year and I said I didn't want to?"

"This is different. It's a job."

"I know, which means I'll be paid to stay away."

"But it's what journalists do."

"I never wanted to be a journalist," she cried, tossing her hands out. "Johnny and Veronica pushed me into it because they saw potential in me. Great. *Fantastic*. And you know what? They were right. Turns out I could do more than work in the café. A lot more, but this offer... I don't think it's what I want because if it was... I'd *want* it more, wouldn't I? And the last thing I need is you putting pressure on me to—"

"I'm not trying to pressure you." He held up his hands. "I just want to help you think it through."

"Well, calling me an idiot and making out like I'm throwing away a golden ticket isn't helping."

She grabbed her toothbrush and disappeared into the bathroom, closing the door behind her. She hadn't meant to slam it, but the door banged into the frame with a definite thud. As she smeared minty foam across her teeth, she studied herself in the mirror. The dark circles under her eyes stood out against her pale skin. How had everything become such a mess?

She thought about what waited for her back home— her small flat above the post office, her desk in the corner at *The Peridale Post* above the nail salon, part-time shifts in the café, and Sunday dinner at her mum and dad's. A life she loved—a life she'd fought for—filled with people she loved. Could she leave it all behind and start fresh in a new country every few weeks?

But then she imagined herself chasing stories overseas. Seeing breathtaking new places, trying exotic foods, immersing herself in different cultures with new people. It was tempting. She couldn't deny that. A chance to spread her wings and challenge herself in ways she never had.

But hadn't she done that already with her brother? One long holiday around the world, and she'd been so glad when it ended.

When she emerged from the bathroom, Dante had pulled on a t-shirt and switched off the lights except for one bedside lamp. He waited on the edge of the mattress, scrolling through his phone.

"Feel better?"

She nodded, climbing under the sheets. She wasn't ready to dive back into the conversation. Silence settled between them, and she could feel Dante's eyes on her in the dim light.

"You know I just want you to be happy," he said, his voice gentle. "Whatever you decide, I'm here for you."

She rolled over to face him.

"I want you to be happy, too."

He smiled back, leaning in to kiss her forehead before settling down beside her. She curled into him, comforted by his familiar warmth. Within minutes, his breathing slowed into the steady rhythm of sleep.

But Jessie's mind continued to whirl. As she listened

to Dante's soft snores, she rolled over and read the email again on her phone. It *was* the opportunity of a lifetime. She couldn't deny that. A second go around the globe while getting paid to do it.

She should be jumping at it.

So why wasn't she?

21

On the small balcony of their new hotel room, Julia stared down at the quaint plaza below as the sun warmed a new day in Savega. Olivia babbled and gnawed on a teething biscuit beside her, and in the small room behind her, she could hear Barker typing at lightning speed on his laptop.

Compared to La Casa, this place felt like a home away from home with its soft yellow walls, homemade quilts of red and purple, and the permanent aroma of cinnamon and fresh bread from Café Rosado beneath them.

Despite the quaint setting, the bizarre events that had unfolded over the past few days consumed her mind. Two deaths, both staged to throw the police off their scent. Someone desperately wanted to get away with murder. And Aunt Minnie was at the centre of it all, unravelling more each day.

The balcony door creaked open, and Barker set

down a paper bag and two steaming takeaway cups; she hadn't noticed his typing stop, but he must have been to Rosado.

"I got you one of those pastry things you seemed to like the other day," he said as he pulled up a chair beside her. Olivia cooed and reached for him. Barker scooped her up, bouncing her on his knee while Julia dug into the warm Miguelito.

"So," Barker said, "now that Ian is in custody, is the case closed?"

"It's not closed until Detective Ramirez says it's closed," she said, licking the flakes from her lips as the cream filling oozed out onto her fingers. "And I don't think she arrested him. Looked more like she took him in for questioning."

"So, three suspects left?"

"Ian, Luca, and Dahlia," Julia confirmed. "Luca is still missing, and I haven't seen Dahlia since just after Helena died. I tried to find her last night, but she must have shut herself away in her room."

"How did she react when you found Helena?"

"Like her best friend had just died."

"You think she could have faked it?"

"I don't know..." Julia said. "Back to the drawing board. New day, fresh approach."

"And what is this fresh approach?"

"Haven't quite figured it out yet."

"You sound like me writing these new scenes," he said, kissing her on the cheek as he whisked Olivia out of her chair. "Whoever has the most to gain from Chloe's death... that'll be your murderer. Back to writing, and this one needs a layer of sunscreen."

She rose to join them, but she noticed a police car pulling up in the plaza below. In almost the same spot where the police had picked him up the night before, Ian unfurled from the backseat.

Julia descended the steps into the bustling plaza, searching the sea of tourists until Ian came into view by the ornate fountain. His demeanour had undergone a transformation since their last, more tumultuous meeting; his familiar serene presence seemed to have reasserted itself.

"How are you?" she asked as they took a seat on the sun-kissed ledge.

Ian peeked open an eye to glance at her before going back to his meditating. She inhaled a deep breath, and she thought he might ignore her.

"I answered their questions. They saw no reason to keep me," he said, dodging her question—but at least he hadn't frozen her out. "And I had a restful night's sleep. There's a peculiar solace to be found in the stillness of a prison cell. No lurking shadows or boogeymen to disturb your peace when you're secured behind those bars." He leaned back, angling his face to bask in the generous rays of sunlight. "Have you talked with Dahlia?"

Julia shook her head. "I haven't seen her since yesterday. She seems to be the latest person to vanish." She wavered before adding, "You hinted at something again yesterday—about asking Dahlia about Chloe's book. Last time I asked her, she said she'd only skim-read it."

"Did she?" He exhaled a frustrated breath, and she thought he might clam up again. He stood and stretched his arms over his head. "Does the name Michael Clayton mean anything to you?"

"Should it?"

"I think you should find out for yourself," he said. "Ask Dahlia."

Ian's parting words lingered in the air as he sauntered towards the steps leading down to the beach. Julia patted her phone to search for the name, but it was still in the room after her rush to talk to Ian. She remained perched on the edge of the fountain, the cool marble grounding her as confusion swirled within. She closed her eyes, trying to pull a Michael Clayton from her memories. Nothing presented itself, and the sound of tiny rushing footsteps disrupted her thoughts.

Her twin nieces, Pearl and Dottie, approached with matching giddy smiles.

"Look Auntie Julia," Pearl said, swishing her braided hair side to side. "We got it done at the beach."

"And tattoos," Dottie said, lifting her sleeve to show a crinkling image of blue waves. "It's real."

"*Temporary*," Sue called after them, heaving herself over the top step. "Fancy seeing you here, Julia."

"Was talking to a man about a book."

Sue's eyes held a softness as she watched her daughters chase each other around the fountain. Neil followed behind, his jaw clenched. He nodded at Julia, his focus on the side street as he marched back towards the hotel.

"Something wrong?"

"We spoke to the estate agent," Sue said with a sigh. "Learned about all the hoops we'd have to jump through to move here now that we're not in the EU. Thank you, Brexit."

Julia watched the carefree joy drain from her sister's face as her shoulders slumped. She sunk onto the fountain ledge and rested her head on Julia's shoulder.

"I am sorry, Sue."

"Are you?" she said in a small voice. "Every time I brought it up, you either said nothing or tried to talk me out of it without making it seem like you were talking me out of it." Laughing, she added, "Sorry, that wasn't fair."

"No, you're right," Julia said, wrapping her arm around her sister's shoulders. "As your big sister, I just wanted to make sure you were sure because I'd miss you. Selfish, I know."

"I'd miss you too, dummy," she said, leaning into the hug. "Neil's taken it worse than me."

They watched Pearl and Dottie chasing each other in circles around the fountain. Their laughter carried on the breeze, at odds with their mother's deflated mood.

"It's not impossible," Sue went on, "just more difficult than we realised. More paperwork, more fees. We'd have to prove a steady income, find a place to rent first. And we don't speak the language."

"Maybe you could still make it work?" Julia offered.

"Take some time to look into all the options. If this is something you want, of course I will support you. Every step of the way. Like you said, it's only a plane journey away."

"I think the bubble may have burst," she said. "I'm getting a little homesick, to tell you the truth." She laughed, taking in the plaza as she looked around. "As lovely as this place is, I'm thinking there's such a thing as too much sunshine."

A wave of homesickness washed over Julia in that moment, and all she wanted was to be standing behind her café counter in her apron, surrounded by the same faces she saw every day.

But there was still work to be done in Savega before that could happen, and if they were going to catch those flights back home in three days, she had to work quick. She'd like at least a few days to relax, and despite being more confused than ever about what was going on beneath the surface, she had a new direction—or rather, name—to follow.

"Ever heard of Michael Clayton?" Julia asked after Sue rounded up the twins. "Ian suggested I look into him.

"Are you serious?" Sue let out a surprised laugh. "*Doctor* Michael Clayton?"

When Julia shrugged, Sue's expression grew sombre.

"They sentenced Doctor Clayton to *life* in prison for murdering a bunch of his patients," she whispered, pulling the twins in close as they tried to wriggle away.

"It was an enormous scandal in the medical community."

"How many is a 'bunch'?"

"A *bunch*," she repeated, leaning in, and adding, "ten?"

"*Ten?*"

"Could have been more."

"Murdered them how?"

"Poisoned them while they were under his care," Sue said. "Then altered records to make it look like natural causes. Arrogant, charming, respected in his field. Typical psychopath, if you ask me. What made your friend suggest looking into *him*?"

"I'm not sure yet," Julia admitted. "But it has something to do with Chloe's book."

"Clayton has been in prison for well over a decade, and *all* of his victims were older women," Sue said, letting the twins go to continue their running around the fountain. "He manipulated them into writing him into their wills and when they least expected it… goodbye Doris, Doreen, and Delilah. Fancied himself as the next Harold Shipman. Unless he tried to kill Chloe when she was a child, I don't think she was a near-miss victim of his."

"But Michael Clayton could be who she based her book on?" Julia wondered aloud. "So, what does that have to do with Dahlia Hartfield?"

Jessie looked up from her phone, captivated by the lively strumming of a Spanish guitar. A festival was in full swing at the plaza, brimming with laughter from families, the rhythmic steps of dancing couples, and the spectacle of street performers juggling and breathing fire.

Worlds apart from the stuffy atmosphere at La Casa. Between the murders and Dante wanting to talk about her job offer, she had needed to get away, if only for an hour, so when her mum suggested meeting at the café, she had jumped at the chance.

She scrolled through comments on a Reddit thread full of speculation about the identity of the killer in Chloe's fabricated memoir. Her eyes flitted over fragmented sentences as she skimmed:

'... echoes the crimes of the notorious Slumber Slasher from 2003...'

'... bears a resemblance to the slayings by the Sunset Strangler along the coast in 2008...'

'... might be hinting at the unsolved murders committed by the Night Nurse between 2010-2012...'

Jessie sighed, shaking her head. It seemed Chloe had pieced together details from many killers to weave her fictional tale, making it impossible to pin down who she'd written about.

Across from her, Dot had yet to stop talking about who she thought the prime suspect was.

"... and *now* the scoundrel has sailed away and fled the country," she announced after a long slurp of her tea. "I knew that chef was trouble from the moment I met him. Shifty eyes."

Julia nodded along as she sipped her coffee, though Jessie sensed her mum didn't buy Dot's theory either. Jessie bit her tongue, still keeping Luca's whereabouts a secret for now.

"Well, whoever the killer is," Julia said, with a much more balanced tone, "they're still out there somewhere. We need to—"

A street musician striking up an energetic flamenco number nearby cut her off as the performer's heels clicked on the cobbles. Jessie watched the mesmerising performance for a moment, but it would be too easy to let her mind drift away from their current mess.

She refocused on her phone, switching to a search on the name Ian had suggested: Michael Clayton. The first result led her to an article titled 'The Angel of Death: The Michael Clayton Story a Decade Later.' Clearing her throat, she began reading aloud:

"'Ten years after his shocking conviction, the case of Doctor Michael Clayton, nicknamed the Angel of Death, still haunts the families left behind. Clayton, a once-respected and beloved family GP, murdered his patients with cocktails of prescription medications, altering records to conceal his crimes, but only after manipulating them into willing him their fortunes.'" She cleared her throat. "'Michael was convicted for murdering thirteen people, though police estimate the true number could be higher. Clayton hasn't uttered a word since his arrest, showing no signs of remorse for his actions.'"

Julia's eyes had gone wide, her hand frozen in mid-air, still clutching her cup. She said, "To think of someone in a position of trust committing such evil against vulnerable people..."

"Well, don't stop there." Dot leaned forward, fingers tapping the tabletop. "What does the rest say? How is this doctor connected to all of this?"

Jessie nodded and continued reading: "'Despite his well-reputed charm, Clayton's downfall came in the form of an eagle-eyed trainee receptionist. Sarah Conway, only nineteen at the time, noticed discrepancies in one patient's files when updating the records and, despite being discouraged by her senior colleagues, Sarah alerted the authorities. Clayton is serving multiple life sentences at Ashworth Hospital, and a six-part *ITV* drama is in production and will air this autumn.'"

"Starring that Sheridan Smith, no doubt," Dot said with a roll of her eyes. "She's in *everything*. Olivia Colman, too. I shan't be watching." She sipped her tea, and added, "What channel did you say it would be on?"

Ethel came shuffling up to their table, weaving around a server carrying drinks and cakes.

"Well, don't you all look cosy," she said. "I wondered where you'd gone."

"We're just going over everything we know so far," Dot said, pulling out a chair for Ethel. "Trying to make sense of it all. Has Luca turned back up at the hotel yet?"

Jessie held her breath. Ethel shook her head, ignoring the chair and swaying to the guitar.

"Minnie's losing her marbles. I think she thinks all this noise in the plaza is in her head. What's going on? It's *fabulous!*"

"Carnaval de Cadiz," the server replied, nodding at a group of men in vibrant costumes dancing around the fountain, making fun with the locals. "They're the chirigotas. They sing songs that—how do you English say—take the pi—

"Another cup of *tea*, please," Dot said, slapping the chair for Ethel to sit. "And I think the word you're looking for is 'satirical'?"

"Sí," the server said. "Tea."

The server left and Ethel still didn't sit down. She shuffled her feet in an awkward dance, itching to join the revellers in the square. But Jessie leaned forward, hoping Ethel could provide another clue.

"Did you ever finish reading Chloe's book?"

Ethel stopped dancing, looking torn between the table and the music. With a sigh, she plopped down into the empty chair.

"I finished it last night, and it was a load of melodramatic drivel."

Julia set down her coffee and said, "Did she mention anything about the killer being a doctor or having a medical background?"

"Hmm, that rings a bell." Ethel pulled the book from her oversized beach bag and thumbed through the pages. "Ah yes, here's the part where she describes being held captive and injected with strange substances." She cleared her throat and began translating an excerpt: "'My captor kept me weak and confused with injections and pills, like a living experiment. I never knew if the next needle would stop my heart for good. He monitored my vitals, drawing vial after vial of blood, as though testing to see how much I could handle. He'd make my death look like an accident. I knew it.'" Ethel snapped the book shut. "Over the top, but I suppose it does sound medical, doesn't it?"

"Frighteningly macabre." Dot shuddered. "What a twisted young lady to make up such a thing. I hope it was worth it."

"That's almost like how Helena died," Ethel pointed out. "An injection in the leg, the detective said."

"It's like Chloe's story is playing out in real life," Julia said, staring off, lost in her thoughts. "First, her own suspicious death after claiming to have escaped death, and now another killed by a method straight from her imagination."

"Well, I wouldn't be surprised if that Doctor Clayton has escaped," Dot said, nodding her thanks as the server slid a cup of tea in front of Ethel. "He probably read that silly book and didn't like some young girl writing all about his misdeeds."

"Escaped prison?" Ethel scoffed. "Don't be silly."

"You see it *all* the time," Dot fired back. "Snuck out in a washing basket, or escaped during a transfer, or—"

"You've been watching too much telly."

Jessie scrolled further in the search results to a more recent article.

"He was still in prison as of a fortnight ago. He's been on hunger strike since his sentencing in 2013. They have to force-feed him through tubes."

"I say let the monster starve," Ethel said before she took her first slurp of tea. "Save the taxpayers some money—we might get all those potholes in Peridale fixed if they let those tubes run dry. I bet he's having liquidised sirloin steak every night on *our* coins."

"Sirloin steak?" Dot laughed, shaking her head. "Now who's being ridiculous? It's frying steak at a push."

"Hmm." Ethel turned back to the festival, her head bobbing along to the music. "You know, I was *almost* one of his victims myself."

"You, Ethel? Don't tell tales."

"It's *true*, Dorothy."

"He only killed people in Wiltshire," Jessie pointed out. "All within a ten-mile radius of his GP surgery. Part of the reason it was so easy to convict him of so many murders at once."

"And I spent a New Year's Eve in some little village *in* Wiltshire the year of the London Olympics," Ethel said. "He was on the loose back then. Had a bit too much bubbly and needed the doctor the next day for my head. Good thing I didn't end up with that devilish doctor."

"Now you sound like Chloe," Dot said, rolling her eyes.

The air between them grew thick before Ethel slipped away, her body swaying to the pulsating flamenco beats. Her announcement of having almost escaped death at the hands of Michael Clayton had stunned them into silence.

"Who'd have thought Ethel was such a party animal?" Dot said as they watched her lose herself in the dance. "I'd have assumed she'd have two stiff hips and three left feet, but she's quite... *rhythmic*."

Julia didn't respond, her brows furrowed in deep thought.

"Mum?"

"We need to focus," Julia said, finishing her coffee. "What does this Clayton have to do with the here and now? Why did Ian mention him to me?"

Jessie leaned back in her chair, watching the revelry in the plaza as she mulled over her mother's words. Julia was right—they needed to focus. With so many tangled threads in this mystery, it was too easy to get sidetracked.

"Maybe we're going about this all wrong," Julia said, shaking her head. "There are too many pieces that don't fit. It's too difficult. Too confusing. Too many angles to look at. The mineral baths... Chloe's book... Helena's shady dealings... Luca going missing... Ian mentioning this serial killer..."

"That Ian is as slippery as an eel!" Dot declared. "I don't trust anyone who can sit still for hours on end claiming they're not thinking anything. Perfect cover-up for hours of murder planning, if you ask me. I bet he told you about the Angel of Death to throw you off his scent. Another wild goose chase to send you off on."

"Maybe," Julia said. "If his plan was to get me

chasing shadows while he slips away unnoticed, it's working."

Jessie glanced back at her phone screen and clicked on an article from the year of Clayton's trial. A picture of a family fleeing from the courthouse dominated the page, their faces knotted in despair as a sea of onlookers jeered at them while photographers snapped every brutal second.

She zoomed in, squinting at the grainy faces captured in the moment of anguish. One woman caught her eye, half-obscured under a black jacket with dark hair falling across her face. But the photographer's low angle had captured her features.

"Look familiar to anyone?" Jessie asked, sliding the phone across the table.

"She looks like Dahlia," Julia said. "But with dark hair instead of blonde."

Dot leaned in, peering at the screen. "I *knew* that wasn't her natural colour. For as holistic as she claims to be, her ends are as split and frazzled as Katie's peroxide locks back home."

"A big change in hair colour makes someone look different," Jessie pointed out. "Look at Lisa going from brunette to black. I didn't recognise her when I first saw her."

"I can't blame the girl for wanting a clean break from Minnie," Dot muttered as she watched Ethel being spun around by a man in a short, embroidered jacket and criminally tight trousers. "But why would Dahlia want to change how she looks?"

"Because she's connected to this doctor."

"His wife, perhaps?" Julia suggested.

"Or sister," Jessie said. "The article says Clayton had a twin sister who testified in his defence at court. Ring any bells?"

"Dahlia did mention she had a brother in passing," Julia said, her face scrunching up as she stared off in the hotel's direction. "We were in the mineral baths together. She was talking about her past. She said she didn't have many people growing up except for her brother. What was it she said?" Drumming her fingers on the table, her eyes shot wide open. "She said he 'went away.' I'm sure of it."

"*Went away*?" Dot laughed. "That's a very polite way of saying 'he went to prison for murder.' That settles it. Dahlia is this psychopath's sister, and I'd say the apple didn't fall far from the tree."

"It settles nothing," Julia said, shaking her head. "I could be wrong. She could have another brother. This doctor might be a cousin or a... close family friend."

Jessie's eyes lit up as a piece clicked into place.

"The passport!"

"What passport?" Julia asked.

"When I was looking for a spare key for Ethel the other night, I found a stash of passports behind the reception desk," she explained. "One of them was Dahlia's, but it had the surname 'Clayton' instead of Hartfield. And the photo looked just like her, but with dark hair. I thought nothing of it."

"She must have changed her identity to distance herself from her brother," Julia said.

Jessie pocketed her phone and stood up.

"Well, sitting here all afternoon gossiping about it like we've got all the time in the world won't help anyone, is it?" she said, pulling a few colourful euro notes from her pocket to stuff under her cup. "Let's get back to La Casa and see what Dahlia Hartfield—*Clayton* —has to say for herself."

"We *will* talk to Dahlia," Julia said, pulling a small business card from her bag—it was the one the detective had given to her. "But first, Detective Ramirez needs to know about this if she doesn't already. The last time we suspected someone, they ended up dead."

"You don't want to wade in and confront a cold-blooded killer on your own?" Dot laughed, stuffing more notes under the cup before snapping her purse shut. "You should go on holiday more often, dear. This break has done you the world of good."

22

In the small, cluttered police station office, a whirring fan stirred the warm air as Ramirez flipped between two phones as she engaged in hurried conversations. Across from her, Julia braced herself, knowing she was about to multiply that stress with her own concerns.

Ramirez hung up and leaned back in her chair, scratching at her thick hair. Julia waited a moment before laying Chloe's controversial true crime book down on the desk.

"Have you read this?" she asked, the shake in her voice betraying her steady hand.

Ramirez glanced at the book and shook her head, not seeming interested.

"I try to avoid that sensationalist stuff. I see too much of the real thing in my job."

Julia nodded in understanding before launching into an explanation of the connections and theories she had pieced together so far. They were tentative links, but clear enough to warrant further scrutiny. She walked Ramirez through the timeline of events, Chloe's questionable memoir, the similarities to the murders of Michael Clayton, and the potential motive for Dahlia to want to silence Chloe before she could threaten to expose Dahlia's hidden past.

Ramirez listened without interruption, nodding and jotting down notes on the pad open on her desk.

"It's an interesting theory," Ramirez said, tapping her pen on the notepad. "But we would need more concrete evidence to back it up before treating Miss Hartfield as a serious suspect. We're still looking for Luca. Have you seen him?"

"I haven't, and I know it's circumstantial right now. But knowing that Chloe might have written this book about Dahlia's brother flips things on its head."

"Motive is important. But we can't arrest someone based on having a motive, as I'm sure you understand."

Julia understood. As convincing as the motive seemed, they needed something more solid to tie Dahlia to the murders, if she was behind them.

"And what about Helena?" Ramirez pushed. "What would be Dahlia's motive for killing her? She seemed distraught when she saw Helena's body on the bed."

"Yes, she did," Julia agreed. "Of that, I'm not sure."

Julia leaned back in the creaky chair. As much as she wanted to be certain that all signs pointed to Dahlia, nagging doubts still lingered.

"What about Ian?" Julia asked. "He was the last

person to see Helena alive when she called him to her room. But I can't piece together why he'd want her dead."

Ramirez scribbled a note. "He said Helena spoke little sense to him during their late-night meeting. She told him she had something to tell him, but went around in circles until she asked him to leave. We haven't ruled him out. But so far, we haven't found concrete evidence linking Mr Fletcher to the crimes, either. And where did *you* hear he was the last person seen in her room?"

"My daughter told me."

"And how does your daughter know that?"

"Oh," Julia said, considering the answer. "I'm not sure. She said he was seen going into Helena's room. I should have asked. There's still so much I don't know," she admitted. "Like those reports Helena had about the healing mineral. Where did she get them? Who made them?"

"I sent a sample of the water to a lab I trust for my own—how do you say—curiosity?" Ramirez flipped a page on her notepad. "My contact said there seems to be a high content of minerals in the water. Magnesium, potassium—"

"Sodium and sulphur?"

"Correct."

"The results might *not* have been fake?" Julia pinched the bridge of her nose. "So, why did Helena go up into the hills to get the results from a man at a rave if there was nothing to hide?"

"More tests are being conducted. And that reminds

me—forensics found Luca Valenti's DNA on the cigarette butt recovered from the pool. Helena's room is being checked for more traces of Luca as we speak."

Julia nodded. If Luca had been at the scene of Helena's murder, it made his guilt seem more probable, especially since he was nowhere to be seen.

"But why would he kill her?" Julia asked. "She'd just helped him by giving him money to leave town."

Ramirez glanced at her phone as it vibrated on a stack of paperwork. She turned it over and leaned across the desk, closer to Julia.

"I know, it's confusing. Perhaps Helena knew too much, and he didn't think he could leave without silencing her? He was engaged to Chloe, and in my experience, the scorned lover is usually top of the suspect list." She rested a hand on the book. "Thank you for making these connections. We'll dig deeper into Dahlia. I'll have her financial records and movements in recent weeks pulled. Who knows what facts will present themselves?"

Frustration bit at Julia. She had pinned her hopes on the book as the key to unlocking the killer's identity, but despite the breakthrough, she was left grasping at fragments of circumstantial evidence.

"I appreciate you not brushing me off," Julia said, standing up from the creaky chair. "I know we don't have all the answers yet, but this connection felt too important to ignore."

Ramirez gave her a tight smile. "That's good police

work—following every lead until we get to the truth. You'd make a good detective, Mrs South-Brown."

They shook hands, and Julia swapped the dark station for the glaring sun. Outside, Barker and Olivia were waiting for her, each making a mess with melting ice cream.

Olivia looked up at Julia, and her ice cream took a tragic tumble off the cone and onto the hot cobbles. Fat teardrops welled up in the toddler's eyes, threatening to spill over in a full-blown meltdown.

"Don't worry, love, we'll just go get you another one."

She met Barker's gaze, and they both suppressed a knowing chuckle at their daughter's dramatic reaction.

As Julia wiped the sticky mess from Olivia's cheeks with a handkerchief, she caught sight of Ian Fletcher in the distance, strolling barefoot up from the beach. His linen shirt billowed in the breeze, and he seemed lost in thought.

Julia considered calling out to him, wanting to press him further about his cryptic allusions to Dahlia. But Olivia let out a pitiful whimper, derailing Julia's thoughts back to the present crisis at hand. Interrogating suspects could wait; a fresh ice cream took priority.

She let Olivia take her hand and lead her towards the bustling ice cream shop. Barker fell into step beside them, slipping his arm around Julia's waist.

"So, how did it go with the detective?" he asked. "Did she think your theory about Dahlia and the book held any water?"

"Somewhat. She didn't dismiss it outright, at least.

But Ramirez made it clear we need more solid proof before treating Dahlia as a serious suspect."

"I think you're onto something with this, love. Dahlia told you herself that she and Chloe were close and they confided in each other."

"She said that," Julia agreed.

"Right. So, if Dahlia went through the trouble of changing her name and appearance to distance herself from her brother's crimes, Chloe dragging all that to light again in the public eye would undermine everything Dahlia had built for herself."

Julia considered Barker's point. He was right—if Chloe had built her memoir around Michael Clayton like they suspected, Dahlia would have ample reason to want to silence her former confidant turned betrayer.

"I want to talk to Dahlia myself," Julia stated as they reached the front of the line. "But first, ice cream."

Jessie arranged the platter of meats, cheeses, olives, and fresh bread on the balcony table. She added two glasses and a bottle of water before stepping back to admire her impromptu picnic setup.

The doors slid open, and Dante emerged from the steamy bathroom, his hair still dripping from the shower. He stopped short when he saw the spread.

"What's all this?"

"An apology," she said, tucking a strand of hair behind her ear. "For not telling you about the email from Johnny. And for snapping at you yesterday. And for being weird since you got here. And for being weird before you got here."

Dante waved it off.

"It's cool. No big deal."

"It is to me." She pulled out a chair and motioned for him to sit. "So, yeah. I'm sorry."

They loaded up plates and tucked into the food. Jessie nibbled on some Manchego as she gathered her thoughts.

"I wanted to explain where my head's been at with this job offer," she began. "I know your reaction was to just take it, no questions asked."

Dante nodded, glancing up from his plate.

"Anyone *would* be lucky to be offered it," she said. "But that I'm not grabbing at it means it's not right for me."

"Maybe you're scared of the leap?"

"Maybe, but I don't think that's it." She gazed out at the lush valley stretching out before them. "When I went travelling with my brother, I *was* terrified. I went back and forth so many times... almost didn't get on the plane. But I'm not scared this time." She turned back to Dante. "I'm conflicted. And the thing pulling me back, the idea of home... it's just too powerful right now."

Dante nodded. "Yeah, maybe I don't get that. I love my family, but not more than a dream job."

"We grew up differently. They've always been there for you."

He gave her a look that made her expect more

conflict. He folded a piece of red meat into a slice of bread with some cheese and chewed it over.

"You're right. I guess I take that stability for granted."

"I was sixteen when Julia took me in, and I know... I'll be twenty-two in a few months. I've had that stability for ages now, but it doesn't feel that long. And after everything that we all went through last year with James and Greg and the Howarth Estate... it made me realise that silly little village... it's important to me. It's the only home I've ever had, and I'm not ready to shake things up again. Not yet anyway."

"I get it, Jessie."

She nodded, but he didn't. Not really. But she wouldn't go around in circles.

"It's not the job for me," Jessie said, "but it's something you've wanted for yourself. The chance to travel and write."

Dante didn't reply right away. He sipped his water, squinting out at the valley.

"Maybe," he admitted. "When I was stuck at the *Riverswick Chronicle* writing fluff pieces, it's the sort of thing I'd dream about. I guess I just assumed you'd feel the same way."

"You wanted to go travelling before Christmas and I said no."

Dante's gaze softened. "I only wanted to go if it was with you."

"That's cute, Dante. But it's not true. You asked me out of nowhere. It must be something you've always wanted to do. And that's fine."

Before Dante could reply, a knock on the door interrupted them. Jessie glanced towards the sound and sighed.

"I'll get it," he said, rising from his chair, the towel around his waist threatening to slip.

Jessie stayed seated at the small table on the balcony, nibbling at olives. Dante pulled the door open to Julia, and her eyes widened at the sight of him wrapped in nothing but a towel. Her cheeks flushed pink as her gaze darted away, searching the room until she spotted Jessie through the open balcony doors.

"I'm sorry to interrupt," Julia called out. "Have you got a minute?"

Jessie set her napkin down and stood up from the table. She met her mum halfway across the sparse room.

"What's up?"

"I told Detective Ramirez everything we uncovered about Dahlia's connection to Michael Clayton. She's looking into it."

"That's something," Jessie said. "Did you find Dahlia?"

Julia shook her head. "That's why I'm here. She seems to have vanished. I thought maybe you would know which room she's in?"

"I think so."

"Do you still have a master key?" Julia asked, to which Jessie nodded. "I should talk to her, try to get some answers. Will you show me where her room is?"

Jessie looked back at Dante, but he gestured for her to go ahead.

"Of course," Jessie said. She grabbed the key card from the dresser. "Her room is right next to Luca's old one. Let's go."

She smiled back at Dante, but he was leaning against the railing, looking out at the valley. Leaving him to his thoughts, she followed Julia into the hallway.

"Everything okay with you two?" Julia asked.

"It will be."

"Decided what you're doing about—"

"The job?" Jessie cut in, wrapping her hand around Julia's. "I'm not taking it. It's not my boat to catch. C'mon. Dahlia's room is upstairs."

She led Julia up the winding staircase to the second floor of the hotel, the late afternoon sun filtering in through the windows to cast shadows on the bare white walls. As they reached the top, she pointed down the empty corridor.

"Luca's old room is there," Jessie said, pointing to the door in the middle. "That's Helena's room next to it, and Dot said she thought *this* one was Dahlia's based on smelling her perfume in there."

Julia made her way to the nondescript white door that Jessie had showed, her footsteps echoing in the hotel's eerie silence.

"Here goes nothing."

Julia raised her fist and knocked on the door. Nothing but silence until a low groan grumbled from within the room. They exchanged a look, and Julia knocked again, firmer this time. Another groan, louder now. Jessie slid the master key into the lock. The door clicked open and patchouli perfume wafted out as they entered the dim, sparse room.

"*Dahlia*?" she called.

She flipped on the light, flooding the room with a harsh fluorescent glare. A gasp escaped Jessie's lips when she spotted Dahlia sprawled on the floor beside the bed, one hand pressed to a gash on her forehead. Blood matted Dahlia's pristine white-blonde hair.

"He's lost it..." Dahlia croaked, wincing as she tried to push herself up. "I asked him if he did it and... he attacked me."

Julia rushed to help Dahlia sit up against the side of the bed.

"Who?"

"Luca?" Jessie asked.

"No," Dahlia said, gulping. "*Ian*."

23

Julia hurried back to Dahlia's room, balancing the steaming cup of tea in one hand and a plate of biscuits in the other. She nudged the door open with her hip to find Dahlia applying a large plaster to the angry red gash on her forehead in a black hand mirror.

"You didn't have to go to any trouble on my account," Dahlia said, wincing as she smoothed down the edges of the bandage.

"It was no trouble at all," Julia replied, setting the tea and biscuits down on the bedside table. "I thought you could use something warm and comforting after what you've been through."

"Such a British response, isn't it?" Dahlia gave a weak chuckle. "Never fails to solve every problem."

Julia sat in the chair opposite the bed.

"I suppose it seems to help in times of crisis," Julia agreed. "Are you sure you won't see a doctor?"

"It's just a scratch," she said, picking up the tea. "I don't drink caffeine, but I'll throw caution to the wind on account of this having been a funny old week."

Julia took a deep breath as she watched Dahlia perch on the edge of the enormous bath—it reminded her of the one in Ian's room.

"It's been a funny few *years* for you," Julia said, keeping her tone gentle despite the confrontation she knew was coming.

Dahlia's piercing eyes narrowed on Julia.

"You know, don't you?" she said. "About Chloe's book?"

The directness of Dahlia's approach took Julia by surprise, yet she embraced the openness—after all, confronting the issue was the very reason she had wanted to find Dahlia.

"Why didn't you mention it when we were in the mineral bath together?" Julia asked. "We were talking about our pasts, and you said Chloe had *no* reason to want to expose you, but she did."

Dahlia tensed, looking down at the tiled floor. When she spoke, her voice was strained. "I was trying to *protect* myself, Julia. What else could I do?" She dropped her head in despair. "That girl had a way of *twisting* things. Of dragging your worst secrets into the light."

Dahlia let out a deep, burdened breath, setting her teacup on the saucer with a soft clink. Her hands, pale against the dark stone, clung to the bath's edge.

"I've got a simple question for you, Julia," Dahlia

began, her fiery gaze locking onto Julia's eyes. "If you had a twin brother... no, forget that... if *your* sister...?"

"Sue."

"If sweet Sue did something like what Michael did... would you want to be associated with her?" Her words hung in the air between them, like smoke lingering after a fire. Dahlia didn't look at Julia as she continued, her gaze fixed somewhere in the distance. "Would you want to have to think about her... talk about her... *explain* her... a decade later?"

Julia leaned back, and she thought of Sue, her tenacious sister. The idea of Sue committing such atrocities was unimaginable. But Julia understood the hypothetical scenario: how far would she go to protect herself from a past that refused to stay buried?

"I..." Julia sifted for the right words. "I understand why you'd want to separate yourself from that."

Dahlia's eyes searched hers, filled with a silent plea for understanding.

"But with Chloe dying," Julia continued, her voice gentle but firm, "it is relevant again. She wrote about him."

Dahlia's fingers danced along the bath's edge as she gave a silent nod. A thick quiet draped over them once more.

"I *know* how it looks from the outside," Dahlia said, her voice a croaky whisper. "I *should* have said something. But you must understand, Julia. The story Chloe spun... the one where she was held captive and tormented by Michael... that all happened... but it happened to *me*."

Julia's heart thundered in her chest. Her eyes darted to Dahlia's bandaged forehead before returning to her ashen face. It was as though the room had skewed, throwing her off balance.

"Why did you defend him in court?" Julia asked.

Dahlia shrugged, a small, sad motion. "I was scared. Terrified of what he'd do if he got away with murder and came after me again." Her voice dropped lower as she continued, her words spilling out in a hurried rush. "When that receptionist who uncovered his crimes started putting everything together, she came to me before she went to the police. I think she wanted to warn me, but I didn't believe her. And I... I went to Michael. I confronted him. I wanted him to laugh it off and say that he'd annoyed her at work. Stolen her lunch or ignored her advances." She inhaled a slowing breath and added, "He didn't deny it."

Julia swallowed the dry lump in her throat.

"What happened next?"

"He locked me in his basement," she said. "Kept me sedated while he tried to clean up his mess. He didn't know the police were already on to him. He threatened me. Said if I ever told anyone the truth, he'd kill me. I told no one the full truth of it all. Not until that trip to Bali last summer."

"When you and Chloe opened up to each other?"

Dahlia nodded, wincing with regret.

"It was a cold, windy night. Luca had just broken off

his engagement with Chloe, and we were both in strange places. She and I got to talking one night by the fire." She let out a hollow laugh. "She told me all about her messy childhood... about feeling unloved... and I confessed more than I meant to. About Michael, what he did to me. I'd locked it away for too long and it all came pouring out. Chloe said she understood, and for a fleeting moment, I thought I'd found someone I could trust."

Julia pictured the two women, their guards lowered, confiding in each other on that balmy Bali night. She could imagine the catharsis Dahlia must have felt, unburdening herself from the weight of a secret carried alone for so long.

"A few short months later, my story was out there for the entire world to see on bookshelves all around the world." There was no anger in Dahlia's voice, only resignation. "My secret was out."

"That betrayal must have hurt."

Dahlia nodded. "It did. But I also believe in forgiveness. After what Michael did, how could I not? I learned long ago that clinging to pain and anger only breeds more darkness." Drawing in a deep, grounding breath, she said, "I *forgave* Chloe. I tried to guide her, to help her make better choices with her platform. The book was already out there—nothing could change that. And maybe it *was* time people knew my side of the story, even if my name wasn't attached."

The silence that followed was deafening. Julia parted her lips to speak, to offer comfort or assurance, but found herself at a loss for words. All she could do was stare at Dahlia, her heart heavy with sympathy and dread.

"And Ian?" Julia prompted. "How did you figure out it was him?"

"It wasn't easy to accept. I trusted Ian, I did. But when I was collecting the towels the day after Chloe died, I noticed Ian had a whole bundle of soaking wet towels in his room, like he'd cleaned up a big water mess." She met Julia's gaze. "I thought nothing of it. But after what happened to Helena, I started going back over everything in my mind. Putting pieces together. That stuck out."

Julia nodded, remembering the afternoon when Dahlia had collected the towels the day they found Chloe.

"Helena must have figured it out too," Dahlia continued. "For all her faults, she was a smart woman."

Julia made a sound of agreement, but something still didn't feel right.

"Do you have any idea where Ian went after he attacked you?"

"No, I'm sorry, Julia." Dahlia rested a hand on her forehead. "I think I need to lie down. Would you mind drawing the curtains and leaving me to get some rest?"

"Of course."

After pulling the curtains together, Julia placed the tea and biscuits next to the bed as Dahlia crawled under the covers. Outside, Jessie was waiting for her. She kicked away from the wall and jerked her head for Julia to move closer.

"I wasn't going to leave you alone with her." Jessie's eyes darted to Helena's bedroom door. "Given who we now know her brother is, I don't trust her. Did she give any more away about Ian?"

"She found wet towels in his room."

"That's it?"

"That's it."

There were missing pieces to this puzzle, but what were they?

The last dregs of the sunset painted the sky in vibrant oranges and pinks as Dot, Ethel, and Percy sat around a small table by the hotel pool playing poker. A gentle breeze rustled the palms overhead. Dot sipped her tea while Ethel slurped the last of her sangria through a straw. Percy munched on a slice of pepperoni pizza from the open box on the table.

"It makes sense the Yogi is behind this," Ethel said, crunching an ice cube between her teeth, throwing a card and a poker chip onto the table. "Remember when we were looking for those baths on our second day here, Dorothy? We saw him whispering with Helena in the dining room. They were talking about being surprised to see Chloe at the hotel."

"Ian could've taken the opportunity after seeing her

here," Percy said with a mouthful of pizza, "to get his revenge for all that online vitriol Julia mentioned."

"Don't talk with your mouth full, dear," Dot said with a wrinkled nose before assessing her cards. "But you're right. It makes sense."

"Though it still could've been Luca," Percy added after washing the pizza down with lemonade. "We found that cigarette butt. And I could've sworn I saw him lurking around the corridors earlier today."

"He left on a boat," Dot said.

"Maybe the place is haunted," Ethel mocked, waving her straw in front of Percy's face. "And if it's not, it will be by the time we leave after all these murders."

"Another glass of sangria and you'll be as bad as Minnie." Dot stirred a spoonful of sugar into her tea. Her ears were still ringing after hearing Minnie's records blaring in her apartment when she checked on her earlier. "I suppose either of them could've done it. Though I've never trusted that Dahlia woman. Something about her rubs me the wrong way. Far too slick and smiley for my taste."

Ethel scoffed. "You think everyone's too slick and smiley. Though I'll admit, I wouldn't put anything past her. A woman willing to profit off magical spring water has to be at least crooked, right?"

"She seemed distraught over her dear friend's death," Percy said.

"Grief... or *guilt*?" Dot muttered into her teacup.

A comfortable silence settled over them as they watched a pair of birds swoop and dart over the shimmering pool. The faint echo of music and chatter drifted from the plaza as the festival continued on into the night.

"Let's just hope we're not the next ones to end up floating face down in the pool," Ethel said out of the blue.

"I'd like to see someone try," Dot fired back as she laid her winning poker hand on the table. "Read 'em and weep."

Ethel narrowed her eyes and slammed her cards down. "I don't *believe* it. You must've had your little puppet, Percy, peeking at my cards again."

"I did *no* such thing," Dot said. "I won fair and square, you old goose."

"You cheated at a game of bridge the first time we met."

"I won because you are as lousy a bridge player as you are a poker player," Dot insisted, dragging the winnings against the table. "I'm better at cards than you, simple as that."

Percy held up his hands in protest. "Now see here, I won't be accused of being anyone's puppet, thank you very much. My Dorothy is right. She's a top-notch player."

Ethel huffed, but she didn't press the matter further. Dot gathered up the cards and began shuffling the deck again, pondering their earlier conversation about the murders. A thought struck her, and she paused her shuffling.

"You know, Helena's actions are odd when you think

about them," she mused aloud. "Faking the water results, trying to pay off Luca to leave town... if she was *innocent*, why would she go to those lengths? It's like she was acting under someone else's instructions."

Ethel perked up, intrigued. "Go on..."

"What if Helena was a puppet?" Dot proposed. "And whoever was pulling her strings cut them loose when she was no longer useful."

"Leaving her to take the fall," Percy added, catching on to Dot's train of thought. "If they weren't so sloppy staging that suicide, it might have worked."

"Precisely," Dot said, resuming her shuffling. "It's something to consider."

Ethel leaned back in her chair, swirling the ice in her empty glass.

"In that case, the question is—who's the puppet master?"

Dot dealt the cards again, the truth just out of reach, like a word stuck on the tip of her tongue.

"Luca," Jessie called, knocking on the door of room 204. "We need to talk."

The door opened a crack, Luca's face appearing in the slim space. His eyes were bloodshot, his stubble grown out. He looked like a caged animal, but at least he'd showered.

"What do you want?"

"Can I come in? It's important."

Luca hesitated, then opened the door wider and let Jessie slip inside. He sat on the edge of the bed, shoulders hunched.

"My mum thinks Ian killed Helena."

Luca's head jerked up in surprise.

"Ian? I don't believe it. He doesn't have that in him."

Jessie explained what Dahlia had told them about Ian's temper and yoga persona being a front. But Luca shook his head.

"I've only had one conversation with Ian, and it was about his father." Seeing Jessie's puzzled look, Luca went on. "He saw me losing my temper after my butter mix-up in Bali. He taught me to calm down. Said he had a father with a bad temper, and my father had a horrible temper too. That's how I ended up living with my nonna."

"Dahlia said he attacked her."

"*Attacked?*" he cried, shaking his head. "He wouldn't. He's a man of morals. You know he turned down big money to teach yoga on *Blisselle*? Didn't agree with her ethos. I wish I'd been so strong and refused her like Ian did." He dropped his head in his hands. "I wouldn't be here if I had."

"What do you mean?" Jessie asked. "Said no to what?"

Luca sighed. "To everything. The fame, the money. I never had enough followers to get on Dahlia's app, but she kept pushing me to grow." He looked up at Jessie. "*She's* the one who forced me to make those influencer accounts. *She* pushed me to propose to Chloe for the attention it would bring me. I thought she was trying to help me, but she was trying to use me. That's what she does. She was trying to mould me into a 'hunky celebrity chef' to front her *Blisselle* cooking section. I was just an asset to her."

Luca walked over to the balcony doors and rested his head against the glass with a thud. A white pigeon hopped off the railing, flying down to the street below.

"I should never have gone along with any of it. She promised me fame and fortune and it sounded so good. But the best things are too good to be true." He faced Jessie again, his features haunted by troubling thoughts. "Dahlia cursed me. And now…"

A loud bang erupted from the adjoining room.

"What was that?" Jessie whispered.

"I don't know."

The banging persisted, echoing as if emerging from within the wall itself. Luca edged closer and pressed his ear to the wall.

"There's someone in there," he said.

"No one's in there. I put you in this room away from the other guests. It should be empty."

"There *is* someone in there."

She patted down her pockets as they walked into the hallway, a sinking realisation dawning. The master key was missing.

"My mum has it. I'll go fetch it."

Luca, propelled by a surge of energy, delivered a forceful kick to the door. It splintered, then caved in with a crash that ricocheted down the empty hallway.

Peering into the shadowed room, her eyes

acclimatised to the darkness. Beside her, Luca stood still, the persistent banging growing closer. She spotted several hefty black bin liners scattered across the floor. She knelt to inspect one. Inside were dozens of plastic tubs, each filled with some kind of powder. She picked one up and examined it, noticing the Spanish label. Though she didn't speak the language, she recognised the word 'electrolitos'—*electrolytes*.

"I found some of these in the kitchen too," she murmured. "There must be enough here to fill... several baths."

The banging started up again, even more insistent than before. Luca whirled around, his eyes darting as he searched for the source of the noise. He rushed to the wardrobe and threw open the doors.

There, crumpled on the floor, was Ian—his hands and feet bound in white linen strips, a gag muffling his cries. His eyes were wide with terror and desperation.

Luca rushed to untie Ian's bindings while Jessie dragged the fabric from his mouth.

"She said she was going to come back to kill me later," Ian rasped, his voice hoarse. "She's lost her mind!"

24

Dot watched with growing unease as Minnie threw clothes into an open suitcase on her bed, heedless of the way silk blouses and leopard print kaftans were being crumpled in her haste.

"You need to *slow* down and *think* this through," Dot urged, wringing her hands. "Running away will not solve anything!"

Minnie glanced up, her eyes feverish, strands of hair escaping from her scruffy up-do.

"I *cannot* stay here. I will not. You heard what the police said—Ian's still out there. Dahlia's the *only* one I can trust."

Dot shook her head, moving closer. She grasped Minnie's arm.

"I know you're frightened, but Dahlia might not be who you think she is. Please, just wait a little longer before you do anything drastic."

Jerking her arm away, Minnie resumed her hurried packing.

"You're *wrong* about her. Dahlia *cares* about me. About this place. She's promised we'll rebuild La Casa together, make it even better than before. Right after a holiday together to reset and recalibrate."

"Is that what she said when the basement flooded?" Dot asked. "When those pipes burst, and you were left with a hotel full of damage?"

"She was *there* for me then. *Helped* me see I needed to change, become stronger. I was *weak* before, letting this place fall apart."

"You weren't weak," Dot countered. "You've always been a fighter, even if you made mistakes. But this— running off into the unknown with a virtual stranger—it won't end well."

Minnie dragged the zip around the bulging suitcase before lifting it off the bed.

"You don't know Dahlia like I do," she insisted. "She wants what's best for me. For both of us. Once we get away from all this darkness, we'll start fresh."

Desperate tears pricked at Dot's eyes. She couldn't let Minnie rush into a calamity, not after all they'd endured already.

"Think of Lisa," she pleaded. "Your family. You'd just leave her behind?"

Minnie's determined expression faltered at the mention of her daughter's name.

"I..." She wavered, the suitcase slipping in her grip

before she tightened her fists around the handle. "It's too late. I have to go."

But Dot sensed the conflict in Minnie's voice.

"It's *not* too late. Stay a little longer and let's sort this mystery out together. I know you're scared, but running away won't make that fear disappear. It will follow you wherever you go." She hesitated at what she wanted to say next, but the words were threatening to burst out. "Have you considered Dahlia might be using you? Using this place to give herself a boost?"

"She'll take care of me."

Dot watched helplessly as Minnie shoved the overflowing suitcase into the hallway. Dot followed her out before Minnie strode back inside her apartment, slamming the door shut behind her. The sound reverberated down the empty corridor like a judge's gavel declaring the end of discussion. But Dot couldn't let it end there.

She knocked, calling Minnie's name. When there was no response, she tried the handle, relieved to find it was unlocked. Pushing the door open, she saw Minnie standing by the open balcony doors, the warm evening breeze ruffling her hair.

"I'm not trying to interfere," Dot began. "But you can't keep running from your problems forever."

Minnie didn't turn, her gaze fixed on the distant horizon where the sun was setting behind the hills.

"I just have to *trust* her."

Dot moved closer, laying a hand on Minnie's shoulder.

"The only person you can rely on is yourself. Dahlia might promise you the stars, but she won't be there to catch you if you fall."

Minnie tensed under her touch, and when she spoke, her voice was cold.

"Don't pretend you know what's best for me. You know nothing."

The dismissal stung.

"I know you can get through this. You've survived worse storms."

Whirling around, Minnie's eyes flashed with anger.

"*Survived*? Is that what you'd call it? I'm treading water most days. The only time I've felt hope is with Dahlia. Her teachings... her healing... the water..."

Dot dropped her hand.

This was useless, but she couldn't give up.

"Hope can be fickle," Dot said. "The only way to stop drowning is to learn to swim."

"Enough with the empty metaphors, Dorothy! You're too busy judging me to understand."

"I'm not judging you. I'm trying to help. Isn't that what family does?"

"Well, maybe you should stick to *your* own family and stop meddling in *mine*." Minnie strode past Dot, yanking open the door. "I think it's time you left and minded your own business. I should never have invited you here."

Dot almost continued, but what would be the point? Minnie had made up her mind. She left the room and staggered down the stairs. How had that gone so astray? Before she could think about it further, she reached the corridor and saw Jessie supporting a dishevelled and shaken-looking Ian as they emerged from one of the rooms. Luca followed close behind, his expression dark.

"What on earth is going on here?"

Before anyone could respond, two police officers came rushing down the corridor towards them. At the sight of Ian, they grabbed him by the arms.

"I've done *nothing* wrong!" Ian protested as they dragged him away.

"We called you to *help*, not to arrest him!" Jessie called after them, but the police ignored her, focused on apprehending their suspect.

Ian continued shouting that he was innocent as he disappeared from view.

Dot hurried over to Jessie, checking that her great-granddaughter was unhurt. Luca hung back, leaning against the wall with his arms crossed.

"What happened?" Dot asked.

"It was Dahlia," Jessie said. "She tied him up and tried to make it look like he attacked her. She isn't who she claims to be."

"I can't say I'm surprised," Dot said, glancing back at the stairs up to Minnie's apartment. "No one in this hotel seems to be."

∿

In the hushed dining room, Julia sat amidst a flurry of photographs, articles, and pieces of potential evidence. Her fingers drummed against the polished wood of the table, a rhythm that echoed the chaos in her mind. Jessie, Dot, Ethel, and Percy were her makeshift investigative team, their heads bent over the scattered array of evidence implicating Dahlia Hartfield.

Julia's gaze swept over the pictures Jessie had printed. Dahlia, hair a stark contrast to its current silver hue, was present at Michael's trial. Snippets from Chloe's book lay juxtaposed with images of Dahlia and Michael, blurring lines between fiction and reality. The damning evidence —a tub of electrolytes found in the same room as Ian, and a scientific paper discovered at the hill-side rave— rested on the table.

On the terrace outside, Luca puffed away at his cigarette as he stared out over the rolling hills. Julia had been shocked to find he hadn't boarded the boat, and even more shocked to learn Jessie had been the one hiding him in the hotel. Though, she couldn't say she wasn't glad to see him when Jessie brought him out like a bonus prize on a game show—they needed every angle on Dahlia they could get. She hoped he'd have something to share once he'd finished chain-smoking.

Dot's voice cut through Julia's thoughts. "*How* did Dahlia try to frame Ian? It makes little sense."

"Dahlia said she collected a pile of wet towels from Ian's room the morning after Chloe was murdered. She said she thought nothing of it."

"Well, for what it's worth," Dot said, fluffing her curls, "I never thought it was Ian."

"You said you didn't trust him and he sent Mum on a wild goose chase giving her Clayton's name *this* afternoon," Jessie said, joining them with more print-outs from behind the reception desk. "Found some more comments on Reddit threads, this time about Dahlia. People are calling her out for selling all sorts of shady rubbish. Apparently, her investors have been running for the hills for years. For all her posturing, she doesn't seem to have an ethical bone in her body. Wouldn't be surprised if those wet towels were hers and she just twisted the story."

Julia's heart pounded as she remembered an insignificant moment from days before.

"That's what happened. Dahlia... she was collecting towels that day. I saw her in the corridor with a basket full of soaking wet towels. I thought it was odd that she was getting on with the laundry so soon after a murder, but she said she wanted to keep on top of things for Minnie."

"Hide the evidence more like," Dot cried. "She drowned that poor girl in her bath and dragged her down to the mineral baths in the dead of night, mopping up with Minnie's towels on her way back."

Julia felt sick as she imagined Dahlia slithering around the darkened hotel corridors under the chilling cover of darkness. She saw her plunging Chloe in the bath, then carrying her body through the halls, dabbing up the soap suds on her way back to her room.

"Could she have carried Chloe on her own?" Julia wondered.

"She's a waif of a woman," Dot said. "I wouldn't be surprised if Helena helped her carry that poor girl's body. Helena was at Dahlia's beck and call, and we didn't notice. She was running around doing the rest of her dirty work like her little puppet."

Luca sauntered in from the terrace—he was a far cry from the handsome vegan chef they'd met on their first day at the hotel.

"Luca," Jessie started, "you mentioned you heard Chloe in Helena's room the night she died. Remember that?"

He scrubbed a hand down his face. "I said that."

"Were they arguing?" Julia asked. "Did you hear what it was about?"

"I staggered into my room," Luca said, shaking his head. "Came back to grab some more cash. That's when I heard the shouting." He mimed opening a door. "I thought the shouting was coming from Helena's room." He turned the other way. "But I'd turned around and leaned my forehead against the back of the door to steady myself. Thought little of it. Just two women arguing. Nothing unusual. Then I went back out, but... it wasn't coming from Helena's room, it was coming from the *other* direction."

"Dahlia's room," Julia confirmed. "What time?"

"Early hours."

"I bet that was moments before Chloe was drowned." He looked down at the table of evidence, avoiding their gazes. "If I'd paid attention, maybe I could've done something. Stopped her..."

"You couldn't have known, Luca," Jessie assured him. "Don't blame yourself."

"I heard what you said, and I can believe Helena helped Dahlia move Chloe's body that night," Luca said. "They were thick as thieves, always whispering in corners together. I bet they were cooking up all kinds of schemes. They'd always say they were talking about the app, but who can say?"

"The room where Dahlia stashed Ian was stuffed with enormous tubs of electrolytes," Jessie revealed. "No question about it... Dahlia *knew* Helena was faking the whole magical mineral water thing. She was in on it. They were adding the minerals in themselves."

"And that's why Helena went to that dodgy doctor at the rave to get the results," Dot added, clicking her fingers together. "Fewer questions asked in that sketchy environment. Helena was being sloppy. We all thought Helena was behind Chloe's death. Maybe Dahlia overheard us talking and realised if the police dragged Helena in, she'd crack and point at Dahlia." Her eyes darted to the doorway. "Ah, Detective Ramirez! You're *finally* here. We called an *hour* ago."

"I was enjoying dinner with my family," Ramirez said through almost gritted teeth. "Please, this better be important. This case has already eaten up so much of my time."

Julia relayed their discovery about the wet towels and Dahlia's ploy to frame Ian. Ramirez maintained her poker face as Julia described the false accusations and Dahlia's evolving web of lies.

"Dahlia tried to set up Ian," Julia pressed on. "It was just another distraction."

"Or," Ramirez countered, "Ian could have fabricated his hostage story to shift blame back onto Dahlia. Who's saying which of them is telling the truth?"

"No," Jessie interjected. "Ian was *terrified* when we found him. And why would he tie himself up?"

"And Dahlia refused medical care when we found her," Julia said. "She just put a plaster on her head and carried on. Surely, if Ian had attacked her, she'd want that documented?"

"You raise fair points," Ramirez agreed, pushing her blazer back to plant her hands on her hips. "However, we must follow protocol." She started towards the door again. "Now, where is Miss Hartfield?"

"In her room, last I saw her," Julia replied.

"Very well. I will speak with her myself and investigate these new leads. In the meantime, I must ask you all to remain here."

"Detective, if we're right, Dahlia is cunning. Don't underestimate her."

As the detective left the dining room, Julia watched her confident strides across the tiled lobby until she disappeared from view, heading for the serpent's lair. More footsteps drew Julia's attention as Lisa slipped into the room. Relief washed over her at the sight of Minnie's daughter.

"I'm so glad you came," Julia said, clasping the young

woman's hands. "Your mother needs you now more than ever."

"I almost didn't come, but your husband was very insistent."

Dot stepped forward, grabbing Lisa in a tight hug.

"You *must* speak with your mother. Make her see *reason*. She's talking about running off with that monster. We're certain that Dahlia is behind these murders."

"Dahlia Hartfield?"

"The same," Dot said. "You were right not to trust her."

"But *murder*?" Lisa looked around the stark dining room as though she didn't recognise the place. "My mother knows how to pick them. I'll talk to her. But she hasn't listened to me in years, if she ever did. Once she gets an idea in her head—"

"Just try," Dot said. "For me."

Lisa departed, and guilt crept over Julia. She turned to Dot and the others.

"I shouldn't have gone along with Dahlia's story."

"She's been manipulating everything from the beginning," Jessie said. "She's tried to set up *every* suspect. She set up Helena's death to look like a guilty conscience killed her. And Luca, you said the money that Helena gave you was from Dahlia?"

He nodded. "Helena wouldn't admit it, but I knew she had little money. Dahlia likes to make her problems go away."

"She wanted to frame you," Julia said. "The more you tried to flee, the guiltier you looked."

"Your daughter made me see sense." He offered a tight smile to Jessie. "And don't be too hard on yourself, Julia. Dahlia is a master manipulator. It takes time to see through her act."

Julia's heart sank as the detective rushed back into the dining room alone, her calm demeanour shaken.

"Dahlia isn't in her room," Ramirez announced, out of breath. "Her belongings are gone."

Dot and Ethel both let out exasperated groans. Lisa followed close behind the detective, also alone.

"My mother's gone as well," she revealed. "And her passport is missing from her bedside drawer, where she always keeps it." Lisa turned to Dot. "Did Mum mention where she was going when you last spoke to her?"

"She didn't."

In a flash, Jessie leapt up from the table and raced over to the reception desk, rifling through the papers and documents scattered across its surface.

"Dahlia's passport is gone too," she called out. "They must be heading to the airport."

"That's where it looks like they're going," Lisa confirmed, tapping at her phone screen. "After everything that's happened these last few years, I hid a tracker in Mum's mobile. I didn't want to risk another abduction."

Ramirez sprang into action, dispatching officers to the airport with the location details from Lisa's tracker. Julia and the rest of them scrambled to join the swift exodus from La Casa, desperate to intercept Minnie and her murderous companion.

As they sped towards the airport, Julia replayed her last interactions with Dahlia in her mind. If only she had been more sceptical, more discerning, perhaps they could have prevented this escape.

25

Dot raced through the bustling airport terminal, her heart pounding as she scanned the sea of faces for any sign of Minnie. The air was thick with stress as police officers hurried past, barking into radios. Ethel struggled to keep up, wheezing as she clutched her side.

But Dot couldn't slow down.

"What if Dahlia has done away with Minnie?" Dot cried, the suggestion running her blood cold. "She could be lying on the side of the road somewhere."

They had all piled out of the minivan in a frenzy upon arriving at the airport, but the size of the place made finding two people near impossible among the crowds. Panic fizzled in Dot's chest as the seconds ticked by. She couldn't let Dahlia drag Minnie further into her mess.

Percy sank onto a bench, mopping his brow with a handkerchief.

"You go on ahead. I'll just catch my breath."

She nodded, grateful to have Ethel by her side at least. Julia and the others fanned out in different directions while officers coordinated the search.

"Lisa? The tracker?"

"Looks like she's somewhere over there by the bookshop," Lisa said, charging ahead. "But I can't see them."

Dot's heart pounded in her chest, a frenzied rhythm that echoed the frantic buzz of the surrounding airport. The sea of faces swarmed past as they hurried to the bookshop, a blur of hurried expressions and hasty goodbyes, but none were the familiar face she sought.

"They've got to be here somewhere," Lisa cried. "The signal is coming from *here*."

"Could it be delayed?" Ethel suggested.

"It's live," Lisa insisted, her finger tapping against the glowing dot on the screen. "It's not exact, but the signal *is* coming from somewhere around here."

A sinking feeling tugged at Dot's stomach as Ramirez pulled two discarded mobile phones from a nearby bin.

"Is this your mother's phone?"

Lisa nodded, pushing her hands up into her dark hair.

"Could they have already left the airport?" Dot ventured aloud, glancing around at the heaving mass of travellers once more. "Maybe this was all just a diversion and they're already off to their next location."

"We keep looking," Ramirez decided, nodding at Lisa to follow as she strode off towards the departure gates.

Dot watched them go, an uncomfortable knot tightening in her chest. It was like watching a television program play out before her eyes—only this wasn't some *ITV* crime drama she could switch off when it all got too much.

"Where could they be?" she muttered as they stood like spare parts outside the bookshop. "If only I had tried harder to stop Minnie from leaving Peridale all those years ago or convinced her to return sooner."

"It might not have made any difference."

"But it might."

"How can you know?"

"This is *all* my fault."

Ethel grabbed her arm, forcing her to stop.

"That's *enough*, Dorothy. I know you love to be dramatic, but you've got to get a *grip* on yourself. How is losing your head going to help?"

"I don't know, but—"

"All this panicking and worrying is useless. It was useless back in Peridale when you thought something dreadful was going to happen on this trip, and it's useless now."

Dot parted her lips to argue, but Ethel raised a hand.

"We can't change what's already happened. Worrying about what we could have done different won't get us anywhere. All we can do is react to what's in front of us and focus on finding Minnie."

Dot's shoulders slumped. As much as it pained her to admit it, Ethel had a point. Her nerves had been frayed since the moment they arrived in Savega.

"You're right, Ethel. You're right."

Dot took a breath and before she could stop herself, she grabbed Ethel close and hugged her tight. Ethel let out a surprised "Oof!" at the sudden embrace. After a moment, she relaxed and patted Dot on the back.

"There, there," Ethel said. "It's going to be fine."

Dot released her and took a small step back, smoothing down the front of her blouse.

"I'm sorry about that," Dot said, feeling embarrassed by her show of emotion. "It's just, well, you've become such a good friend to me, Ethel. So much better than I deserve after the way I used to treat you."

"I gave as good as I got."

"Even so, I don't know what I'd do without you here," Dot continued. "You're always able to talk sense into me when I get carried away. Percy tries his best, bless him, but he doesn't have your backbone. I think I've always needed someone like you in my life."

"Likewise," Ethel said with a nod, her mouth curling into a smile. "It's good to have someone who can match my temperament. Keeps me on my toes. You know I've got your back."

They shared another brief, heartfelt hug. As they pulled apart, Dot felt her nerves settle.

"Right then," Dot said, her voice firmer. "Enough of the mushy stuff. We need to come up with a plan to find Minnie."

Ethel nodded. "I agree. Those coppers are chasing their tails. We need to put our heads together and think."

As Ethel leaned against a pillar to catch her breath, Dot's gaze landed on a desk near the bookshop. On the unmanned desk there seemed to be a microphone for the loudspeakers. An idea sparked.

"Minnie was wearing that horrid leopard print earlier," Dot said. "Someone must have seen her in that outfit. If I put out an announcement, maybe we'll get a lead?"

Dot strode towards the desk with purpose, but as she approached, a realisation dawned on her.

"Oh, I don't speak a lick of Spanish," she muttered. She turned and called over her shoulder, "Ethel, if you don't mind?"

With an exaggerated groan, Ethel peeled herself away from the pillar and shuffled over.

"If I must." After clearing her throat, Ethel rattled off the message and her voice echoed over the airport's speaker system. "I said if anyone has seen a lady in wild animal print with a silver-haired woman, they should come and tell the two daft old women by the bookshop."

"Excellent," Dot said with a firm nod. "I suppose now we wait here and hope someone turns up."

They positioned themselves closer to the bookshop entrance, scanning each face in the streams of passers-by. As they stood guard, a display in the shop window caught Dot's eye—a book with a High Priestess gracing the cover—it was the leather book Dot had bought when they first arrived and Ethel had thrown into the same bin the detective had fished the phones from.

Unable to resist, Dot picked up the book. She flipped

through and found the page describing the Ten of Swords—the very card that had so unsettled her back in Peridale.

"Ethel, come read the full meaning of this wretched card that started this whole mess."

"I'm regretting revealing that I could speak Spanish. I'm like a performing translation monkey."

Ethel's lips traced her the words.

"Oh," she said, her bottom lip curling out. "It's not all bad. There's more to the card than just betrayal. It says here that—"

"*Señoras, señoras!*" a woman in a cleaning uniform called out, gesturing for them to follow her. "Please... this way..."

Dot and Ethel exchanged a surprised look before hurrying after the woman as she wove through the crowds. Dot's heart leapt—could this be the breakthrough they needed?

The cleaner moved as fast as a whippet, despite her short stature, never glancing back to check if Dot and Ethel were keeping up. Dot wheezed as she tried to match the woman's brisk pace, but determination propelled her forward. Up ahead, she spotted Julia and waved. Julia shot Dot a questioning look as she caught up to them.

"Any sign of Minnie?" Julia asked.

"Not yet, but this woman seems to know something."

The cleaner led them through a door marked 'Staff Only' and outside of the terminal building. Dot blinked against the glare of a stark floodlight, shielding her eyes.

They emerged into a small courtyard area, hidden from view of the public and ringed with barbed wire. Empty food carts and piles of luggage lined the space.

There, nestled against the wall in a stationary wheelchair, sat Minnie. An oversized visor and sunglasses shielded most of her face.

"*Minnie*!" Dot cried, rushing over.

She didn't respond as her head flopped to one side.

"A funny time for a nap," Ethel said.

"Minnie, dear," Dot said, shaking her shoulder. "Can you hear me?"

Minnie stirred, letting out a faint groan. Her words were slurred when she said, "Dorothy... that you?"

"Yes, it's me," Dot said, clasping her hand. "What's happened, Minnie? Where is Dahlia?"

Minnie's head lolled again.

"Either she's had too much sangria," Ethel said as she leaned in close and sniffed, "or someone slipped something into her drink."

Julia nodded at the bathroom door near where Minnie was parked and said, "If Minnie's here, maybe Dahlia's inside?"

Julia thrust the bathroom door open. Ammonia fumes assaulted her nostrils, a potent sting. Streaks of dark hair dye stained the sink in reckless smudges. Behind a closed stall, a woman hummed 'The Winner Takes It All' by ABBA, as though she didn't have a care in the world. An icy shiver traced Julia's spine, but a resolute spark ignited within her.

Despite the choice of song, this winner was trapped.

Julia knocked on the stall door.

"*Occupado*," came Dahlia's sing-song voice.

"Please, I'm bursting. I'm... pregnant."

There was a heavy sigh as the lock clicked. The door swung inwards, and Dahlia's jaw dropped at the sight of Julia. Dark dye caked her hair, and she held a copy of *Hola!* magazine.

"What a surprise," Dahlia said. "I didn't have you down as a liar, Julia."

"I'm just reusing a past truth in a different context... isn't that what you've been doing?"

Dahlia's face hardened. She made to push past Julia, but Julia stood her ground.

"We need to talk." Julia crossed her arms, nodding at Dahlia's hair. "Strange place for a make-over."

Dahlia's gaze darted around the bathroom, avoiding Julia's stare.

"Oh, you know, just felt like a change."

"A change? Right before fleeing town unannounced?"

Dahlia's composure cracked as she forced a smile.

"I wouldn't say *fleeing*..."

"Then what would you call it?"

"A break." Dahlia's hands trembled, rustling the glossy pages of the magazine before she tossed it onto the closed toilet lid. "I wanted a fresh start somewhere new."

"With Minnie in tow, barely lucid from whatever you've given her?" Julia countered.

"Just a little sleeping pill. She was feeling anxious about the flight."

"Dahlia..."

"I think Ian's attack has confused me," she said, lifting her hand to her head. Her fingers grazed the plaster still stuck to her forehead. "I'm not feeling myself."

"Drop the lies."

"It's the truth."

Julia sighed. "Give it up, Dahlia. We found Ian tied up in the wardrobe. We found the electrolyte tubs. The fake water results. Chloe's staged drowning. Helena's supposed suicide. You've been orchestrating this from the beginning."

As calm as anything, Dahlia walked up to the mirror and checked the progress of her hair dye, as though nothing was amiss.

"I know you killed Chloe, Dahlia. She stole *your* story... *your* secrets... and broadcast them to the world. You thought you could trust her. Maybe if she hadn't betrayed you, you'd never have resorted to murder. It's not as if it runs in the family."

Dahlia's eyes flashed with anger, but she kept running her comb through her hair.

"Except maybe it does. Your brother seems to have inspired you," Julia continued. "Injecting Helena, trying to make the deaths look like accidents... it's very similar to how Michael killed his patients."

Dahlia whirled around, her features twisted in a bitter snarl. She brandished the dye-covered comb like a weapon.

"How *dare* you compare me to *him*!"

"Then tell me I'm wrong." Julia waited, but nothing came. "Explain how two people ended up dead."

"I... I don't have to explain anything to you."

"Maybe not to me, but you'll have to explain it to the police when they get here."

Panic flashed in Dahlia's eyes. She glanced around the bathroom as if plotting her escape, but Julia blocked her path to the door.

"You want to know *why*?" Dahlia cried. "Because Michael's legacy of evil has defined my life. No matter where I went, who I became, people saw me as an extension of him, as if his sickness flowed in my veins too." She swiped at her tears, smearing her cheek with dye. "I changed my name, my look, tried to start fresh. But it was all for *nothing*. Chloe dredged it all up again with that wretched book, and I knew no matter how hard I worked, I'd always be *his* sister."

Julia listened, allowing Dahlia's pent-up torment to spill forth.

"Don't you *see*? I had *no* choice!" Dahlia cried, her voice growing more desperate by the second. "*She* gave me *no* way out. It was me or her."

"There's *always* a choice, Dahlia." Julia took a deep breath before answering Dahlia's question from earlier. "If my Sue had done the same as your brother, I can't say for certain how I'd cope. Not well, I'd imagine. I have this friend, Roxy, and her sister is in prison for murder. Long story, but I know Roxy has struggled with the aftermath, and still does."

Dahlia nodded, her gaze fixed on the dripping tap.

"But," Julia continued, "I couldn't imagine continuing that cycle, no matter how betrayed I felt. My friend, Roxy... she's had her problems and her speed bumps, but she hasn't killed."

"Then you are both better women than I am," Dahlia said with a sigh, still avoiding Julia's eyes in the mirror. "Believe me, I gave Chloe a *choice*."

After a moment, Julia asked, "What happened that night in your room before you drowned Chloe? Luca said he heard raised voices in the early hours."

"After that disastrous dinner, when she was acting like a brat and rubbing everyone the wrong way, I couldn't sleep. Thoughts of Chloe's memoir kept swirling through my mind. That wretched book was everywhere—talk shows, bestseller lists, book clubs, this damned airport—and everywhere it went, my darkest secrets went with it. Reliving my trauma had become a public spectacle, all for Chloe's gain."

Dahlia's gaze grew distant, lost in the memory.

"And what happened next?"

"Around two in the morning, I went to confront her. I knocked on her door, but she didn't answer. I could see the light on under the door, so I knew she was awake. I knocked again, louder, and she opened it."

Julia pictured the scene—the darkened hotel

corridor, Chloe silhouetted in her doorway, her eyes rolling, phone glued to her hand.

"At first, she tried to laugh it off. She said, 'Can't this wait until morning? I need my beauty sleep.' She made it sound so *trivial*. Unimportant." Dahlia's tone darkened, and she said, "She slammed the door in my face."

"You fought your way in?"

"No. I returned to my room, and ten minutes later, she knocked on my door. Said she'd thought about what I said and was ready to talk. Had her tail between her legs. I demanded that she admit to her followers that she fabricated the story. That she'd never been a victim of any serial killer." Dahlia exhaled with a shaky laugh. "She *refused*. Started spouting some nonsense about how the details didn't matter, only the message of empowerment and survival. I told her my life was not hers to exploit for empowerment, and I..."

Dahlia's voice broke from the raw emotion before she collected herself again.

"I said if she didn't tell the truth, I'd expose her lies myself. She just laughed. Said no one would believe me over her, that I was 'just a crazy old lady with an axe to grind.' That's when I lost it."

Dahlia fell silent, her eyes downcast.

"Go on," Julia urged. "What happened after she said that?"

"She said she'd tell people I was obsessed with her, that I'd been stalking and threatening her for months. That *I* was... *unhinged*. Dangerous, even."

Julia considered this. She could picture how the

media would seize onto such a narrative, spinning Chloe as the tragic victim of a deranged woman's vengeance.

It would destroy Dahlia's credibility.

Just like it had Ian's.

But it wasn't like Dahlia was doing a good job of proving Chloe otherwise.

"I saw red," Dahlia whispered. "All I could think was how she'd already taken so much from me, and now she planned to take my sanity too. I couldn't let her do it. Before I knew it, my hands were around her throat."

Dahlia mimed the action, her fingers curling.

"She fought me," she said, her eyes clenching shut as her hands tightened into claws, "but I was too strong. In those ten minutes before she came to my room, I'd run myself a bath to relax. I plunged her into it and…" Her fingers loosened as her body sagged against the counter. "It happened so fast. Before I knew what I was doing, the bubbles stopped. She wasn't fighting me. I'd killed her. I always thought it would be more difficult, but there she was… *dead*."

A heavy silence fell between them. Julia processed Dahlia's account, disturbed, yet somehow feeling some sympathy for the murderer before her.

"What did you do after that?" Julia asked.

"I woke Helena up and we moved her body to the mineral baths. She was so desperate to sell her vitamins on *Blisselle*, I knew she'd do anything I asked. The alcohol was Helena's idea to make it look like an accident. I cleaned up the water that we dripped everywhere and then I went back to my room. I was expecting she'd be found in the morning, but of course, Minnie couldn't resist having a middle-of-the-night soak."

"And you still went on to kill Helena. Did you put Luca's cigarette ash in Helena's room?"

Julia's stomach churned as Dahlia's face twisted into a smile, relishing the chance to boast about her cunning scheme.

"Just in case they didn't buy the suicide route. I thought about forging a note, but I could never imitate her doctor's scribble. They do have awful handwriting. Michael did, too." She smiled at some far-off memory, staring through Julia. "If I'd known Ian was spotted going into her room, I would have tried to frame him first. I didn't *want* to kill Helena. She did work hard for me. When the pipes first burst, it was her idea to add the electrolytes to the water. It was plain old tap water with a little sulphur in it. Minnie was old and desperate for someone—*anyone*—to save her from having to run the hotel. It was too easy to drive a wedge between Minnie and Lisa."

"And you got Minnie all to yourself." Julia's disgust grew with each callous admission. "You manipulated and used these people who cared about you."

Dahlia shrugged. "I gave them what they needed. Minnie was lonely. Helena wanted what I had. Luca and Ian were desperate for fame and redemption. I delivered that. With the right story, we could market the hotel and profit. With a doctor on my side, it was a sure-fire win.

She gave me credibility, and I let her flog her vitamins on *Blisselle*."

"Helena wasn't a doctor. Not anymore. You knew that."

Dahlia examined her fingernails. "I didn't. Not until you told me. But it didn't matter by then." She glanced up, her eyes cold. "She was already dead. I injected her with all the vitamins I could liquidise and fit into a syringe. She tried to fight me. Didn't stand a chance. I was too determined. You could say I had the... taste for it. She knew too much and was drawing too much attention. She promised she wouldn't, but she'd crack under pressure, so she had to go. I gave her a choice."

"What choice?"

"How she wanted to die," Dahlia said, as though it should have been obvious. "She could have jumped from the balcony. That would have been quicker."

Any sympathy Julia had felt dissolved.

"It would only be a matter of time before people connected the dots back to Michael... back to *me*," Dahlia insisted, searching Julia's eyes for a shred of understanding. "If Helena hadn't been so reckless, she could have lived. If Chloe had been honest, I would have *respected* her. *Forgiven* her. She *chose* to die, too. She'd learned nothing. She was the same reckless, selfish girl I'd opened my heart to in Bali. And she admitted she had another book in the works," she confessed, her voice as hollow as her gaze. "She was planning to use 'us' as the foundation. She wanted to tear down the wellness industry... our livelihoods. She'd taken my past, and she wanted my present too. The stage was set. I did what I had to."

"The stage was set," Julia echoed. "You just made it sound like you killed Chloe as a spur-of-the-moment thing, but... you *planned* this from the start, didn't you?"

Dahlia didn't respond.

"Luca and Ian..." Julia started, piecing together Dahlia's manipulations. "You invited them here because they each had their issues with Chloe. They were shocked that you invited Chloe... they wanted *nothing* to do with her."

Dahlia remained silent, staring at the floor.

"It was the perfect cover for you," Julia continued. "They were here to throw suspicion off yourself."

Dahlia's silence was all the confirmation Julia needed. Her intricate plan unravelled further with each passing second. Dahlia had played them all, manipulating the situation to pin Chloe's murder on anyone but herself.

The bathroom door swung open, and Julia let out a deep breath as Detective Catalina Ramirez strode into the bathroom, out of breath but with purpose, firing her eyes as they closed in on Dahlia.

"Got here as fast as I could," Ramirez said.

Dahlia's gaze flickered with a brief flash of fear before she gave a resigned sigh. She held her wrists out.

"I won't put up a fight," she said. "My brother made a fool of himself trying to flee the police. I won't repeat *that* mistake."

With a curt nod, Ramirez stepped forward and cuffed Dahlia's outstretched hands.

"I never meant for everything to go this far," Dahlia said as she checked on her hair in the mirror one last time. "But now I think I understand how my brother got so... *carried away*." She gave a hollow laugh. "When you're in desperate situations, it's funny what you'll do to save your own life."

"I wouldn't call it *funny*," Julia said.

Detective Ramirez marched Dahlia out of the bathroom, leaving Julia alone. She leaned against the counter and let out her biggest breath yet. Her hands shook as she clung to the marble behind her back—she wasn't sure how she'd held herself together.

A moment later, Jessie poked her head around the door. "She spilled the beans?"

Julia nodded as Jessie entered, followed by Dot.

"Well, I can't say I'll miss her," Dot huffed, wrinkling her nose at the pungent odour. "No matter how charming they seem, you can never tell what darkness lurks inside a person, even the ones who claim they're 'well.'"

"I'll second that," Jessie agreed. "She fooled everyone with that spiritual guru act. I feel bad for Luca getting tangled up with her."

Julia sighed, staring at the copy of *Hola!* she'd been reading while waiting for the dye to process.

"I still can't quite believe she was capable of cold-blooded murder. The whole thing was premeditated."

"Regardless, we can close the book on this dreadful

business," Dot said. "They've rushed Minnie to the nearest hospital. I hope she'll bounce back after all this betrayal."

"I'm sure she will be," Julia said. "We'll stay until she needs us to."

Jessie nodded. "No more flimsy miracle cures."

As they made their way out of the bathroom and through the crowds towards the airport's exit, Julia felt a lightness enter her heart. Despite the darkness and deception they'd uncovered, she had her family beside her, and they still had a few days left of their holiday.

"Anyone fancy a glass of sangria when we get back?" Julia asked. "I think we've earned it."

26

Later that evening in La Casa's reception area, Julia stood with Detective Catalina Ramirez, the atmosphere relaxing now that the chaos had ended.

"I have to say, the confession you got from Dahlia was remarkable," the detective said, rocking back on her heels. "Especially considering her brother took a vow of silence after his arrest."

"Dahlia knew she had nowhere left to run. The noose was tightening. This was the end of the road for her."

"That seems to be the case," the detective agreed. "After obtaining warrants and digging into her finances and records, it's clear La Casa represented a last-ditch effort to regain control. Her *Blisselle* app has been losing investors for months. People were losing faith in her strange offerings. It seems taking over your aunt's hotel under the guise of a rebrand was a way for her to pivot into a new industry while still peddling her pseudoscience claims. A desperate attempt to start over."

Julia sighed, thinking of her poor great-aunt being manipulated by Dahlia for her own agenda. She hoped she was feeling better in the hospital.

"Just like Helena. It seems Dahlia was a shapeshifter."

Ian arrived in the hotel lobby with a bag slung over his shoulder.

"That's influencers for you," he said, having caught the tail end of their conversation. "They'll be whatever they need to be, with a little help from the smoke and mirrors." He turned to Julia and bowed. "Thank you for putting an end to things just in time. For a moment there, I thought I was going to become Dahlia's next victim."

"All in a day's work."

"You're far too modest, Julia," Ramirez said. "You were one step ahead of me on this one. An extra day, and I might have pinned Dahlia down with the paperwork, but it would have been too late. She would have left Savega with your aunt and gone who knows where."

"I'm just glad it's all over," she said, resting a hand on Ian's arm. "And I'm glad you're alive. I'm sorry for believing Dahlia's lies about you, even for a second."

"No matter," he said, pulling her into a hug. "You're a light, Julia. Don't forget that." He stepped back, hoisting up his backpack. "Am I okay to leave town now, Detective? I feel as though I've long overstayed my welcome here."

The detective nodded. "You're free to go."

"Then I shall. There isn't a flight until the morning, but truth be told, I think I'd rather sit meditating in the airport than spend another second in this hotel." He took in the reception area with a frown deep in his beard. "Far too white and stark for me."

"Where will you go?"

"Onto the next retreat," Ian said, pulling open the front door. "Los Angeles, here I come... can't be any weirder than what happened here."

Julia and the detective watched as Ian strode through the hotel doors into the night. A wave of relief washed over Julia as she witnessed him reclaiming his freedom—a sight that eased her heart. Now sure of his innocence, she found comfort in the fact that he had survived to face a new dawn.

Detective Ramirez turned to Julia and said, "What will you do now that you've saved the day? I could organise a press call. You deserve the credit."

Julia peered into the dining room where her family clustered around a table, laughter and candlelight mingling as they shared a meal together.

"The credit is yours to take, Detective Ramirez." She stepped back from the detective, her exhale turning into a wide, heartwarming smile. "I'll do what I came here to do—try to have a nice family holiday."

Jessie slipped her phone into the back pocket of her jeans and leaned against the white wall of the hotel, gazing up at the stars twinkling above Savega. The phone call with Johnny had been bittersweet, but a weight had lifted from her shoulders now that she'd decided.

The door creaked open behind her. She turned, anticipating Dante, but Luca stepped through, a duffel bag slung over his shoulder.

"Planning to sneak out?" Jessie asked.

Luca jumped, glancing at her as he lit a cigarette.

"You're like my shadow."

"Or your conscience. Just call me Jiminy Cricket." She laughed, refusing his offer of a cigarette. "Where will you go?"

Luca stared up at the moon as he puffed away.

"Home," he said, looking down at the cigarette before tossing it after only a few drags. "I've been running for too long."

"Back to your nonna?"

"She died a long time ago," he said, staring at his shoes as he stamped out the glowing tip. "She left me her house, but I haven't been back. I thought there were too many ghosts there, but... after what we went through here." He turned to look back at La Casa, "I think it won't be so bad."

"I think you're right." She saluted him as he backed away. "There's no place like home."

"Click my heels three times?" Luca saluted back, clicking his shoes together. "Thank you for believing in me, Jessie. I know I didn't make it easy for you. How did you know it wasn't me?"

Jessie thought about it, but she wasn't sure. Maybe it was because he'd shared his story and she'd seen herself in him, or maybe it had been a gut feeling. She shrugged.

"I didn't," she admitted. "But I hoped you were innocent. Stay out of trouble, yeah?"

"I'll try."

Luca disappeared into the night. She retrieved her phone to follow him on Instagram, but he'd deactivated his profile.

"Good for you," she whispered to herself, putting her phone back.

Stamping out the still smouldering cigarette, she hoped Luca would find what he was looking for. Without Dahlia trying to push him into a box he didn't want to be in, she felt he'd find his way.

As she turned to return to the hotel, the abrupt purr of an engine and the sweep of headlights slicing through the darkness stopped her in her tracks. A taxi had pulled up at the top of the steps. Minnie emerged from the backseat. She edged out like every movement hurt, a hand clamped to her lower back, declining the driver's extended hand for help with the stairs.

"Here," Jessie said, rushing over to offer Minnie her arm.

"You're too kind, dear," Minnie said, a croak in her throat. "These old bones just aren't what they used to be."

"How are you feeling?"

Minnie pushed forward a wobbly smile and said, "Much better now that the sedatives are leaving me. Doctors said there were alarming amounts in my system. Wanted to keep me overnight, but I've never wanted my bed more. I can't believe that mad woman was slipping me things this whole time. No wonder I've been in such a fog."

They entered the lobby, passing by the front desk.

"Should I wake the others?" Jessie asked.

"I've caused enough drama for one holiday. Let them get their rest. Get yourself to bed. I can manage."

But Jessie didn't let go and guided Minnie to the stairs. They climbed together, Minnie's laboured breathing echoing in the stairwell. When they reached the top floor, Jessie swiped the master key card and held the door open to Minnie's apartment.

"I should give you this back," Jessie said, handing the card over. "It came in handy."

Jessie helped her over to the zebra-print sofa before she went to open a window, letting in the faint sounds of a guitar player in the plaza down below. When she came back, Minnie was eyeing a bottle of sangria, but she didn't reach for it.

"I've been such a fool," Minnie murmured, dropping her head into her hands. "To think I trusted that woman."

"She played a good game."

Minnie shook her head. "But I should have known *better*. The things she promised... the nonsense she whispered in my ear... I allowed myself to be blinded by mirages in the desert... by minerals in the water. I thought they were helping me. The *hours* I spent down in that basement."

"You must have really wanted to change."

Minnie heaved herself to her feet and shuffled over to her bedside table, picking up the bottles of Helena's vitamins lined up in a neat row. For a moment, she stared down at them, her expression unreadable. With a sudden force, she hurled them into the bin.

"Good riddance," she declared.

Jessie perched on the edge of the snakeskin-print duvet as Minnie settled back against the plush pillows. For a moment, they listened to the guitar.

"I've made such a mess of things," Minnie said, staring up at the ceiling. "If only I'd learned my lesson the first time." She tilted her head to meet Jessie's gaze. "That's the trouble with getting to my age. You repeat the same mistakes over and over. Let me give you some advice, my dear." She reached across and patted Jessie's hand. "Learn your lessons *young*. Don't end up like your Great Aunt Minnie."

Jessie offered her *great*-great-aunt a sympathetic smile.

"What do you think I should do?" Minnie asked. "About all of this? The hotel, the business..."

"Oh, I don't—"

"I need a *fresh* perspective. A youthful perspective."

Jessie paused, wrestling with the notion of whether to offer guidance. But the raw desperation in Minnie's eyes tipped the scales, and she took a moment to think about it. She surveyed the room, resting on the stark wall which Julia had mentioned was once adorned with photographs of Minnie's glamorous heyday.

"The hotel means a lot to you. It's been there for you through so much."

Minnie gave a faint nod.

"A rebrand and relaunch is a great opportunity."

An even heavier nod.

"But maybe not the right opportunity for *you*." Jessie clenched her hand. "It might be time to let it go. Sell La Casa and move on to something new."

Minnie's eyes widened at the suggestion, and Jessie could see the conflict behind them. The idea of leaving her beloved hotel behind filled Minnie with uncertainty, even if she had been ready to flee it under Dahlia's influence only hours earlier.

"You honestly think I should sell?" Minnie asked.

"It seems like the hotel is too much for you. This could be your chance for a fresh start. You've redecorated and created a blank canvas for someone else to put their stamp on it. Jump on the boat while it's passing."

"Maybe you're right." Minnie paused, and added, "I'll sleep on it."

She stifled a yawn, and Jessie took that as her cue to leave. She stood up from the bed and left Minnie to drift off, hoping her words might guide her to make the right decision. As Jessie shut the door behind her, she hoped Minnie would emerge from this mess stronger. At her age, she'd hate for her to spin around in the same cycle again.

Jessie slipped back into her room, the faint glow from Dante's laptop the only light in the darkness.

"Must have been a long phone call," he remarked, glancing up from the screen. "Everything okay?"

Jessie nodded, peeling off her jacket and draping it over the back of a chair.

"Johnny can talk for England. We were having a catch-up."

She climbed onto the bed beside Dante, nestling against his shoulder.

"So, did you change your mind?" he asked. "About the job?"

"No."

"That must've surprised him?"

"A bit," Jessie admitted. He had been very surprised and spent fifteen minutes trying to sell it to her. "But in the end, he understood where I was coming from. And besides, he said he might have found someone better suited for it."

Dante let out a contemplative hum.

"What are you working on?"

"Just some edits for a fluff piece about the field vote for Veronica," he said, setting the computer on the bedside table. "But it can wait until morning."

He shifted down, and Jessie curled against his chest. She pressed a tender kiss against him as he wrapped his arms around her. She wanted that moment to last forever, but it couldn't—what she had to say next would change everything.

"You might want to check your emails," she said, snuggling closer. "I have a feeling a golden opportunity is coming your way."

27

After two peaceful days in the hotel following Dahlia's arrest, Julia and her family were enjoying lunch with Minnie on the patio under the glorious sunshine. It reminded Julia of their first meal upon arrival, except the atmosphere had completely changed. The tension and insincerity had vanished, replaced by a relaxed familial warmth.

And Lisa was there, sitting by her mother's side. Mother and daughter reunited after everything. Lisa refilled Minnie's water glass as a gentle breeze rustled the colourful umbrella above.

The food had returned to what Julia remembered from her last visit, featuring paella loaded with prawns, mussels, calamari, and saffron rice. A refreshing warm soup made from vine-ripened tomatoes, and golden, fluffy tortillas sat beside small plates of marinated olives. From the satisfied expressions around the table, Julia knew she wasn't alone in enjoying the return to form.

"I want to thank you all," Minnie said, raising her water, "from the bottom of my heart, for everything you did to bring an end to the dreadful nightmare here at La Casa. If it wasn't for your persistence and courage, I dread to think what more damage Dahlia *Clayton* may have inflicted."

Dot reached over and gave Minnie's hand an affectionate pat and said, "You don't need to thank us. You're family. We look out for our own."

"Even so, you went above and beyond. And you helped open my eyes to many things I'd been blind to," she continued, turning to Julia and raising her glass higher. "Especially you. You never gave up searching for the truth. I'm in awe of you for doing this for me not just once, but now twice."

Julia felt her cheeks flush. She'd only done what came naturally to her—keeping her ear to the ground until the full picture emerged.

"I'm just relieved you're safe," Julia replied, smiling around the table. "We all played a part."

"What will you do next?" Dot asked. "Are you coming back to Peridale with us? It's still your home."

"It's not been my home for a very long time."

"But it could be," Dot insisted. "You're staying here?"

"I'm not doing that either." Minnie inhaled with a smile, reaching across the table to grab Lisa's hand. "I've made a big decision. It's time to move on. Time to catch the boat." She closed her eyes, and when she exhaled, she peered up at the building looming over them. "The time has come to sell La Casa."

"Cheers to that," Jessie said, toasting Minnie, who tipped her head in return. "What's next for Minnie Harlow?"

Minnie looked around the table, her gaze settling on each person, a stark contrast to the distant gazing that characterized her demeanor when Julia and her family first arrived at La Casa.

"This whole ordeal with Dahlia," she began, her voice wavering, "has made me realize that my willingness to let her take over, and my reliance on Lisa before that, stemmed from exhaustion. I'm tired of the responsibility, the routine, the pressure… it's all too much."

"So, you're going to move to a retirement place?"

"Goodness, no, Dorothy! I've never been one for knitting and pottering around a garden," Minnie said with a laugh. "It wouldn't suit me. I already told you about my plans. I'm catching the boat. *Literally*. I've spent my last bit of savings on a three-month cruise. I won't have to lift a finger!"

"And I've agreed to manage the sale of this place," Lisa said, looking up at the hotel with surprise fondness. "It's time for someone else to make La Casa their home."

"And when they do," Minnie said, clutching Lisa's hand tighter. "I'm cutting the profits down the middle and giving you half."

"Oh, Mum, you don't—"

"Money won't change that I was a useless mother to you for as many years as I was. I'm sorry that I can't change the past because if I could, I would… and I'd make a few of the same mistakes again." She laughed before pulling Lisa's hand up to her mouth to kiss the back of it. "But what I can do is change your future. I won't be around forever, and I'd rather die knowing that you won't be struggling to make ends meet working in a grimy rock bar."

"I do like working there," Lisa admitted, batting away tears with a napkin. "But thank you. That will... that will change my life."

Julia smiled as she raised her glass. "I'd like to propose a toast. To new beginnings."

Glasses clinked around the table, and as Julia sipped her sangria, the sweet wine bursting over her tongue, she felt a swell of contentment. After everything they had endured, it was a relief to sit in the dappled sunlight and share a celebratory meal together.

"And to leaving the past where it belongs," Dot added, lifting her glass again.

"You'll have to stop by Peridale on your travels," Jessie said. "It's always there. Not much changes."

"Except the field," Ethel grunted. "I wonder how the vote is going."

"Neck and neck last I heard," Dante said.

"We'll find out when we're home, I suppose," Julia said. "I still need to cast my vote. Couldn't decide before we left, and I got a little distracted."

"My fault," Percy said.

"*My* fault," Dot corrected. "And how glad I am that you convinced me to come. Minnie, Lisa... I couldn't be happier for you."

"And who knows, I might love it so much I'll keep going forever. Well, for at least another few years. I'll give Dahlia credit for one thing... her strict diet made me shift all those pounds I've been carrying around. I'll toast to my waistline."

Laughter rippled around the table. Julia smiled as she looked at each dear face—her family, whole and happy again. She wished they could stay suspended in this moment forever, basking in the Spanish sun.

But life moved forward. Their time here was ending.

After lunch wound down and the table was cleared, Julia stood in the airy reception area, suitcases gathered around her feet. She checked her watch as the minutes ticked by, wondering what was keeping her gran. Their transfer van would arrive any moment to take them to the airport.

Out on the patio, Jessie and Dante leaned against the railing, chatting as they admired the breathtaking valley one last time. Dante said something that made Jessie laugh, and Julia smiled at seeing the glow on her daughter's face.

The sound of the front door opening drew Julia's attention. Sue and Neil entered with the twins behind them.

"All set for home?" Julia asked.

"Home does sound nice," Sue admitted. "The kids are getting restless cooped up here."

"Not ready to stay behind?" Julia asked. "You and Neil could buy this place. Start afresh abroad like you wanted."

"Pipe dream. I think we got a bit swept away with the place. Maybe we just need more holidays abroad."

"And Peridale's not such an awful place to raise a family," Julia said.

Sue smiled. "You're right. We fought hard enough to protect its charm. Where's Gran?"

"Not sure," Julia said. "I hope we're not having a repeat of when we set off. The transfer will be here soon."

Barker walked over with Olivia, and Julia pulled her daughter into a tight hug, breathing in that sweet baby scent.

"Sorry that I wasn't much help with your writing. But with everything going on..."

"Don't be silly." Barker kissed Julia's forehead. "All the chaos was inspiring. I got more writing done than I have in ages. The new book's almost finished thanks to this holiday."

"Small mercies," Julia said, kissing him properly. "Well done, love. Can't wait to read it."

Outside, a van pulled up. Their airport transfer had arrived. Julia checked her watch again. Where was Dot?

"We're picking them up on the way," Jessie said, as if reading Julia's mind when she walked inside. "They had something to take care of first."

Julia nodded, and she took one last look around La Casa, thinking how much would change for the hotel when it passed to new owners.

But for her family, normality awaited back in Peridale. And after everything they had endured here,

Julia was ready to return to the comforting familiarity of home.

Dot took a deep breath as she stepped through the creaky wooden door frame into the dilapidated villa. The morning sun streamed in through gaps in the crumbling walls, illuminating the swirling dust. This was the place that had haunted her dreams—the site of her and Percy's traumatic kidnapping ordeal.

Now, seeing it in the light of day, it seemed ordinary. The dark memories clung to the space like cobwebs in the corners, but the villa itself was just a sad, abandoned building.

"It's not scary at all," Dot said.

"And it's smaller than I remember," Percy said, ambling over to a rickety table in the centre of the front room. "This is where we played cards."

Dot pictured them huddled around the table, using a deck of cards and laughter to distract themselves from their dire situation.

"We found the lightness in the dark, didn't we?" Dot said.

"A little magic makes the world go around," Percy said, producing his trick bouquet of plastic flowers, never too far away.

She accepted the flowers, slipping her hand into his. He gave it an affectionate, reassuring squeeze.

"I'm so proud of you for coming on this trip, my dear," he said. "For facing your fears."

Dot's eyes welled up, but the tears weren't from sadness or fear now—they came from the overwhelming love she had for this man.

"You know what, Percy? If I wasn't already married to you, I'd marry you all over again."

A blaring car horn from the road interrupted their tender moment.

"That'll be our lift to the airport," Dot said.

"Ready to go?"

Dot gazed out across the landscape, drinking it in. The darkness she'd experienced here hadn't diminished the beauty of the place. She realised now that the past couldn't overcome her if she didn't let—she was in control of her present.

Memories were just memories.

And a building was just a building.

With a satisfied smile, she turned to her husband.

"I don't think I've ever been more ready to see our little village."

Percy's eyes crinkled as he grinned back at her. Arm in arm, they made their way down the winding path back to the road, where the minibus awaited them. Dot thought about taking one last look at the villa, but she didn't need to.

"Did you do what you needed to?" Ethel asked, the only one off the bus.

"Yes," she said. "I think we've put an end to this cycle."

Ethel's lips curved into a knowing smile. "Funny you should mention cycles. Reminds me of what I read in that tarot book at the airport."

"Actually, Ethel, I don't think I need to hear this."

"It's not bad," she said. "The ten of swords—it's not just about betrayal, you know. That book said it can also represent the end of a *cycle*. And the potential for new beginnings once one has faced their troubles or challenges."

Dot stared at Ethel for a moment before breaking into laughter. The sound echoed around them, warm and hearty against the stillness of the Spanish countryside.

"Well, I never..." she said, shaking her head in disbelief. She turned to Percy, who was grinning at her side. "Evelyn predicted something right for once."

The van started with a rumble, pulling Dot from her thoughts. As they drove away from the villa, she didn't look back. Instead, she turned her gaze forward, towards the winding road that led them home to Peridale.

For all its charm and warmth, Savega couldn't hold a candle to their little village. It was time to go home.

Jessie rested her head on Dante's shoulder by the large windows on the edge of the airport, watching the planes move around on the concourse. She used to love doing this with her brother when she was travelling, the sight of the slow-moving planes and the low hum of the engines calming amidst the chaos of constant travel.

Dante exhaled, his breath tickling her ear.

"Jessie, I need to tell you something."

She knew what was coming next.

"Hmm?"

"I'm not coming home with you," he said. "I accepted the job from Johnny. He wants me to start right away."

Jessie clenched her eyes, her chest tightening. She nodded, forcing down the lump in her throat. Her heart ached with a strange mixture of emotions—pain at Dante's impending departure, but also a grudging happiness for him.

He wouldn't have stood in her way if she'd wanted it.

She didn't.

He did.

She wouldn't stand in his way.

"Where are you going first?" she asked, her voice small.

"Amsterdam," he replied. "I'm going to review a new hotel there—a new health spa, of all places."

Despite everything, Jessie laughed—a hollow sound that echoed in the vast space of the airport.

"Another wellness retreat?" she said. "Good luck."

Dante laughed with her, the sound soft and comforting.

"If the bodies pile up, I'll know who to call. You ever been to Amsterdam?"

She nodded. "You'll like it. Just keep an eye out for the bikes."

Their laughter died down, leaving behind a silence. Jessie stared at a plane as it ascended into the sky, her heart aching despite being the one who'd told Johnny all about Dante's talents.

"What do we do now?" he asked. "Do we... do we try the long-distance thing?"

Jessie didn't answer.

"You're right," he said, sighing. "It probably wouldn't work."

She cuddled in closer as another silence fell between them, with only the chatter of the airport behind them. She hoped the moment would stretch out forever.

"What do we do now?" he whispered.

"When's your flight?"

"In two hours."

"Let's live in the moment," she said. "Almost a lifetime."

As Dante smiled at her words—that same cheeky smile that had caught her attention at that first press conference at the library in Peridale—Jessie didn't stop the tears running down her cheeks and onto his shoulder.

She already missed him.

28

The familiar scents of home enveloped Dot as she stepped through the creaking wooden door of her cottage. Lady and Bruce yapped at her heels, almost tripping Percy as they raced up and down the hallway.

"Down, down!" Dot called, but a broad smile crossed her face. She knelt down to lavish the wriggling dogs with scratches. "Oh, I've missed you both, too."

"You're back!" Evelyn exclaimed, appearing from the sitting room. "Look at you both. You've caught the sun. You're positively glowing!"

Dot straightened, brushing dog hair from her pleated navy skirt.

"It was just what we needed."

"No... trouble?" Evelyn asked.

"Not a lick."

Evelyn breathed a sigh of relief as Dot dragged her

suitcase past her. She dumped it on the coffee table, unzipped it, and flung it open.

"Presents from our travels," she said, pulling bags out to hand them to Evelyn. "Fridge magnets, soaps, crystals, and some funny smelling tea that had your name written all over it. And this." She extracted a flowing kaftan in an eye-catching leopard print. "It's secondhand from someone very dear to me, but I put it through the wash to get rid of the energy or the juju or whatever it is you believe in."

"How exotic!" Evelyn exclaimed, holding the animal print up to her plain blue kaftan. "I love it! What do you think?"

Dot smiled. "Suits you."

They settled onto the sofa, Dot sinking into the familiar cushions with a contented sigh. She fanned her arms out against the back, stamping her feet on her carpet.

"It's so good to be home," she said. "Don't get me wrong, Spain was beautiful, but there's no place like Peridale."

"Too much sun and sangria, not enough rain and cups of tea?"

Dot laughed. "Something like that."

For a while, they talked about the trip—the winding streets of Savega, the lively plaza, the chaotic hotel. Dot avoided mentioning the murders. She focused on the lighter moments, describing the picturesque views and lively music that filled their last few days.

Once Evelyn left to get back to running her bed-and-breakfast, Ethel popped by after unpacking at her cottage. They settled in the back garden with tea and cards while Lady and Bruce ran around the blossoming flower beds.

"I'm looking forward to my own bed tonight," Ethel said, finishing her tea. "I might finally enjoy some peace, though I must say, my cottage is going to seem rather quiet after spending so much time with you two."

"We've always got a spare room," Dot said, nodding at the cottage.

Ethel snorted, brushing a stray curl from her face. "Isn't three a crowd?"

"Not at all," Percy chimed in, his eyes twinkling. "A triangle is the strongest shape."

"What will people say?" Ethel laughed. "They'll call me and Dot your sister wives."

"And we'll just have to set people straight," Dot said. "This is Peridale. People will talk no matter what we do. Fancy another cup of tea?"

"Sure, why not," Ethel replied with a grin, sinking back into her chair. "I suppose there's no rush to get back to an empty cottage."

"How about another round of cards?" Dot suggested. "I fancy beating you again."

"You wish." Ethel rolled her eyes, topping up their tea. "But you're on."

Percy glanced at his watch and said, "Just one game, mind you. We need to be at the café before closing for Katie's ballot results."

Jessie sat at her desk in the cramped office above the nail salon, with Dante's desk sitting empty across from hers. The office door swung open, and Veronica breezed in, clutching a steaming takeaway coffee from the van at the bottom of Mulberry Lane.

"Ah, you're back," she sang out, settling in at her desk with a groan. "I know he only worked here for a few weeks, but it feels empty in here, doesn't it?"

"Yeah."

"You okay?"

"I will be."

Veronica started peeling a satsuma, and it was as if Jessie hadn't been away.

"I'm sorry," Veronica said, as awkward as ever when it came to talking about romance. "It seems like you wanted different things, but I know you cared about him."

"I did." Jessie avoided Veronica's tilted head stare, tracing a water ring left behind by a cup on her desk. "If you love someone, let them go, right?"

"Right." She tossed a satsuma across the office as Jessie looked up, and she just about caught it. "You want to talk about it?"

"Not much to say."

"You sure?"

"I'm sure."

Veronica excused herself to the small bathroom. Alone, Jessie rifled through the stack of mail on her desk until she found the postcard pouring out her conflicted feelings about Johnny's job offer. She already felt so different from that girl—she should have put it in a text message.

The toilet flushed, and Veronica emerged, flicking water from her fingers. Jessie pocketed the postcard, turning back to her desk.

"I already read it," Veronica said as she settled back into her chair, pulling her keyboard close. "Who do you think recommended you to Johnny?"

"*You* did?" Jessie frowned. "You trying to get rid of me?"

"It was an incredible opportunity, and I see your potential," Veronica said, shrugging without a hint of apology. "There's no way to sugar-coat it... *The Peridale Post*... Peridale... it's small. If you stay here, your career as a journalist won't go too far. You might end up sitting in my chair as editor one day, but that's it."

"That's good enough for you."

Veronica bobbed her head from side to side as she tossed in a satsuma segment and said, "Fair point."

Jessie looked down at the postcard, a storm of emotions swirling through her. She wanted to be mad at Veronica for meddling, but she couldn't muster it.

For now, at least. Who knew what stories awaited around the corner? Peridale was many things, but it was never boring. There would be another mystery, another campaign, another revelation that only *The Post* could uncover in their quaint little village.

And she and Veronica would be ready.

"It's good enough for me, too," Jessie said as she booted up her computer again. "And you really think I could be the editor?"

"I'm not dead yet." Veronica winked. "I have an ad drafted ready to go to replace Dante. Should I post it, or do you think we can pull it off with just the two of us?"

Jessie considered this as she logged herself back into the system.

"We've got this," she said. "The dynamic duo."

"Good, because before we go to cover the ballot results, I've had some ideas for new features..."

As Veronica launched into outlining her latest editorial vision for the paper, Jessie relaxed, comforted by the familiar enthusiasm. Veronica was right—she and Dante wanted different things. He was off chasing his travel writing dream while she was still finding her journalistic feet.

This was where she needed to be.

Home.

Julia couldn't resist donning her apron and jumping behind the counter, even though she'd only returned from Spain that afternoon. She'd missed the cosy warmth of her café and seeing the familiar faces of her fellow villagers gathered inside.

The small space buzzed as more customers filtered in, even though the café was due to close in ten minutes.

Everyone was excited about the reveal of the ballot results. Julia scanned the crowd, spotting her daughter Jessie with Veronica, poised with cameras from their seats at the nearest table. Dot, Ethel, and Percy had claimed the centre table and hadn't stopped talking about how they 'single-handedly stopped a murderer in Spain.'

In the kitchen, Julia's stepmother, Katie, was shaking out the pink glittery ballot box, counting each slip of paper while Sue monitored the oven timer for the baking celebratory biscuits Julia had thrown together—the temptation to bake had been too strong.

Julia savoured the aroma of her peppermint and liquorice tea as it steeped. The gentle clatter of cutlery and the murmur of conversations provided a comforting soundtrack. But something was missing—or rather, someone. Her husband, Barker. He had a habit of disappearing into his office whenever he was working on a new book, but he had promised to be here for the announcement.

Just as she was contemplating going to find him, Sue emerged from the beaded curtain that separated the kitchen from the main area.

"Katie needs you," she said, beckoning Julia to follow her back into the kitchen.

Julia left her tea behind on the counter and followed Sue through the beads. Katie stood over the ballot box, chewing her plump glossy lip. Her face brightened as she spotted Julia.

"We have a bit of a problem," Katie said, gesturing to the four neat piles of voting slips. "Unless I've counted wrong *three* times, it's almost a straight tie between the four options."

Julia's heart sank at Katie's words. The fate of the field hinged on this vote, and now it seemed they were no closer to a decision.

"The market has won by *one* vote," Katie continued, "but the gardens and play park for the kids have tied and 'leave it alone' are only two behind."

Sue chimed in, "I think the market should win... but then I might be biased because that got my vote."

"What do you think, Julia?" Katie turned to her, eyes filled with worry. "Why is nothing ever straightforward?"

Julia walked towards the back door, needing a moment to think. She stepped out into the courtyard. From there, she could see across to the contested field.

Few had wanted James Jacobson's Howarth Estate houses there. But if the villagers were so split over what should replace those plans, choosing one option would disappoint three-quarters of the village. As she stood gazing at the vast expanse of grass, a solution occurred to her.

"Katie, how many acres is it again?" Julia called over her shoulder, not taking her eyes off the field.

"Fifteen."

"How big is one acre?"

"About the size of a football field."

Julia nodded. She had never been much of a football

fan, but she knew those pitches weren't small. Bigger than the village green in front of the café. Smaller than the graveyard behind the church.

She turned back to Katie and Sue, an idea forming.

"I reckon we could fit a market, a garden, *and* a play park—which got my vote—on a football field. That would leave fourteen acres untouched."

Katie's eyes widened as she let out a squeal of excitement.

"You're a genius, Julia! With the grant money from the council, we could build all three and make everyone happy. Peridale's brand new community square... Oh, I need to announce this right away!"

Julia smiled as Katie burst through the beads, relief washing over her.

This was a solution that could satisfy everyone, bring something new to the village, and protect their open spaces.

Now they just had to make it happen.

Barker leaned back in his creaky leather chair in the basement under the café, phone in hand. Above, the muffled sounds of celebration echoed around the café. He cared little about the outcome—he was just relieved it wouldn't be those dreadful houses.

He pulled out the phone number scribbled on a torn

piece of notebook paper given to him by Ethel before they left Spain. It belonged to Hilary Boyle, formerly the housekeeper for the late Vincent Wellington at Wellington Manor, and a former member of Ethel's defunct bridge club.

Katie might have been distracted by the result—and he'd been distracted by working on his novel in Spain—but Barker had promised Katie that he would help her find her birth mother. He glanced at Vincent Wellington's old 1979 diary on his desk—he still hadn't figured out how to tell Katie they were looking for more than just her birth mother.

Barker picked up the phone, took a deep breath, and dialled. After two rings, a familiar gruff voice answered.

"*Boyle*," the woman said on the other end of the line. "Who am I speaking to?"

"Ms Boyle, you might not remember me, but we met several times when you lived in Peridale," Barker began, adopting his politest voice. "My name is Barker Brown and I'm related to your former employer, Katie Wellington-South."

"I remember you," she said, giving no more away. A seagull squawked in the background—she must have moved to a coast.

"I was hoping you could help me with something regarding Katie."

"What's that wretched girl gone and done now?"

Taken aback, Barker wavered before responding. He'd never liked Hilary with her bad attitude, bulging eyes lined in black, and scraped back white bun, but that didn't matter now. He'd hit too many dead ends and Hilary might be his only hope.

"I work as a private investigator between writing books and—"

"I didn't ask for your life story, Mr Brown. What's the purpose of this call? I've long since moved on from my life at Wellington Manor, so if she wants me back, that ship has sailed."

"Katie doesn't own the manor anymore, and it's not a manor anymore, it's apartments," Barker said, looking at Vincent's diary. He was getting side-tracked, and he wasn't sure Hilary wouldn't hang up on him at any moment. "Katie has asked me to help find someone. Her birth mother, and... given that you were a housekeeper at the time Vincent Wellington *adopted* Katie, I was hoping you might be able to help..."

Thank you for reading, and don't forget to
RATE/REVIEW!

Find out what happens when Julia and Barker go digging into where Katie really came from in...

LEMON DRIZZLE AND LOATHING
COMING MAY 28th 2024

But before then, don't miss **DOUBLE ESPRESSO DECEPTION**, the 10th book in my **Claire's Candles** series, which will see Claire visiting Peridale and crossing over with Julia and the gang! **PRE-ORDER NOW! Coming April 23rd 2024!**

Sign up to Agatha Frost's newsletter at AgathaFrost.com to be the first to hear about its release!

Thank you for reading!

DON'T FORGET TO RATE AND REVIEW ON AMAZON

Reviews are more important than ever, so show your support for the series by rating and reviewing the book on Amazon! Reviews are **CRUCIAL** for the longevity of any series, and they're the best way to let authors know you want more! They help us reach more people! I appreciate any feedback, no matter how long or short. It's a great way of letting other cozy mystery fans know what you thought about the book.

Being an independent author means this is my livelihood, and *every review* really does make a **huge difference.** Reviews are the best way to support me so I can continue doing what I love, which is bringing you, the readers, more fun cozy adventures!

BONUS! SANGRIA RECIPES

You've heard all about it, now it's time to make it! For the first time *ever* in a Peridale book, here are some recipes for you to try! Minnie's homemade sangria (with or without alcohol)...

Going to give it a go? Don't forget to take a picture and tag @AgathaFrost when you post!

Minnie's Sangria

This recipe balances the floral notes of elderflower with the crispness of white wine and the fresh, vibrant flavours of summer fruits. The addition of sparkling water right before serving adds a celebratory fizz, making it a perfect drink for warm evenings or festive gatherings. Feel free to adjust the sweetness with more or less agave syrup according to your taste.

BONUS! Sangria Recipes

Ingredients:

- 1 bottle (750 ml) of dry white wine (e.g., Sauvignon Blanc or Pinot Grigio)
- 1/2 cup elderflower liqueur
- 1/4 cup brandy
- 2 tablespoons agave syrup (adjust to taste or substitute for simple sugar syrup)
- 1 ripe peach, thinly sliced
- 1 cup fresh strawberries, hulled and halved
- 1/2 cup blueberries
- 1 lemon, thinly sliced
- 1 lime, thinly sliced
- 2-3 sprigs of fresh mint
- Sparkling water or club soda (optional)
- Ice cubes – to serve.

Instructions

1. Prep the Fruit: Prepare all your fruits by washing and slicing them as indicated. This not only ensures they're ready to infuse the sangria with their flavours but also makes your beverage look irresistibly inviting.

2. Mix the Base: In a large pitcher, combine the dry white wine, elderflower liqueur, brandy, and agave syrup. Stir gently to ensure the agave syrup is well dissolved and the liquids are thoroughly mixed.

3. Add Fruits and Herbs: Add the sliced peach, strawberries, blueberries, lemon, lime, and sprigs of mint to the pitcher. Stir gently to combine, being careful not to bruise the fruit too much.

4. Chill: Cover and refrigerate the sangria for at least 3-4 hours, ideally overnight. This allows the flavours to meld and the fruit to infuse the sangria with its essence.

5. Serve: Just before serving, gently stir the sangria again. Fill glasses with ice cubes and pour the sangria over them, making sure to include some of the fruit pieces and a sprig of mint in each glass. If desired, top each glass with a splash of sparkling water or club soda for a fizzy touch.

6. Enjoy: Serve immediately and enjoy the refreshing, nuanced flavours of your unique sangria!

Minnie's Sans-Alcohol Sangira

This version maintains the balance of flavours found in traditional sangria while omitting the alcohol. Adjust the sweetness to your liking by adding more or less agave syrup.

Ingredients

- 1 bottle (750 ml) of grape juice
- 1/4 cup apple juice

- A splash of vanilla extract
- 1/2 cup elderflower syrup
- 2 tablespoons agave syrup
- 1 ripe peach, thinly sliced
- 1 cup fresh strawberries, hulled and halved
- 1/2 cup blueberries
- 1 lemon, thinly sliced
- 1 lime, thinly sliced
- 23 sprigs of fresh mint
- Sparkling water or club soda (optional)
- Ice cubes

Instructions

1. Prep the Fruit: Prepare all your fruits by washing and slicing them as indicated. This ensures they're ready to infuse the sangria with their flavours.

2. Mix the Base: In a large pitcher, combine the grape juice, elderflower syrup, vanilla extract, and agave syrup. Stir gently to ensure the syrups are well incorporated.

3. Add Fruits and Herbs: Add the sliced peach, strawberries, blueberries, lemon, lime, and sprigs of mint to the pitcher. Stir gently to combine, being careful not to bruise the fruit too much.

4. Chill: Cover and refrigerate the sangria for at least 34 hours, ideally overnight, to allow the flavours to meld and the fruit to infuse the sangria.

5. Serve: Just before serving, gently stir the sangria again. Fill glasses with ice cubes and pour the sangria over them, making sure to include some fruit pieces and a sprig of mint in each glass. If desired, top each glass with a splash of sparkling water or club soda for a fizzy touch.

6. Enjoy: Serve immediately and enjoy the refreshing, nuanced flavours of your unique virgin sangria!

Going to give it a go? Don't forget to take a picture and tag @AgathaFrost when you post! And let me know if you want more recipes in future books...

WANT TO BE KEPT UP TO DATE WITH AGATHA FROST RELEASES? *SIGN UP THE FREE NEWSLETTER!*

www.AgathaFrost.com

You can also follow **Agatha Frost** across social media. Search 'Agatha Frost' on:

Facebook
Twitter
Goodreads
Instagram

ALSO BY AGATHA FROST

Peridale Cafe

33. **Cruffins and Confessions (coming soon)**
32. **Lemon Drizzle and Loathing (coming soon)**
31. **Sangria and Secrets**
30. Mince Pies and Madness
29. Pumpkins and Peril
28. Eton Mess and Enemies
27. Banana Bread and Betrayal
26. Carrot Cake and Concern
25. Marshmallows and Memories
24. Popcorn and Panic
23. Raspberry Lemonade and Ruin
22. Scones and Scandal
21. Profiteroles and Poison
20. Cocktails and Cowardice
19. Brownies and Bloodshed
18. Cheesecake and Confusion
17. Vegetables and Vengeance
16. Red Velvet and Revenge
15. Wedding Cake and Woes

14. Champagne and Catastrophes
13. Ice Cream and Incidents
12. Blueberry Muffins and Misfortune
11. Cupcakes and Casualties
10. Gingerbread and Ghosts
9. Birthday Cake and Bodies
8. Fruit Cake and Fear
7. Macarons and Mayhem
6. Espresso and Evil
5. Shortbread and Sorrow
4. Chocolate Cake and Chaos
3. Doughnuts and Deception
2. Lemonade and Lies
1. Pancakes and Corpses

Claire's Candles

1. Vanilla Bean Vengeance
2. Black Cherry Betrayal
3. Coconut Milk Casualty
4. Rose Petal Revenge
5. Fresh Linen Fraud
6. Toffee Apple Torment
7. Candy Cane Conspiracies
8. Wildflower Worries
9. Frosted Plum Fears

Other

The Agatha Frost Winter Anthology

Peridale Cafe Book 1-10

Peridale Cafe Book 11-20

Claire's Candles Book 1-3

Printed in Great Britain
by Amazon